STEPHEN DAVIS

THE MERLIN LEGACY

STEPHEN DAVIS

THE MERLIN LEGACY

MEMOIRS

Cirencester

Published by Memoirs

25 Market Place, Cirencester, Gloucestershire, GL7 2NX
info@memoirsbooks.co.uk www.memoirspublishing.com

First published in England, October 2012

Book jacket design Ray Lipscombe

ISBN 978-1-909304-56-7

Printed in England

CONTENTS

For my wife Phil. You are amazing and the best nurse ever.

For Rebecca , Rob, Ellie and William.

For Toby, Laura and Charlie ('Badger'), and of course Huw.

For my mother and John, and Libby and Matt.

Thank you for being strong.

My thanks to Chris Newton at Memoirs for his help in editing the manuscript.

HOW IT ALL BEGAN

Some years ago, we bought and moved into an old, neglected longhouse in Netherbury, Dorset. It needed a great deal of remedial work. At the rear stood a range of old stables and animal feed rooms. One stable was piled to the eaves with logs cut from old trees, so many that it took us ten winters to burn them all on the fire.

One spring as the pile was coming down somewhat, I set to work to sort the logs out, restacking them and clearing the floor. Concealed behind them I found a large and dusty tin box, sealed with what looked like candlewax. When I managed to open it I found it contained a pile of yellowed paper.

I took all this into the house to study it, to find that in my hands I was holding the manuscript of a book; in fact, two books. I was stunned by what I read.

This is the first volume. I wonder what you will make of it.

Stephen Davis, 2012

CHAPTER 1

A BOY AND A BUZZARD

A swirl of leaves and dust danced unnoticed by the side of the Beaminster road, on a bend just above the village of Netherbury in Dorset. Not one of the drivers taking their sunburned families home that day paid it any attention. They were all concentrating on the winding road, lost in their radios, tapes or CDs or distracted by squabbling, tired children sitting in the back.

The swirl danced on, still fixed to one place. It rose and fell, shimmering in the hot, humid air. It seemed to kiss the verge, rattling an old sweet paper and lifting a wisp of hay dropped by a passing tractor and trailer.

A droning, dozy bumble bee wandered into it - and found itself spinning. Its buzz got angrier until the hairs on its body bristled in fury. It floundered to the other side, and with more of a fall than a flight crashed on to a white clover head. Then, calmer, it resumed its previous happy drone.

A passing lorry, laden with tractor parts, flattened with its wash the stalks of dry grass on the verge, and heads of cow parsley swayed back and forth as if bowing to its passing. Yet the swirl of leaves and dust stayed put, as if anchored to the road. It danced on as a caravan passed, with its attendant cavalcade of cars behind.

There were cars laden with surfboards and one towing a dinghy. Dogs' heads lolled out of estate cars, tongues panting. Many of the cars were full of sunburned children, sand in their pants or still wearing damp swimming trunks, their tummies full of chips and ice cream. Mothers fretted about sunburned noses and some had to soothe grizzling babies who had not yet been lulled to sleep by the car's motion. Further back, one held an elderly grandma fanning her face with today's paper. Even with the window open she found it hot. Urging her son not to drive too fast, she looked out at the rolling hills and the sinking sun. It was sending long shadows over the stubble fields and turning the sky to the west a bright red.

This grandma had struggled with her knitting on the beach, trying to read a paperback and helping her granddaughter with sand castles. She was now giving her a grandma-type cuddle and lulling her to sleep. We will forgive her tired eyes for missing the swirl of leaves fixed to the road edge as they drove past; but Lucy, her granddaughter, did not. She, along with Mewlic's ancestors, saw something, or rather someone, else.

Lucy had tried to get in the front for the journey home and was forced to have a loud complain and a bit of a sulk as her mother clipped her into her child seat. Initially she was feeling put out, but with thumb in her mouth and Granny next to her she began to get in that dreamlike, sleepy mode the young adopt so well. As the car slowed to join the long line and go around a bend, her eyes had been squinting into the sun. Her thumb was being noisily sucked as Grandma hummed her favourite nursery rhyme.

Then out came the thumb with a pop. Her eyes opened wide and her head twizzled around. Her little arm pushed against the side of her chair, helping her to turn and look. She needed a better look at the funny, strange man standing by the road edge…

'Funny man!' she called out to the rest of the car, but her words were lost in the general noise. As the car had gone past she had seen his long brown boots and tatty black jacket. His hair had made her giggle and then cry out. It was really quite long and the ends danced about as if tied to pieces of string. He was leaning on a long stick and appeared to be looking up into the hill. His long fingers were wrapped around the stick shaft.

As the car drew away he shifted his gaze and looked at her. He had given her a piercing, frightening look, followed by a friendly smile. His eyes were bright blue and his face a nut brown. Lucy nearly cried out in alarm, but as she was about to do so he took one hand off his stick and put a finger to his lips as a shush sign.

The car went round the bend and he was gone. She did not see him ever again, nor did anyone else, at least not that afternoon. The onlooker would only have seen that swirl of leaves and dust by the road edge.

If you had been standing on that bend on the Bridport to Beaminster road that hot late afternoon and looked up into the bowl between the hills, you would have seen a small figure lying across the upper slope. The setting sun warmed the back of his head as he lay face down on the sheep-cropped grass. The ewes with their nearly full-grown lambs wandered up to him, suggesting that he had been there for some time.

A far-off observer that day might have assumed the boy was getting ready to roll down the hill in a form of crazy game.

However, getting closer, you would have seen that his eyes were tight shut. Alarmingly, a trickle of blood flowed from the back of his head through his blond hair and down on to his grey shirt collar

Cropping the grass never more than a few yards away was a dark bay gelding. While slowly chewing a mouthful it would raise his head and look towards the boy with tired old eyes.

The boy mumbled and groaned in his sleep, bringing the horse over to him. The horse lowered his head and blow a load-vibrating snort towards the boy's ear, stamping a foot. After waiting a while it resumed its chomping, tearing at the weeds and grass.

The noise of a car hooting or a lorry in the valley below would cause him to lift his head into the light wind and stare into the valley. Nothing happened to warrant his attention, so he resumed his grass cropping, one eye on his fallen friend, moving around him as if tied by an invisible string.

The gentle wind that late afternoon started far out to sea with the gulls and crossed the shingle beach. It touched the last few holidaymakers finishing their day. Then it pushed its way inland, over the small town and into the rolling hills. It almost seemed that it was trying to get as much distance it could from the sinking sun. A vague hint of winter to come could be felt, despite the final heat.

The combines had long finished with the corn and great slabs of baled straw stood in field corners. The sweet smell of hay teased your nose along with the faint smell of newly turned earth. Standing beside the boy, your eyes might roam to see a far-off tractor struggling to plough the stubble back into ground baked hard by the long hot summer. A long brown scar was left behind, with a tumbling-twisting plume of following rooks, crows, and gulls. Further around the hills of Pilsdon and Lewesdon, majestic beech crowns seemed to march in a row towards the sunset.

Sitting quietly by the boy, you would have heard laughter from the farm below. Two small children splashed and played with a bright yellow inflatable on the farm pond. Any conversation they had was lost by the distance, along with the odd catch of cows lowing and the hum of traffic.

If you had looked into the branches of the oak on the far side of the hill, your gaze would have been met by a buzzard, one of Mewlic's ancestors; his name I have not been told. His yellow eyes were fixed and rarely blinking. He had managed to escape from the attention of his two sons and wife for most of the afternoon, considering himself lucky. He had spent the morning soaring above the hill faces, riding the updrafts. By late morning he had had a bit of luck, spotting not one but two dead rabbits on the road edge. He had lifted one up the hill to a quiet spot and gorged upon it. After, this with a full crop, he had flown with the some of the rest of his kind and mewed a call to his wife and sons.

He had never felt the desire to work terribly hard these days and this summer the work of feeding three growing sons had exhausted him. It was getting near his time to build up fat for the winter. He had left them squabbling and made his way from the fence post to the dead larch and finally to the oak. On the way he had snapped up an unlucky frog, more out of boredom than hunger.

As usual he had to endure the irritating scolding of two blackbirds, which pinked their alarm calls at him and were just brave enough to try to dive-bomb him occasionally. He had seen and ignored them many times before.

Relaxing, he roused and shook his wings roughly. He meticulously started to preen, his eyes half shut in happy mode. Now well into his moult, some of his new flight feathers were still buried in their waxy protective sheath in his skin, and they tormented him. He was standing with his head buried in the feathers under his wing, nibbling at these irritations, when he started with alarm. Human laughter, the barking of a dog and the noise of galloping hooves made him pull his feathers close. His eyes became slits and his heart pumped. He shifted, trying to see.

He searched with his eyes, then relaxed. He knew this threat, having seen it many times before. His feet widened, talons lifting, feathers puffed, and although he did not rouse or start preening again, he was happier. He could wait and watch the boy ride up the hill. The boy was me.

Some of you will think I am brave to write this down. Some will think I am stupid to put my life at risk. I have been thinking long and hard as to whether I should, and on balance have come down in favour. This account is it.

As a boy I had no idea that the figure who forms the central focus of this story actually existed. As I grew older I met him and certain other characters in films and on television and read many books and stories about them. One thing that clarifies the need to put it down is the fact that I know in advance, as a condition - call it a perk if you will - the year when I will pass on. Then a successor will take over. Maybe you will say I am lumbered with the task, the honour, the responsibility, the title, the history.

What on earth, you are probably thinking, am I going on about? I will try to explain.

I have to write first that following my first injury, my early memories are nil. To fill that part in I have asked good friends to help. It has not been easy for them, as these initial times were when their great-great grandparents were still alive. Hang on, you are saying, how was I around then? You have assumed that I am relying on human memory, but I am not.

We are not alone. Animals, bird and others can communicate and keep history that they find relevant. I bet you are thinking, this is going to be one of those weird stories. It will all be about talking to spirits, animals, being in touch with yourself - how wrong. This is as true as I can make it. It will sound, I suppose, far fetched, and possibly if you do not stop to think, improbable.

My memories are I suppose from the hospital, some six months after my fall to now. They are as complete as I can recall, but possibly sometimes out of chronology, and of course are messed up by my later fall. You will also need to know that following my first accident I have never fully regained some functions. I am sure that the term 'trapped in a body' is one you are familiar with. Initially, as you will read later, I could not walk or talk properly or see very well out of my right eye. I am typing this with one finger, as the fingers on my right hand do not work too well. I am sure my left eye is overworked. But I know that compared to some, I have been lucky.

It is pouring down outside, cold and dark. This winter is one of the worst we have had - so much for global warming - but at least it is dry under the thatch. I can concentrate on remembering.

Every now and then I get exasperated with my speed at getting my memories down. A cuppa, a chat with my mates, who are now in and waiting for their tea, restores my sanity.

At the end of the day I have to remember who I was made to be, and what I have seen; remember what I am and what history I have apparently helped to make. I take it for granted now, yet all the things in my life that you will perhaps be stunned by are different.

It is not at all easy for me to tell this story. I can vividly recall being scared silly at times, in fact petrified as never in my life before. You could say that at times I have been honoured, amazed and horrified in turn. It is fair to say initially I thought this very unfair. After all I was given no choice.

I am now aware that Shola had already chosen my replacement. If only he knew. This is what I meant when I said earlier that I know the date of my death. A weird thought, which I find hard to get used to. I suppose I realise that I have been honoured to be chosen. I have continued possibly 700 years of function, tradition and duty. I have obviously learned many things I would not have without it – strange, and still after all these years I am trying my hardest to comprehend the task.

My parents told me how some of it began, and tales, the legends of good friends, filled in the gaps. I will now elaborate to you. My mother reluctantly gave in and told me, I do remember, some two years after my initial fall. I nagged her relentlessly for answers. I have hinted earlier that I have needed spoken histories from other friends too.

It is perhaps easier for you and me if I tell that story straight as it was told to me. This first episode I tell right from my mother's memory, with Mewlic's help. His account is woven and integral to his family's memory and maintained as a solemn duty from generation to generation.

I need to explain that with many names, beings and folk I write about I have had to guess the spellings. They have no written history, and having been introduced to them I had to get their names down on paper phonetically. Let me say that this is not because they are uneducated, less bright or in some way missing. It is just because they have never had the need for writing.

For those of you who are unfamiliar with Dorset, it is one of the prettiest and least spoilt counties in England. Of course it has some built-up areas, some shopping malls, some housing belts - after all, life goes on. However it is mainly unspoilt, with gentle rolling hills and beech-tree-laden valleys. Its fields tend to be small, with some cereals and other crops, a lot of dairy cattle and of course sheep. Thomas Hardy's Wessex is slow to change, its people being linked mainly to the land. Think of Dorset and you think of green as the dominant colour, tucked-away villages with thatched, cob-walled cottages and narrow twisting lanes with high hedges. The people are genuine and in times of stress support each other wonderfully.

My mother tells me that I slipped away from the house that afternoon on my father's old horse, going through Netherbury. The thatched houses appeared deserted that afternoon. Very little traffic moved and the hooves must have rung and echoed along the main street. There were far fewer cars back then, when I was still in my teens.

I often rode that way to the hill. It meant crossing the main road, but traffic was much less of a problem when I was young. The family wolfhound, Milly, was used to the trip, tucking herself at the side of the horse if a lorry should come by.

My mother remembered that I must have had a boring morning, waiting for her to return from shopping. I was waiting for confirmation of my A level passes, which meant the post. I was staving off my normal adolescent hunger by eating the odd handful of biscuits or a banana.

The real nuisance of course was seeing the wolfhound lying across the door with one eye on me all the time. The hound and I had grown up together, although it was a sad fact that given the short lifespan of these great dogs she was already old. Milly was ancient in comparison to me, but we were inseparable. The rest of the family said it was often hard to tell who shadowed whom. Indeed one night my mother had been woken from a deep sleep by the sound of grumbling and growling. On sneaking into my room she had found us both asleep together, the big dog with his head on the pillow. The dog and I were obviously sharing a dream, with the whole bed twitching and moving. My mother often smiled at the memory of waking us, wondering who was more relieved, with Milly wandering back to her bed in the kitchen.

After lunch I must have wandered out of the kitchen, grabbed a slice of the fruit cake which my mother always had, and gone to the stable. I made horse talk to the hunters waiting there as I had heard my father do many times. The old hunter stuck his head out and whickered back.

The other dogs, both pointers, wagged their stumpy tails in the dust and fell back to sleep. A few hens wandered about in the yard, scratching in the dust.

Looking down into the top field I could see my father schooling a young horse. The air was warm and a few swallows screamed overhead. Now and then a pheasant called.

By the stable door I rubbed noses with our old hunter, Caspian. He had served my father well for nearly twenty years and was now in semi-retirement. As I was lighter than my dad, exercising had become my great job. It kept the gelding's interest, health, and fitness, and without me being aware it taught me a lot, which if truth be known is what my father intended.

He had apparently at times watched from a distance, sometimes chuckling and sometimes concerned as I tried increasingly higher jumps in the field, then laughing out loud as I managed them.

Of course, to Caspian these jumps were nothing at all. He had spent most of the previous twenty years carrying my father over the most amazing hedges and gates. To me, however, the gates must have looked immense, and it took a special horse to give me the bottle to do a five-barred gate. The horse, as my father knew, would teach me well.

Once saddled and tacked up, the horse, the hound and I trotted out of the village heading up into the hills. Having crossed the main road and gone through the gate, we were free of the risk of traffic and on the smooth cropped grass of the sheep fields that run above the main road and up into the hills. The fields here were smooth grass, free of holes, and all three of us, to get rid of the morning boredom, charged up the sloping hill.

Caspian cantered with a loose rein, my fingers just making

contact. The wind was making me watery-eyed, pulling at my billowing shirt. Milly lolloped behind, a little wide of us. She would soon catch up.

A small clump of hawthorn bushes grew on the right as the slope eased off, and wind-blown branches gave me a few low jumps to play with before I slowed to a trot and finally a walk, then stop.

The view of the distant sea was like shimmering glass in the late sun. The wolfie rejoined us to lie down and on the other side of the valley the buzzard stretched a wing, roused and carried on watching us.

I must have stayed looking at the view for half an hour or so. I stretched in the saddle and Caspian lifted his head from the bracken he was picking at.

'Come on, it's not that hot now.' I shouted to the big dog. She looked up, wagging her long tail, and got to her feet.

So far I have added to my mother's and Mewlic's story as I have seen fit, but now I will borrow mainly his family's account, which has been preserved from generation to generation. His ancestor saw the drama unfold from his aerial perch in that old oak. He saw the boy on the dark horse with dog at his side gently slowly cantering along the hill top edge by the wood fringe. A fallen beech trunk gently jumped and all seemed well. Then, with a flashing speed and ferocity of movement, everything changed.

The wolfhound had been ranging a few yards in front, and from a clump of gorse and nettles on the far side a roe deer exploded and virtually ran into the horse's front legs. The hound gave a baying bark, jumping sideways, and Caspian tried desperately to avoid a collision, raising his forelegs desperately.

The final stroke of fate was that as the horse tried frantically to avoid the deer with its forelegs, his hind leg found a rabbit hole, previously hidden from view.

Apparently it was obvious that I tried to regain some balance, with the hound coursing off after the deer. In a sort of slow motion, horse and rider fell.

I did not find out until later about my injury; I was knocked unconscious. Caspian struggled to his feet and had a good shake.

The buzzard saw everything. He saw the heavy fall and heard the sickening noise as my head hit the ground. His talons instinctively gripped the branch, his eyes yellow slits. Later that night he would tell his sons how the falling horse had tried to avoid the fallen boy, the horse being winded and suffering as well for some time. It had struggled to its feet with stirrup irons hanging and the boy flat on the ground. He would also describe how after a few minutes the wolfhound reappeared on the far side of the valley and barked once. It ran across to the horse, which whinnied back.

The buzzard's hunger was beginning to get the better of him at this point and he noisily flapped out of the oak. He had ridden the valley wind to the cold upper levels. Looking down, he had watched the tired hound run to the fallen horse and prostrate boy. He drifted on his broad wings watching the drama, soaring along the woodland edge.

In that strange communication animals have with each other, the old horse appeared to call the hound, both peering at the boy. The hound's tongue hung out as he gasped for air. It looked as if they were both trying to raise the boy, the horse snorting by the boy's head and stamping a hoof. The hound tried licking the back of his head, whimpering and even scratching at one of the boy's arms with his great black nails.

Then the horse looked at the hound, and the hound left, running straight as an arrow for Netherbury village and home.

The sun had nearly set and the shadows were long. The moon appeared and a single fox called to it. The countryside knew that night was coming, and a few lambs called bleating to their long-suffering mother, rushing in and nearly lifting her off the ground as they both had a last suck. I remained ignorant of these sights and sounds, though with mental straining I can recall some of them. I do recall the smell of the grass and blinding lights, though my eyes were shut. I heard a hissing noise in my head and found it impossible to move any part of my body. As I drifted in and out, I do remember a feeling of warmth as though I was wrapped in a thick blanket. I also felt I was lying on a ledge, or sitting on a plank with softer ground either side.

I remember strange new voices talking about putting me in a pond, of all things. I could not move. I can remember a firm but friendly voice saying 'Peter, don't try to move, stay as you are'. On reflection I know who this was. I could feel his presence and warm breath on my neck. Even though I was pathetic, in my few lucid moments the closeness was relaxing.

I remember how my hearing improved so much that I could hear mice moving in the grass near me, the faraway cawing of rooks, distant conversation, and the far-off sea crashing with surf. I remember that everything was black. My eyes, for some reason, did not seem to be working at all.

'A dewlap caused the fall, a bad place, the hound has gone, sleep' said the deep voice.

The buzzard getting ready for roost could see the horse standing on the hill, the prone form of the boy and the far-off figure of an old man leaning on a stick watching and not moving. Darkness fell, and the horse was visibly anxious. The buzzard heard a fox barking, and then through the night the wolfhound calling and people noisily coming.

'Over here, he has not changed.'

'Hurry, quick!'

I remember trying to move again and a firm, friendly and deep voice ordering me to be still. The buzzard's story tells of the flashing blue lights arriving on the valley road, people with torches and a stretcher, the general noise.

My mother told me, a little emotionally, that Milly had arrived barking crazily in the yard. She kept running to the gate, then back again. To cut a long story short, she and my father put two and two together, quickly locked the house and set off at a jog after Milly. She ran ahead, repeatedly turning to make sure they were following. They reached the top road and looked up into the valley. In the dusk they could just make me out, and the outline of Caspian beside me. My father sent my mother up to me while he sprinted as fast as he could back to the first cottage, where he used their telephone to call an ambulance.

The buzzard's story adds a little, as Mewlic told me. It tells of the ambulance being watched by the wizened old man leaning on his stick as it sped off. It tells of the worries of the hound and horse as they were led off the hill and back to Netherbury and home.

What has not been recorded anywhere until now is that Milly

and Caspian were truly worried that they had somehow understood the few words I had spoken. This shocked them, leaving them petrified and anxious.

As my mother cradled my head in her lap, waiting for the ambulance, I apparently muttered 'I am OK' and a few other words. The horse had reared back and the hound had shot away, tail between its legs.

Horse and hound had looked at each other because for the first time they had understood in exact terms the words I had said. The sad thing was that for my mother it was just an unintelligible grunt.

Finally the ambulance sped off to hospital with me and my distraught mother on board.

The tumbling swirl of leaves and dust by the road edge had stopped. An old man with a stick wandered back to his tumbledown house near the river. It had not been exactly as he had imagined.

My father led the horse and hound home, very worried.

CHAPTER 2

A DISTURBING LEGACY

I can tell you almost nothing of my first few months in hospital, but if such things intrigue you, I will try to tell what I can. This is mainly my mother's tale, as she told it to me after much persuasion.

I was admitted to Dorchester Hospital and was then moved to Southampton. They were worried about me bleeding into my brain, as I had managed to fracture my skull in several places. My coma lasted a few weeks. Like all trauma cases, my recovery to a conscious state was slow, and involved garbled incoherent speech. I was intubated, fed through a tube and nursed by wonderful nurses twenty-four hours a day.

I can remember vague things, ridiculous things, like needing a bottle to pee in, people visiting, hospital food, which occasionally was not too bad. However my early memories are limited and do not add much.

I can remember fighting to talk and walk again, but particularly I can recall an elderly man visiting quietly one afternoon. I am afraid that at this stage I struggle to describe him at all; what he said or did is gone. Try as I can I cannot remember much, though we have talked many times about his visit.

He came in when I had no visitors one afternoon, when I was particularly sleepy. What he said I cannot remember. I do however remember the senior nurse leaving her desk and coming over to my bed when he had gone. She asked who he was, with a worried look on her face. I had no idea, so I could not help. This did not ease her at all and I remember her face as she walked back, showing fear. It is strange that I remember his visit then.

I was soon out of a wheelchair and doing simple tasks around the hospital ward, always under the watching eyes of the nurses. Hospitals generally by their nature are clinical, impersonal places. They do make the odd effort for patients - a few obscure pictures on the wall, the odd pile of out-of-date magazines, the compulsory hopeless coffee machine.

I spent my early days wheeling myself up and around the corridors in my wheelchair and then clinging to walls and chairs, trying to move around. My nursing staff, the physiotherapy team, speech therapist and consultants were wonderful.

At that point I had been left with a right arm that did not work well and a hopeless right eye, I could not walk at all well, and sounded as if I was drunk when people could hear me at all. After two months it was considered all right for me to be allowed home for a weekend, and this I have every reason to remember.

My nurse drove me home for that one-night stay; my mother was to drive me back. I can remember my pleasure and relief as the long thatched house came into view. Even though by then it was getting well into winter, the borders along the front of the house showed my mother's care. It was simply wonderful to be back home, and the village looked really welcoming.

My parents were waiting by the gate, along with the dogs. I remember that it was a drizzling wet day, and leaving the car I was helped inside by one and all with many smiles. It smelt so good to be home. My parents had converted the sitting room into a temporary bedroom for me, as stairs were still impossible for me then. Though I knew I was going back to the hospital on the Sunday afternoon, I can still easily recall my immense joy at progress, and being home again. It felt I was getting somewhere at last.

The house and its home fields looked as I remembered, and the village as we drove through looked unchanged. It probably sounds automatic, perhaps trite, but on walking into my home I could feel myself improving. Though I am so grateful for the hospital for keeping me alive, boy, it was good to be home.

After a fantastic welcome home with lunch cooked by mother and all the family there to see me I was helped outside, with all in attendance watching my progress. Then a new aspect to my life made its presence felt, and arrived with a vengeance.

Up to this moment the dogs, including my beloved Milly had been shut outside in the garden and yard. As I appeared at the door they went mad with excitement, jumping and bounding in the air on the spot. Their tails nearly fell off with wagging.

'Careful, down' said my father, lifting his hands jokily to protect me.

Then the moment I will remember all my life. I simply said to the dogs how great it was to see them and that I was home again. The effect of this was, to say the least, dramatic. It made my parents initially roar with laughter, but it made the dogs shoot away, tails between their legs. Why? Because I had spoken to them in their own language!

My parents thought I was mucking around with the dogs by pretending to bark and growl. To be honest I did not at that point realise what was happening, or that I was making the noises.

I may have been marginally brain damaged, but it took me a few seconds to realise what I had inadvertently done. Reverting to human speech saved the moment.

I managed to bend over a little, calling the dogs to me in soft tones. They approached, cowering low. After a few moments, which seemed at the time like ages, peace, harmony and welcome resumed, though Milly remained what is best described as a touch guarded.

Another episode during that first home visit was equally unpleasant. After settling the dogs and getting them back to normal, with one reinvestigating an old bone and the others charging around the garden, I was taken through to the horses in their stables by my father.

In I went, and again, my father tells me, I whinnied a welcome. He had two horses waiting, to be ridden later. They both jerked their heads up, badly panicked, and shot to the far side of their stable. They pushed their heads over the stable doors on the far side, threatening the hinges.

My father, ever the horseman, went past me, calling loudly and reassuring the horses, pushing through the internal doors. He laid a big hand on each horse's neck and scowled at me.

'That's a weird trick you learned in hospital. I don't think we need you doing that again.' His eyes looked at me with concern.

I apologised and felt dreadful, but was held by Caspian's eye. He had obviously completely understood my welcome. His eyes rolled white and he flung his head up, forelegs trembling. I turned and tried to run, but failed badly, and left the stable for the kitchen. Frankly, I was petrified.

After supper, which admittedly was a bit strained, my grandma arrived to see me and eventually the normal household harmony returned. She was brilliantly supportive, I remember even now after all these years. To be honest I got dreadfully tired in those days and with my mother's help I was, shall we say, tucked up early into my temporary bed. I am sure that to be kind to my parents they too were pleased to see me going to bed early as well.

One other thing happened that weekend, and it is vitally important to this whole remembering exercise. I woke early, and managed to get clothes of some description on. At this stage I was unable to walk too well or very far. I wanted to see outside. I struggled into a jacket and without waking anyone I pushed open the back door. I slowly made my way to the orchard, past the flowerbeds. I should say at this point that of course the dogs, and in fact both my parents, had heard me moving. They all listened carefully, very much aware of what I was doing.

The grass was sopping wet from the drizzle the day before. It was really still, one of those late winter mornings. It was cold, and my breath fogged the air a little. There was a thin reddish glow from the rising sun, and looking down to the river I could see a low mist hanging over the water.

I went down through the orchard gate, then came to a sudden stop, for standing there was a stranger. It was the man I had seen in the hospital some weeks before, the man who had worried the nurse.

'Can I help you? Are you lost?' I asked him.

He said nothing, just raised his eyebrows.

'The path is over there' I said, pointing over to the orchard edge. 'This bit is private.'

He still said nothing, but moved toward me. I began to tense.

He was dressed in a black waxproof jacket, brown corduroy trousers and big black gumboots. What worried me somewhat was that he held a long gnarled beech stick in his brown hands. His face is best described as wizened, with many lines. Running down from his hairline was a truly hideous scar. I did have the strength to stay put, though I wanted to turn and run.

CHAPTER 3

JULES

Now the next part I do remember clearly, and probably will forever. As he came towards me he began to speak.

'How are you, Peter? I watched it happen. You had us all worried.' He paused.

'Hang on just there a moment' I said, lifting my hand. 'Sorry, but I don't think I know you.'

He stopped by the side of a plum tree. 'No, I'm sorry' he muttered. 'I forgot.' But he still did not say who he was.

At this point my mother called loudly from the house, asking if I was all right. Obviously from the half-open back door she could not see this fellow.

The dogs arrived in a mad charging rush, sliding to a halt at my feet in a big doggy pile. They had obviously just been let out of the kitchen. Just before they got to me I heard the man say, 'We will talk soon' and as I turned he had gone. But where? The orchard is not that big and no leaves blocked the views, it being winter. Yet there was no sign of him at all.

'What's that scent, who is that?' I heard from the kitchen. I wandered up to find my mother cooking up bacon, eggs and rounds of toast for beans.

'There was a chap in the orchard, I've no idea who, think I have met him before' I said, grabbing a piece of toast.

'Get off that!' she said, waving a spoon at me and looking out of the window, trying to see. 'Tell your father.'

Over breakfast later my father thought the chap had been a recluse who lived for free, in return for helping now and then, on the farm along the river valley. The old cottage he lived in was virtually derelict, he thought, and he was not seen very often as he kept himself to himself.

The rest of that Sunday went horribly quickly. My mother was taking me back after lunch later and before that I tried to get around a bit, hopping and lurching along on my stick. I had many get-well cards and letters to read, in particular one from the university. I had managed to get the A level grades I needed for a place, but having been in hospital that had all gone west. The college Dean had been very kind in holding my place for a year to see how much improvement there would be. In other words, having missed the place, and now the first term, a place would be held for me in the next year. In fact I never improved enough to take up the place then, and had to do it several years later instead.

I sadly remember saying goodbye to the dogs and waving towards the horses in passing so as not to upset them again. Then my mother and I set off on the horrible journey to the hospital.

I will not dwell on the last two months in hospital. Don't get me wrong, they did a brilliant job. The nurses and staff were really kind, but I hated being there.

The physiotherapist in particular realised this. She arrived by my bed one day with her coat on, while the staff got me dressed.

'We're going out', she said. 'You have had enough of this place.'

She then pushed me in my wheelchair out along the beach for nearly an hour and a half. So observant, kind and wonderful.

At last that final meeting and review with my consultant. I was promoted to outpatient that day, and not a moment too soon. I would have numerous visits for review, speech therapy and occupational therapy, to the local hospital gym and so on, as an outpatient in the year that followed.

When I had been home for possibly two months I started wandering around the village. My parents had come around at last to allowing me to do this unaccompanied, the only provisos being they knew the route I was taking, that I always had Milly with me and that I used my walking stick.

It was one of those fine early spring mornings. The air was still, with a hint of warmth. A woodpecker drummed now and then, and birds squabbled over nest material. The village was peaceful that morning as Milly and I made our way down the main road to the bridge over the river. The stream's flow was already very low, as we had had little rain that winter. I could just make out the shape of a trout as I looked down the stream. Milly was on a lead by the road edge, just in case the odd car came past.

Children were protected from the river by an old white-painted fence. I leaned on this, smelling the spring air. Without thinking I looked at Milly and said in a whisper, 'Great, you all right?'

She nearly pulled the lead out of my hand. Half growling she looked at me, wagging her tail but very wary.

I will never forget what happened next.

'Too loud, you did it again' she said.

I bet you didn't believe that. It wasn't speech and you wouldn't hear it. It was more of a quiet noise with thought behind it. Now I am not very scientific, call it subliminal if you will, but my communication with Milly began that morning by the river.

I sat down by the road edge, holding my head. Milly started whimpering, then pushed her head into my lap, shaking but moving her tail slowly.

'What's this, why me? It's impossible, rubbish!' I said, half sobbing.

Milly pulled her head back and stared me straight in the eye. Her dark brown eyes held me, the gaze fixed as only a questioning dog can.

'You can and I can' she said.

You might think this is all a load of made-up rubbish, straight from a Disney film. Well - just wait.

Milly and I were able to – well, have a chat. Why was I so upset about that? Just imagine for a moment. One day you are a fit adolescent, playing rugby, riding, hunting. I was doing all the things young men do. Then I was made to feel useless, could not walk properly, speech was difficult. My eye did not work properly and my future looked completely changed.

Then to crown it all, I found that I could understand my beloved hound on a new level. I felt then that madness was overtaking me.

As Milly and I found out that morning, we now shared many thoughts completely. But she was, after all, a hound. We simply did not share names for things, a language to make it sensible or easy. Yes, we had simply phrases to share - where's that, what's that, walk, garden, dinner, bed and so on. That lovely wolfhound is now four dogs ago, and it has been easier with each.

I started crying, holding that big dog's head by the side of the road that morning. A car stopped and the driver leaned over with the window open.

'You all right mate? Is your dog all right?'

I was able to smile at him, waving him on. I got to my feet, holding the lead.

'Do we need that?' moaned Milly. She had a pained look on her face

'It's just in case a lorry comes.' I looked at her.

'Take it off, I am not stupid.'

I never did put her on the lead again.

We walked on, without really being aware of it, along the river. It follows the road for a while through the village. Walking against the flow, you reach the remains of an old weir which goes back to the flax-swinging days, when this area added to the miles of rope produced for the Navy in the square-rigger days. After that the river is lost from view as it fights through vegetation. The path rejoins it in a clearing where cattle drink.

That morning, if I had been concentrating on what was going on, I would have seen a dipper bouncing in the flow. I could hear ducks on the river higher up, and watched a flight of gulls going overhead.

Milly and I wandered on, lost in our shared amazement, both stunned by our situation; not really chatting but sharing thoughts together on lots of things. As I try to remember how I felt that morning, I cannot find the words to describe my – no, our - wonderment. Just imagine it, if you can.

We wandered aimlessly on, my leg just beginning to be a bore and starting to hurt. I needed to sit, and recall feeling slightly lost. It had, after all, been nearly a year since I had been remotely near here, and we were a long way off the path.

As I negotiated a muddy patch, trying to move from one grassy bit to another, I was made dreadfully aware how poor my balance was. Then I saw a sign, tucked away by the side of a grass track to what appeared a ruin. It said 'WARNING – beehives - keep your distance'. I am really allergic to stings, so I changed track right away, back to the main tractor track. This would lead back to the river path, I was sure. But on turning round, we were surprised.

'Found me, have you?'

I looked around and standing there, in a green moleskin shirt and jeans, was the man from the orchard who I had seen at the hospital. To say I was confused would be an understatement.

'I'm sorry' I muttered, starting to walk on.

'Wait, I want to say hello. Frankly, we need to talk.' He fixed me with a look, and then a grin.

'Don't worry, I'm not a lunatic you know. I have followed your progress for probably – well, how old are you? It must be nineteen years.'

I was aware of the media stories that had cropped up about what sometimes happened to unlucky kids when they met strange men. I was on guard.

'I saw you in our orchard a while ago, one cold morning' I said.

'You did, but I also saw you in hospital, and before that on the hill. I watched you being whipped off in an ambulance. How are you now? No, don't tell me.' He waived a hand in the air. 'You look worn to a frazzle, come and sit down. I think you have overdone it. Come on, it's quite safe. I'm not dangerous you know.'

He turned and began to walk to the barn, not looking around. Milly looked at me. 'Go on' she thought to me. 'I can take him on if we have problems. He's skinny and weak. I will look after you, don't worry.'

You may think how lucky I was, with a great wolfhound as my mate and bodyguard. Looking back on it, I can't say enough how she helped my recovery.

I followed on, into the remains of the barn. It was hard to imagine that anyone lived in it. It appeared to consist of falling slabs of stone. An old blue door, with paint falling off, led inside. We stopped at the door. I called 'hello' and went in.

The man was bent over an open hearth, above which, on a hook, hung a kettle. The room was full of deerskins and smelled of newly-crushed bracken. It was a strong and pleasant enough smell, though try as I could, no bracken met my eye. There was some old, heavy furniture, including an old oak table in the corner with a pile of newspapers. In the corner a hen was sitting contently, on eggs presumably. A curtain crudely hung on pegs in the riverside corner and through it could be seen a rough bed of sorts. The roof had obviously been thatch originally but was now lashed up with tin sheets.

My new friend looked up.

'Find a pew' he said. 'Your mate is fine wherever she wants.' He waved at Milly. He returned to the pile of sticks in the hearth, picked two of them up and held them. Then he began muttering. He started to half-sing something, rocking a little. Slowly at first a small wisp of smoke began, then a handful of flame caught the wood. He shoved the burning sticks under the kettle, looking at me.

'Tea?'

I nodded, stunned by what I had just seen.

It would be fair to say that my memory is poor after forty-odd years. I know I stayed there talking to him and listening for perhaps an hour; it would be best described as chitchat. He asked me a lot of questions and listened quietly to the answers. The tea, I do remember, had an odd taste. After it I remember feeling great.

After we had been nattering for an hour my cellphone went off, the ring tone making its normal joke noise. It was my anxious mother.

'Where are you Peter? I've been getting worried, what are you doing?'

'Just having a rest, that's all. By the river. Don't worry, I'm fine.'

'I'll come and pick you up, you've been ages. Are you by the bridge?'

'I could be' I said.

'I'll be there in half an hour.'

Like all mothers, her voice gave away her worries.

'I have to go' I said.

He nodded, raising a hand. 'There are a few things we will need to cover' he mumbled. He seemed reluctant to look at me, but then he seemed to pluck up courage and his eyes fixed me. The scar on his face was almost crimson.

'Now is not the time, but there are some private things you should know' he said. 'Important things. You and I are different from others.'

To say this confused me was another understatement. He seemed to be stuck for words. Then came the remark of all remarks.

'Your hound?'

I held Milly's head. 'What of her?' I said, a little annoyed and very protective.

He paused, as if gathering strength. 'Well, I watched you earlier by the river. You can talk to her, is that right? She told me by the river. Milly, isn't that right?'

The dog stood between us, wagging her enormous tail.

'Sorry, I forgot to tell you' she half thought and half mouthed to me.

I was amazed and rather frightened. I looked at him in fear. He understood Milly as well.

'Come on. You had better go. Your mother will be here.' He smiled at me, getting slowly to his feet, his joints cracking, pulling an old jumper over his head.

'This is not fair, how do know?' I stammered, my damaged speech coming back with a vengeance. 'Who are you? I don't even know your name.'

'No need to worry, you and I are the same thing. I have been known as Myrddin, but if you want to call me a name you are more familiar with, my predecessors were better known as Merlin.'

He cocked his head on one side, giving me a quizzical look. His eyes seemed to hold me. 'No one calls me that now. I was christened Julian. Jules will be fine.'

I went through the door, Milly ahead of me. Outside it was beginning to drizzle. Pulling the collar of my jacket up, I looked across at him, walking with us. Ever polite, I found myself automatically thanking him. I was trying to outwalk him, but at that stage a slow amble was all I could manage.

'I need to see you again, there is a lot to tell' he said.

'I haven't got long, when? I've got the hospital over the next days. There's my mum.' I was trying to run.

'Come and see me, as soon as you can' he said. 'I'm always around here. Bring Milly.'

I hurried on to my mother's waiting car and bundled Milly in through the tailgate.

CHAPTER 4

SPECIAL POWERS

It was two weeks before I saw him again, two weeks during which there were many hospital visits. I was driven to the outpatients at the local cottage hospital. Wearing tracksuit bottoms, I was persuaded to hop and stand on one leg. I went on a running machine and was taken to the point of embarrassment many times. The speech therapist got me talking louder and slower, and to say the least was very thorough.

One fine morning with the smell of cut grass hanging in the air, I had stopped on my limited walking at the village bridge. The river here is no more than a few yards across, varying in depth between four feet and four inches. It is divided in a few stretches by bars of shingle and weeds. This morning it was gin clear, and I stopped to lean over the metal bars that edged it where the road crossed.

I watched a crayfish slowly working the margin, its pincers trolling the stream. Further down the stream I could see a trout waving slowly in the flow.

A woodpecker drummed a tree in the distance. The lambs called for their mothers and a young girl rode her horse by. I was a bit lost at the time, not really concentrating, when a deep voice said, 'Good morning again.' A brown, thin hand grabbed the rail I was leaning on.

I turned to look straight into his face. He was now wearing an old T-shirt with the words of a well-known fizzy drink on it and old jeans and a pair of trainers, and leaning on a massive stick. I could not help noticing that the skin on his face, neck and hands was virtually translucent, veins coursing under the surface. He was deeply tanned with piercing blue eyes that held me, try as I might to avoid them

'I thought you might come and visit me, Peter.'

'I've had the hospital' I replied.

He started to make small talk; I cannot remember exactly what we talked about. After a while he lifted a hand and said. 'Don't be worried, but I have to show you something.'

He went very quiet. Then he began to murmur. At the time I could not understand a single word.

After a few minutes he lifted a hand to the river and with a fine, sharp, whistling call a bright blue kingfisher arrived in a flash of lightning. The bird landed on his outstretched hand and whistled to him. Then it flew back the way it had come. I can remember to this day, thirty years later, how it amazed me, though now it is easy for me to do the same. But his next trick stunned me.

'They are pretty things' he muttered. 'Now watch this.' He sounded as if he was ordering something or someone.

Even on telling this sounds ridiculous, but now I can do it. This does not really help you at this stage of my memoirs, but as I will explain, there is a purpose, need, or power.

I am aware that we live in a world of space travel, electron power, gene splicing and so on. This memory is painful for me. It brings back my absolute fear at the time and I am aware it will test your credulity. There is more to come that will need your concentration.

'Look at that cloud, the small one' he ordered, somewhat fiercely. I looked up.

'Which?'

'There is a gap, between the small one in front of the big lump of blue.' He pointed.

'Sort of over the farm' I said.

He nodded, and I watched. He appeared lost in thought, both arms raised skywards. Many strange words half emerged from his mouth. He was humming, with a rocking motion. To be honest, being young I felt amusement rising, then a touch of boredom. After a while I must admit I felt a slight fear for him, for what he was doing to himself and for what I was seeing.

There was a reasonable wind blowing, pushing the clouds seawards. Then I saw the small cloud stop. It froze in the sky. I froze myself, not believing what I saw. If I am honest, I wanted to run in terror.

My eyes shifted rapidly between the cloud jammed in the sky and him. He was very obviously in some pain, gripping the rail with both hands. His eyes had lost their colour and his body shook violently. His eyes flickered back to normal and he shuddered and half fell towards me. I can remember to this day looking back skywards; the cloud had resumed its course. He collapsed into my arms, muttering many words that were incomprehensible.

We stayed possibly for ten minutes like this with him panting and worn out.

'I know I asked before, but what or who are you?' I whispered.

After a while longer he stood up. 'This is difficult to explain' he whispered. I almost had to bend my head to hear.

'Peter, you and I are the same, No, don't be frightened, you were chosen, like me.'

It is difficult for me to find the words to describe the next half hour. He whispered, obviously worn out, 'There is so much to explain, so much. And I have so little time.'

'What on earth are you getting at?'

'Do you believe in a god?' He seemed to change track.

'Look, believe in a god, that's fine, necessary for some. However for many many years, in fact forever, there has been a much more relevant force. A god, call it what you will. It is being badly neglected at the moment by one and all.'

He paused again for what seemed an age. 'Look, promise you will come and see me. Tomorrow at say three, any good? I have to go and rest now.'

'Yes, fine.' I looked at him as he shuffled off, dragging his stick. His body was racked; he shuffled away, almost bent double.

'Are you really ok?' I called after him. He did not turn or answer, just lifted a hand.

I can remember thinking, who is he, and why me? I learned in time what he meant and I am trying to remember for you the order in which the rest of my life changed.

CHAPTER 5

MEMORIES OF WAR

Over lunch the next day, I inadvertently-on-purpose asked my father about Jules. Over shepherd's pie and then rhubarb crumble, he admitted that he did not know much.

'He keeps himself to himself, that chap. I know Tom uses him occasionally.' He seemed to pause with a mouthful. 'He gets his cottage for free. Been there for years, well at least since we moved in here, which has got to be fifty years. I don't really know much about him, seems harmless. Why? You met him?'

I replied that I had, in a non-committal way. The chat went in another direction.

After coffee, Milly and I left the house. We walked down through the orchard into the field. Overhead a few house martins screamed about and I watched them charging about the sky. The day was fairly warm already, with the hedges and trees greening up.

On the far hill new lambs ran about as the valley felt summer coming. We walked down to the river and through the gate on to the lane. On this route we went past the old school house, which has since been bought and done up. Leaving the edge of the village, we went up the nearly overgrown track to the ruined barn where Jules lived.

A small plume of smoke was emerging from the chimney. I called out by the door and heard him reply. We went in. Inside it was nearly dark, and in a corner under a blanket was Jules.

'You all right?'

Milly went over to him, getting her head rubbed, her tail going nineteen to the dozen.

'I'm all right, just been having a kip. I'll put the kettle on.' He threw back his blanket, and went over to the fire, slowly.

'No, I'm fine, not for me, just had a late lunch' I responded.

'Yes, but I could do with one, I'll make it anyway.'

I did not argue, and let him get on with it. My eyes wandered around the room, seeing more bundles of skins, piles of clothes, plates, and in the corner lots of newspapers.

'It's cosy in here, been here a long time?'

'Oh, a while.' He came over we two mugs of tea. 'There is no sugar I'm afraid, but you won't need it with this.'

He wandered round the room, drawing back the odd curtain. More light entered and I could see him better. Milly, having sniffed around, had obviously settled down in front of the glowing embers and was nodding off.

For all the visits and meetings to that date, I remember that this was the first time I had been aware of his age. His eyes looked rheumy, his body more than usually bent. I noticed that he had a fine tremor to his hands, and was walking around with a more shuffling gate than I remembered.

He caught my eye and smiled,

'We need to share a few things' he said. He grinned, then almost scowled. The scar on his face, which looked purple and quite dreadful, blanched with his grin.

'Don't think I'm being nosey, but that scar, how did you get it? It must have hurt a lot. Looks dreadful. You don't have to tell me, I'm just intrigued.'

He looked at me, half serious, then half smiling.

'Don't worry, you are not nosey. Funnily enough it's more than half relevant to what you have to know.' He looked almost sternly at me. 'I need to sit to tell you a bit' he muttered, moving to a beaten-up old chair in the corner.

He began by asking me if I had heard of the evacuation of Europe through France during the war. Of course I had. It had been ghastly, he said, his eyes getting even more watery.

'All the troops had to be taken off. A call went out on the radio and it became imperative that any boat was needed to help. I was like you, possibly even younger and had, let's say a friend, who could fly over.'

At this stage he looked at me, a firm look on his face. I must admit to being rather worried by his look. I now know what he was meaning and who he was referring to.

'Shola got us over there, and it was truly horrible. It was impossible to fly anyone back, so I spent the time talking to and comforting the badly injured and dying. I had to be careful the odd soldier wondering who I was and how I had appeared. The shells were going off, explosions, men crying out, all around the dead.'

He paused, silently replaying the horrors he had seen. I kept very quiet, not wanting to intrude. After a time he continued. He said he had stayed there for two days, helping as he could. I did not ask at this point who Shola was or what he or she had done.

All around him had been dead or dying men. Men waded into the sea to waiting boats which got as near as they could.

He shook his head, and I remember his eyes filled and his hand holding his tea shook.

'After two days we could do no more. In any case the Germans were nearly there. Shola took off and we looked down at the dreadful confusion. Without warning a shell went through her right wing and burst above us. I felt immense pain in my head and passed out. I came around after perhaps thirty minutes to find we were still flying and far out over the channel, Shola fought to fly, her wing only just working. I was covered in blood. I tentatively explored my face and head. I could not see out of my right eye, and I could feel bone from my hairline to my lip.'

He looked at me.

'The rest is boring. We somehow got back and I spent three months in hospital. This face is the result. Shola stayed here, keeping as still and hidden as she could.'

'Hidden?' I said. 'Why? She had surely done a brave job.'

'Yes, she had.' He looked at me. 'She did recover. You will see her soon.'

I must admit that at the time my admiration for him was immense. He was so matter of fact. I was more than marginally intrigued to meet this Shola lady, who like him must be getting on a bit.

'Look' he said. 'There is a lot to tell you. I am not sure how, where or what to begin with. I cannot really remember how it was all explained to me. I will need you with me in three weeks, a month before the longest day. Will you remember to come? Be here late evening, I have to show you something.'

He looked urgently at me. I nodded and said that I would. I can remember wondering how I would get out of the house.

I picked myself up to go, signalling with my outstretched hand for him to stay put.

'I'll be back here somehow, I promise. On that Thursday.'

He half smiled to me and nodded and I left, Milly sniffing ahead.

I remember how he had said or implied that we were the same. What on earth did he mean? I was beginning to get alarmed.

CHAPTER 6

A VISION IN THE WOODS

From what I remember, those three weeks went really quickly. Although I was limited in what could be done physically, a little was possible.

My family, as you may have gathered, had a small farm. Lambing started at that time. We only had forty sheep, which had been brought in for their safety, if nothing else, from fox predation of newborn lambs. This meant numerous day and night visits to feed water and check the ewes. My parents were now happy for me to wander up the hill on my own to do this.

Unfortunately I still had no strength at all. If I ever tried to kneel down to help out a ewe, I had to crawl to a nearby hurdle to persuade my annoying body back up into an upright standing position. I often walked back home with muddy, straw-coated knees.

This was the time when we began planting an extensive vegetable garden. You will have to imagine me crawling along planting seeds on all fours. I had to drag the bag of seed potatoes along, dropping one in each hole as I went.

CHAPTER 6

I followed the calendar closely, determined to meet Jules again as he had said. Finally that Thursday arrived. It was drizzly and cold. The wind was from the north west, which always brings a temperature drop, and we had nineteen newborn lambs to worry about. Over supper with my mother (my father had gone away on business), I told her to go to bed later and said I would happily check the ewes. I did have my phone, I reassured her.

Later, I must admit that the ewes and lambing sheds got, shall we say, a hurried look. All was well. Ewes were feeding their new lambs and the four left to lamb were not looking at all imminent.

As I walked off the hill and down through the village the rain was just beginning again, a fine drizzle. The hedges on the way were now fully greened, and in the air I could smell new-cut lawns mixed with that sweet, not unpleasant smell of wet dust. Overhead a small but noisy flock of swallows screamed after gnats, their twists and turns defying the laws of physics.

Two cars past me on the lane and I had to move in and stop to let them past. They waved thanks and accelerated on.

The river came into sight, winding along, still very low but now gin clear. A moorhen strutted along on the surface, almost jumping from one patch of weed to the next. Its head was jerking backwards and forwards as it walked, its long yellow legs and wide toes working in rhythm. Soon it went under the bridge and was lost from my view.

The lane bends here by the gamekeeper's house and I stopped to have a transient moment with his two labradors as they jumped up to the fence. Tails were wagging. Now I find it easy, but then I was still unnerved by the new way I could for some reason talk, in a limited way, with dogs.

I had left Milly at home. If I had taken her to check the sheep, Mother would have smelt a rat.

From what I remember Milly and I were getting used to our new thoughts, which were still limited. We were just learning the new, shared language. I vividly remember how my father found Milly and me absorbed with each other. He looked at me very oddly, saying eventually 'That dog gets on with you well', and leaving it at that.

I carried on walking up the track to Jules' barn, shack, shed - call it what you will. In the yard I found him with three children in tow. They all looked at me, the youngest shooting behind him.

'Ah, Peter!' he smiled. 'Come on you lot, home time, it's getting late.'

He bent down to give each a playful rub on their head. They skipped about, saying their goodbyes to him, all playing about. The two bigger ones said goodbye to me. The little one was too shy. She jammed a thumb in, twizzled around to smile and ran on.

'They are the boss's kids, in case you wonder. I have seen them grow up, like my own.' He looked proud for a moment. 'Anyway, you and I have a fair way to go, blessed weather. Let me get a jacket.' He shot off towards his door at a half run. Then he reappeared, thrusting an arm into his old coat and looking at the sky.

'We've got about half an hour's walk. You'll be about three hours. All right for time, no one to worry?' He began to walk briskly out of the yard.

'No I'm fine. What on earth are we doing?' I was struggling to keep up. I still had trouble walking then and was rather too good at falling over. Sadly, all these years later nothing has changed.

'Look, I'm sorry but since my accident I just can't do fast, can you slow a bit?'

He looked around at me. 'Sorry I forgot, we have enough time I think. Look, as we walk I'll start.'

I know I said I would not butt in any more, but it occurs to me that at this point in my life, my memories, my reality, begins. I promise you I will not do this again.

We walked or half ran out of his yard into the lane and up the hill. As I walked after him I struggled to do my jacket up. The drizzle was now the all-penetrating kind. The light was beginning to go, and we heard a fox calling. He looked at me.

'How you doing?'

'Fine. I am just wondering what the heck we are doing and where we are going.' I caught him up and walked alongside.

'I know, I owe you an explanation. The trouble is, what I have to tell you is a bit tricky.'

We turned off the lane and walked to an old five-barred gate.

'Hang on a bit, I am not very good yet with climbing. My right leg is still rubbish' I said.

'I'll help' he offered.

One aspect of my recovery which annoyed me most then was how useless I was compared to the way I used to be. I climbed up the gate eventually. Then his help with my feet got me over, generating, I have to say, a fair bit of humour.

'The next one unfastens' he reassured me.

We set off across an old, untouched meadow, with the odd suckler cow looking at us, avoiding the numerous cowpats. Then the gate, and onwards towards the local manor house, sitting surrounded by a beech hanger. Rather than go right up to the house, he turned off, down a track on the right. At the bottom many pheasant release pens could just be seen between the trees.

We walked past them, giving a polite 'evening' to the under-keeper we met doing his last rounds.

The track now narrowed, becoming shingled and in places slippery.

'We will need to stop on the side of that small valley there' he said. He pointed down and across a small pond and up the other side.

'Now come on, tell me this is daft, talk to me.'

'Right, I will' he said, looking round. 'But we are a bit pushed for time, so keep walking, and please keep your voice down. I have been thinking how I would get some ideas over to you. There is no easy way. Because you have realised that with Milly things are now different, you just need to listen. Don't butt in. Ask when I'm done.' He was uncharacteristically firm.

I must admit that at the time I was more than a bit wary. I was alone with a comparative stranger. True, I had seen already amazing things. I was aware that my life was now different. I was not able to run, I had a job shouting, and I was now a long way from people. Yet he had always been kind, and I had seen that he was trusted with little kids. I did wonder what on earth would be happening.

'A while ago I asked you half-heartedly how you felt about a god' he said. 'No, don't bother answering.' He raised a hand without turning. 'It is fine to believe in any god, people do, and it helps them. Older than that though, there have been ancient forces, gods, spirits, call them what you will. They have run the world and still do. This will sound completely mad, ridiculous, far-fetched. But as I will show you now, it is true. What you are about to see has been going on for centuries. My job and your job is to witness and hopefully make sure it always happens. Without it – well, who knows?'

We had reached the edge of the pond. We walked around the

muddy edge before tackling the climb up. He put a finger to his lips in a 'keep quiet' gesture.

'I will just explain that I have already seen this for fifty-odd years' he said. He bent towards me and whispered 'I know that you will see it for the next fifty, after me.'

To say I was dumbfounded would be inadequate. To this day I can remember exactly what followed.

'Now, we must be quiet. Sit down on the other side so we can look down. I will explain everything you see on the way back. Be quiet, not a sound. We have, looking at the light, perhaps twenty minutes.' He nodded at me and I nodded back. He stressed again that on the walk back I would understand all that I would see. He would, he promised, explain.

We rounded the small crest of the hill and half slithered down, possibly ten yards, to a big holly bush. He beckoned to me to go in. By the time we were settled on the dead leaves below it, it was almost dark. I heard a pheasant calling, and then a rabbit cried out at the pounce of a stoat. The wood on the edge of the valley was in night mode.

Almost above us, a tawny owl screeched. Jules looked across at me and smiled, pointing up.

After what seemed ages, but in reality was perhaps ten minutes or so, he nudged me. Putting a hand to my ear, he whispered 'Three forwarders'.

I looked below and could make out three fallow deer making their way silently along the valley floor. I sat up a bit more to see, but Jules' arm came across to push me back down. We carried on watching as the deer moved on, their ears twitching to and fro, their heads turning. You could see them scenting the air.

After a few moments, Jules rubbed my arm and pointed down. To my amazement two foxes and three badgers were following, perhaps eighty yards behind. I stayed still, watching. They went after the deer, walking slowly, their noses on the ground then back in the air.

Then a faint sound of bells sounded, not in harmony but very musical. I felt Jules tighten his hand on my arm. The noise of the bells got louder and sweeter and then, for a fleeting moment, I saw an amazing vision.

There appeared a very tall, slender woman with long blonde hair. Her hair would have reached the small of her back and was so fine that it flew out behind her. She was dressed in a long white gown with a brown leather belt. It was impossible to see her feet, hidden by the gown, but they made no noise. She seemed to glide. Try as I may I cannot describe her face; she never looked directly up.

All around her was a blueish white light. It travelled with her, enveloping her and spreading for two or three yards around. All the time, to right and left, her arms and hands seemed to be throwing things about. I could not see what they were, but I have assumed that they were blessings or charms. Whatever they were they made no noise as they landed on the dead leaves. I wanted to cry out, to say hello, but I resisted.

She glided on until below us, then half looked up to Jules. To my amazement, with his left arm he took my right and lifted it, at the same time touching his lips with his right hand. He then raised his own right hand straight up in acknowledgement. I knew our presence was noted and acknowledged.

In all too short a time she had crossed the valley floor and gone. The music of the bells faded to silence and the strange light went.

I can remember how overcome I was, how stunned.

I could not believe what I had seen. She was an achingly beautiful woman, spirit, being, goddess; even now I have no words to describe her beauty.

Slowly Jules got to his feet, giving me a hand to pull me up. It was now very dark under the trees. My balance was not marvellous and I was grateful for his help.

'Who or what was *that*?' I stuttered. 'She is beautiful! Where does she live, where is she going, where has she been? Quick, tell me, please!'

'I had the same reaction' he said. 'Isn't she amazing? I will tell you as promised, but we have got to get you back.' In the darkness I could make out his grin.

We made our way back around the pond, which was showing a moon shadow. Then back up the track to the side of the manor, with me trying desperately not to slip.

'I'll talk for a while, you listen' he said. 'I want to begin telling you in a sensible order. I still remember the first time I was shown her. All those years ago.' He stopped as if remembering.

'I was stunned. Still am. I have seen her many times as I said, but still am simply in awe. Have you ever heard of Beltane?'

'Isn't that some pagan thing?'

'Pagan is a ridiculous word, it implies all sorts of things. No, before it got hijacked. It is remembered or venerated; I suppose that's the word, to mean a blessing. The May Queen, that sort of thing. Rightly so, it is imperative she happens. It is admittedly ancient, but for most it has become a ritual, an excuse. The meaning, the true significance, has been lost.'

I wondered where this conversation was going.

'You have just seen the person, spirit, goddess, call her what you will, who ensures the land wakes properly after the winter. She walks on all the land I believe and always comes through this part of Dorset on this night. She has done so since time immemorial and will do so forever. I was told to witness her and was shown her like you, many years ago.'

He looked at me. 'You were chosen, if I recall properly, when you were about six, to follow me.'

He stopped talking for a while to allow this to sink in.

'This is how the word Beltane arose. Now you also know the true significance.'

We walked around the edge of a new cereal crop.

I paused, thinking. 'But what on earth do you mean, chosen? Who by, and why? And don't I get a say in it?'

'No, but you will hear from Shola the full situation very, very soon, for sure.'

He paused, again as if thinking what to say next. 'Yes, that name again, but I simply cannot say more, it is not my job.'

He paused again as if struggling to find the words. 'It is enough to say that you and , are have become different... without blowing your mind.'

He playfully turned and squeezed both my arms.

'We, or shall I say you, will now carry centuries of force, tradition, lore, call it what you will. Yes, weird isn't it? It will not affect your future too much.' He pulled a sarcastic face.

'You may think... no... but seriously, you have become vital to the continuity of the future. I do not want to sound too dramatic, but you are different now, linked to your past and involved in the future. You are my replacement.'

I can remember clearly that at the time this sounded vaguely frightening, not what I wanted. The future I thought was mine was gone, taken away from me, controlled by… what?

'Look, I don't want to sound pathetic or a kill joy. I had plans. Limited, admittedly now' I said.

We carried on walking, without talking. The church clock in Netherbury chimed the quarter. I looked at my watch and was stunned to see that it was nearly midnight.

'We have to check the ewes still' I said.

'I'll help, I'll come with you.'

We walked on, helped by the moonlight and a myriad stars. Jules said again that I had been chosen as a young man, like him. That believe it or not, my own replacement had already been chosen. He hinted that the trade-off was some extra powers - gifts - call them what you will.

'You can, like me, talk to your dog, but have you tried asking her about horses? She has told me something you perhaps have not tried yet' he grinned.

'Look, I know that tonight has been an awful lot.' He took my arm. 'But there are long traditions lined up for you. You may not feel it, but you are about to be even more honoured. You have joined a long unique story. And no, you do not get any choice. Apart I suppose from killing yourself.' he laughed. 'Look, these ewes are fine, lets get you back.'

We walked away from the lambing sheds down the hill.

'Finally I want to say that Shola will explain everything. She did for me. All will be clear then. In the morning, tackle your dog Milly - promise. She knows more than you can imagine, and she's waiting for you to ask. We will meet Shola a month after midsummer, not long, just a while.'

'She will be back then? Is she away?'

'Not really away… you will see though. It will all make sense then, I promise. One thing though.' He looked intently at me. 'We are seriously talking about an honour here, not for everyone. If you mention anything to anyone from now… well, I shall not say what will happen, but it is not good. And don't worry, it's never yet been done. All your – our - past holders have been fine.'

I promised, said goodnight and went on in. Jules watched me until I opened the front door. I can imagine he walked back as I did forty years later, wondering if I would reject or go with the story.

CHAPTER 7

BACK IN THE SADDLE

As you can probably imagine sleep came fitfully that night, in fact it was virtually non-existent. I gave in and got up early, grabbing Milly, and we left the house to check the lambing sheds. Milly agreed to make her own way when we got nearer, and keep a field away so not to worry the new mums.

The morning was one of those marvellous early summer ones, everything still, the new light already bright, no one about. The rooks on the far village edge were busy and already house martins were hunting the air. At times they flew breathtakingly low over the hay lay, catching the odd fly, or going high to yell at each other and for the joy of life.

The new mums and their lambs were all quiet, lying deep in their straw. The last due ewes were no different, all peaceful. At that time I had none to feed on the bottle, so I called Milly and began to walk down the hill and home. The wolfie trotted at my side. We had developed a way of thinking and whispering thought and we began to chat.

'Last night I was told that I should ask you about a horse' I said. I paused as we walked. 'It's mad that you and I can talk as we do – it's limited I know, but wonderful. No one would believe it.'

The wolfie did not answer, but trotted along at my side.

'Have you gone deaf?' I joked, playfully pulling at her tail.

'No, just trying to think what you mean by horse.' She half turned. If you are a dog person you will understand when I say that she was grinning.

'I see, you know Caspian and my father's other horse, in the stables at home?'

She thought back 'All right, now I know. That's what you call them - I see.'

We walked on, Milly agreeing to make the initial contact. She said she did vividly recall my accident on the hill, and later when coming first home from the hospital. Caspian had been scared silly. She was worried how he would take a similar concept. I would leave it to her, I promised.

Over breakfast mother asked about last night, and I got away with it by saying that it had taken a while to settle the ewes. In any case she had gone to bed early. She cleared up the bowls, cereal packets and marmalade jars and I wandered into the garden. The horses were now turned out into the home paddocks, on their holidays you might say. No rugs were needed, shoes were taken off. They were just checked and talked to daily.

I wandered into the orchard, to see Milly trotting to find me.

'How did you get on, any luck?' I thought to her.

'Come on it's fine, done it, should be all right, not happy though.'

I followed the hound to the paddock. Now I will cut this short for you, but imagine it if you will. The old horse stood twitching his tail under a tree, shaking his head to get the flies off. His head turned to me as Milly and I approached and I could see his legs stiffen and his head come right up. He looked ready to charge off.

Milly sent strong thoughts of reassurance to him, which I too picked up on.

'It's all right, big boy' I said softly, walking up to him.

There followed one of the strangest meetings I have ever had, which is saying something, as you will realise. Suffice it so say that Jules was dead right. My injury gave me gifts in compensation, reward for the job, call it what you will. You cannot imagine how marvellous it has been over the past thirty years, having this ability to talk to animals. It is not really talking, nor thought alone. In fact it's impossible to describe, but it means we have no barriers once some initial phrases are known and shared. In a world where money is vital, this gift has meant that on finishing university I have been able to earn a living using it.

The horse, the hound and I stayed together all morning and I eventually left when I was called to lunch by my mother. She found me with my arms wrapped around his old head, bent down towards me. If she had got closer she would have seen, and I remember it well, that I unashamedly cried again with joy, just as I had with Milly.

Milly, Caspian and others are now long in the ground, but as I said earlier all the hounds and horses I have had since have been stunned that I can talk to them in this unique way.

After lunch Caspian and I met again, me carrying his bridle. I made sure that I was not visible from the house. Gently I put it on.

It is relevant to this part of my memories that at this point I had no strength. I could not really bend or weight bear to well on my right leg. On realising this, to my amazement, Caspian got down on the ground, folding his forelegs under him. Milly watched, willing me on. By lying on his back and turning I ended up sitting on him. I was so pleased. Then, with my hands locked in his mane, he started to his feet. I lay flat to meet his rising fore end and then back as he got his enormous back legs under.

After a bit of walking and about ten yards of trotting, I simply lay flat on his back, laughing out loud. I could not believe my luck.

Without a saddle Caspian said he could control my balance more easily, reacting to any shift in position. I lay with my face buried in his mane. Both horse and hound were ecstatic.

After perhaps an hour the horse lay down with me clinging on, then allowing me to roll off. Hanging on to his mane, I pulled myself to my feet and gave him a massive hug. If you ride or love horses you will understand that having ridden all my life, having this accident and then this happening was simply wonderful.

I walked back up to the house carrying the bridle.

'I saw you doing that. It was stupid and dangerous!' said my mother. 'You must be mad. What would your consultant say? He would be cross to say the least!' she shouted.

I tried to explain that Caspian was really safe and that I had only walked.

'You have been told that another bang on your head will kill you.'

'I'm careful, don't worry.'

There followed perhaps half an hour of me defending myself. She was obviously more than worried and this drove her conversation. Peace returned only when I promised to try it again only with my father present. I made tea for us both, grovelling, and gave her a hug. I realised though that damage had been done, some trust lost.

The following day father had Caspian tacked up. He was not aware of course how the horse had helped me to get on the day before. By climbing on to an old water trough I was able to get into the saddle. Caspian was so well schooled that in fact he was easy to ride.

As he was without shoes, we were limited to the top field. My father stood in the middle as around in a big circle we went, initially limited to walking and finally a small trot.

After a while we walked back to the stable yard, with me promising faithfully that progress would be limited. I had one fairly major problem though - getting off. On the way Caspian had reached the same conclusion.

'Wait here while I get your mother to help get you off' said my father. As soon as he left the yard, Caspian simply thought to me 'wait'. Then he dropped his forelegs like an animal in a circus, bringing me low enough to lie down and rotate myself off. He had just got up when they appeared.

'No problem, there we are.' I lifted both arms and gave a mock bow.

'Well' said father, looking across at mother. 'Put him back in the field, then come in.'

Later some sort of harmony returned. On reflection it must have seemed mad to my parents for me to be riding again after my injury just eight months before.

Over the following months the time I was allowed to ride increased, until with Caspian reshod I was allowed out. It was heaven, and to ride a horse I could talk to was unreal.

CHAPTER 8

JULES EXPLAINS MY DESTINY

I met Jules again out walking with Milly three weeks later. If I am honest I had tried to keep some room between us for a while, following the events of that night.

'Hello again, how's things?' he asked, rubbing the wolfie's ears.

'Oh, not bad' I answered, looking at him.

He seemed to have aged. His chin carried uncharacteristic wisps of stubble. His eyes looked baggy and sunken.

'Everything all right with you?'

'Yes, all right… but we have so little time.'

He stopped talking, looked anxious and stayed quiet.

'Time for what?'

'You will see.'

Again he paused, one of those long silences that would become common. I waited, not wanting to say anything.

'Did you find that night makes sense now, you happy with seeing that?' he asked, looking straight at me.

'I wasn't sure' I replied. 'I need to know more. Such as why me? What's it all for?'

'Look, I remember when it was first explained to me' he said, holding both my shoulders and standing in front. 'Remember that like it or not, you, like me, have been chosen. We are different, we have a position, if you like to call it that. You are now part of a history that goes back seven hundred years.'

He paused and smiled at me. 'As I have said before, Shola will get it all straight to you.'

'Her again.'

'Yes, you must wait… I am forbidden to say more. But I can say, explain… more about what we saw together.'

I called back Milly, who was wandering forward. 'All right, go on then' I said, turning to him. 'Start at the beginning.'

As we walked together he did so.

He had been witnessing her progression, vision, call it what you would, for many years. It was always the same date, come rain or gale. No, he did not know where she came from. He knows she never stopped walking, from very early spring until late summer.

At this point he stopped, as we had met an elderly lady walking her dog. On passing her he began again.

One of the sad facts he had come to realise was that the forwarders, as he called them were vital. He was not sure, but felt that the lady vision or goddess, call her what you will, did not recognise the presence of roads. They did not figure in her world at all. He paused as if lost.

'The forwarders went ahead. They made sure all ahead was safe. Over the years I have seen many, many… '

He paused again, then turned to me and asked if I had ever seen roadkill animals. Of course - a deer, many foxes over the years, badgers too. Like a revelation, it dawned on me.

'They are her forwarders, protecting her?'

He looked at me with sad eyes,

'Yes, I believe some are. Of course some really are road accidents - it happens. Many have given their lives to guard her way, make sure it is safe, I am certain.'

I was stunned. Milly wanted to know what had been said. I thought the story to her while we walked.

'That has been known for ever among us' she thought back,

I was stunned.

'What, are you joking?'

'No it's true, our lore, call it that. We know about and honour them.'

After a long wait he carried on. 'She is beautiful and does not age at all. She always looks the same age, always equally beautiful. Now I have shown her you, as my replacement. That night was exactly as it happened to me at the start, and I can confidently say that you will do the same for your replacement one day.'

He looked at me and gave me one of his enormous smiles. Then he went on to say that many people had realised that some things were happening, needed by the world. They had formed rituals, ceremonies, some of them laughable. Some, though, were well intentioned. Always the dates were wrong, which in a way was a blessing.

Then he said something I will never forget.

'You have seen our land health guarantor, call her the White Queen if you like. As the year rotates you will see air and water forces as well. This witnessing will be your necessity, your job until you die.'

At this point he went very quiet again, obviously thinking.

'We only have a given time, which is why I know I have to show and teach you a lot from now on, before mine is used and yours begins.'

Pointing at the valley, the sky with its scudding white clouds and the river down below, he turned to me.

'Can you imagine? Feel the force behind all that. Look again at those trees, the bushes, the grass. It cannot be taken for granted. The forces controlling it all are ancient. It wakes up bees and badgers, drives flowers from the ground, wakes oaks, organises the winds, sorts out the rain.'

He looked straight into my eyes again. 'You saw a fraction of it with me the other night, and with Shola's help and wisdom you are going to see much more. Physics, chemistry, biology at school and university are fine, vital... but behind it all is something you will learn and see. Now I really must not say more, it's not my job.'

He turned and looked away to Milly.

'She, or rather they, know more than you imagine. Look, like it or not, I have shown you your beginning. From now on it is even more real. In a way I am sad that I am so limited in what can be said at the moment.'

He looked kindly at me, holding my arm in his usual manner and smiled.

'Next year you will go with me for my last time, at Midsummer's Day evening, to a special place that my predecessor ordained should be built. Before the year ends you will be with me for recognising the power behind the wind, then the water force. However, in a month you will meet Shola, and all will be explained.'

'Does she have something to do with this?' I asked, kicking at a tussock.

'Oh, very much so, very very much, she chose you all those years ago.'

He paused, looked into my eyes as he said this.

'What is she, some government agency then?'

'No.' he laughed, 'far from it, very far from it.' He almost laughed out loud and had to momentarily turn away. 'No, not an official... older than all regulation, government, officialdom, you will see. I will be with you, just like my beginning. I cannot say more. Will not say more. Wait. Just remember, exactly a month after Midsummer's Day. Come to me late afternoon. Don't worry, we do not have to go far. I will be with you.'

We had reached now the centre of the village, outside the village hall. A group of small children played by the road edge. Jules looked at them and smiled.

'Come on then, home time for you, I am going this way.' He turned towards me.

'Do not forget our meeting. Be safe until then. Enjoy your riding. Yes, Caspian told me this morning when I walked through your footpath.'

He laughed and walked off. Milly and I wandered home, her thinking of supper and me wondering about it all, particularly Shola.

CHAPTER 9

A RIDE ON A DRAGON

The time around midsummer that year was unbearably hot. The ewes had to be sheared, which was a sweaty job to say the least. Every year my father had a local contractor in for the job. They had to be dry, so if rain looked likely it was postponed, or they had to be got in under cover. The shears were sharpened and the ewes dragged one at a time from their adjacent temporary hurdle pens for their annual haircut.

There was only a small number, but it was still backbreaking. I have to admit to feeling guilty for many years for not being able to help properly. Sweeping the yard of daggings, rolling the new shorn fleeces, filling the woolsacks, did keep me feeling useful, I suppose, that year.

With it over, cash changed hands and very welcome cans of beer took over.

Every day the vegetable patch needed watering and weeding and woodpigeons driven off. We had become virtually what you would call self-sufficient and every day we were freezing and pickling, and the jam, chutney and jelly making did not stop.

CHAPTER 9

The day Jules wanted me at his house arrived. Now before I tell you about this I want to say that writing this memory down is extremely difficult for me. I know it was thirty-odd years ago. I have met her many times since, even worked with her, as you will hear. The memory of that first breathtaking visit still makes my hands shake; so much so that it is difficult to type. If you have ever been seriously frightened you will have a rough idea what I mean. Multiply that fear by ten and you will get a better idea. Even now the memory haunts me.

I also need to stress most firmly that I am telling this account, as I said before, because I think it important that people should know. But I have unashamedly censored it so that after reading this you will not be able to replicate it. It is for my successor to carry on, but I have no qualms about you knowing a little, the bare bones. This position carries a long history, and will be secured until the world's end. Now I will finish interrupting by saying that you may find the next truly frightening, for which I apologise. Some will wonder, some may try to dismiss it, some will try to hide by calling it farcical.

That lunchtime went slowly for me. Mother did not usually cook at midday, but as father was out that night she did. The food was tasty, she was a good cook, but it took to me what seemed like an eternity to get through the meal. The chatting was always light, with the odd joke, then coffee followed a dessert. I helped wash up, left Milly asleep in her bed by the stove, and left.

I walked down through the orchard and picked up the path to the bridge over the river. The field this path went through was ours and had been cut earlier in the year for hay. It was still a deep yellow colour with just a bit of new grass showing. We had been seriously short of rain that year, and the fields needed a good soaking.

Overhead a few straggling house martins hunted, adding noisy cries to the sky. These were northern birds working down, gently starting to be drawn on their migration to warmer sites. The rooks from the village edge cawed and spiralled above their old nests in the beech and Scots pines. It was still very warm for that time of year, and you could almost sense thunder coming.

I made a large detour around the buzzing beehives and strolled into the yard. Jules was sitting in an old beaten-up deckchair waiting for me.

'Hello, I was a bit held up by mother's cooking' I apologised.

'Don't worry, she comes only when I call anyway. With her there is no such thing as late. Good lunch?'

'Fine, what about you, you fed, had your grub?'

He nodded a reply, went to shut a loose chicken in and shut his front door. It occurred to me that I had never seen him lock it. He carried an old rucksack by one of the straps, the other missing,

We began walking up the lane out of Netherbury. It joins the main road at the top and we walked along for perhaps thirty yards, keeping in single file against the oncoming traffic. Soon a farm gate allowed us to leave the road, thank goodness, and start our climb up the hill.

We climbed up using an old sheep track, reasonably inclined, up to the bracken-covered edge. A few surprised ewes ran off, one making a noise like castanets, its backside well clinkered up. Jules and I laughed and walked on. Near the top, he stopped for a breather

'Not as fit as I was, getting old' he wheezed. 'You are doing well now yourself, how are things?' He put a hand on his knee and took a few big breaths, leaning forward.

'Oh, getting there' I replied. 'My consultant tells me it will take me another three years to get anywhere near the way I was. I am running a bit – well, fifty yards.'

We stopped making small talk for ten minutes, taking in the fantastic view. We were not high enough up the hill to see over it to the sea yet, but could look back down on the village and the small wriggling road we had walked up on. One or two cars made their way to and fro below us, just audible.

Before moving off, his breathing now normal, Jules looked rather fiercely at me. I remember that look to this day.

'Look, when we get to the top Shola will meet us. Don't ask why' he said. 'But it is really important that you do not look at her eyes. You will see why.'

'Fine' I quickly replied. 'But why? Are they disfigured, is she worried by the look of them?'

'No nothing like that. Shall we say they are dangerous to you. Don't worry, just don't catch them directly.'

Even more mystified, I said that I definitely would not. He appeared reassured, smiled again and we carried on walking to the very top of North Warren hill.

'Anyway' I said, 'How will she know where to find us?'

'She will know' he said.

We got to the top and the views were wonderful. The sea just shone back at us, looking at East Lewesdon Hill. Turning north you could just see over the adjacent escarpment running west-east, over down into the land north of Beaminster. It is not really that high, in the scheme of things, but the view silenced us both for a while.

'Now remember, do not meet her gaze' he said. 'I've got to tell you that normally she just is a few yards away, but as you have not met her before she will take a while to get here, so… how can I say, you adapt, get used to her. All right? She is being very kind to you.'

I nodded. What else could I do? Frankly I was thoroughly mystified, to say the least.

I remember what followed exactly. He cupped his hands together and faced the north east, I suppose roughly in the direction of Wales. Standing very upright he began what is best described as a song, or chant, into his cupped hands. After perhaps five minutes the song got louder. Now it was more like the chants made during a Roman Catholic mass; intense, reverential and never repeated.

All the time his eyes were tight shut, and I stood to one side watching. He began to rock on his heels a little, and the chant increased in speed and volume.

Then, without any warning, he dropped his hands.

'She comes' he said, pointing low in the sky.

Far into the distance I could make out a faint dot against the sky. It seemed to be getting closer.

'She is only doing this for you. Normally she is here now.'

I remember the next thing only too well. Soon the dot took shape, growing into something with flapping wings, making no noise at a distance, still vague. Now imagine my horror, as this dot got bigger and I could see its enormous scale. Two vast wings beat slowly in the air. Its body was rounded, with what looked at a distance to be a tail. As it got nearer I saw that there was no one flying it. It was truly terrifying. I do not mind admitting that I have never been so petrified, to this day. But Jules began to smile. I thought him mad.

The flying shape got nearer and nearer, taking form; I saw a pair of leathery wings, beating with no noise. There was a long neck with a large pointed head. Just in time I remembered that I must not look at the eyes. The upper half was covered in what looked like green leather and the underneath a softer yellowy–gold. The front legs were shorter than the big, powerful hind legs which trailed behind. In all it, or rather she, was huge, as big as a whale. Her skin appeared to be covered in scales, with thorns or spikes running down her back.

'Shola! Welcome again!' shouted Jules.

This was too much for me. I looked around trying desperately to see somewhere to run, to hide. I turned and ran as hard as I could to the side of old stone workings on the ridge, and tucked down as best I could. I do not mind admitting that I peed myself in abject fear. I painfully remember to this day how nauseous every thing was.

Shola was… a *dragon*.

I stayed in a quivering heap, petrified and shaking. I could not believe what I had seen. The stuff of films, children's books and folk tales had answered a call. She had flown in and landed just yards away. I was petrified with the vision. I could not believe any of it.

'Come on, no need to worry' said Jules. 'Your response is normal.' I felt his hand on my shoulder. 'Look, I promise, it's all safe, you are fine.'

I remember lifting my head and looking down to where Shola stood Her eyes were shut. Great wings spread out and the enormous tail was moving from side to side. My eyes were drawn to her enormous sword-shaped claws. On her front legs they were shorter, but I could make out that they were bloodstained. The claws on her back toes were massive and greyish ivory in colour.

She seemed covered in scales, great saucer-shaped plates that moved with her breathing. Her right wing had a large white section, and I recalled that Jules had said it had been damaged during the war.

He noticed where I was looking and must have read my mind.

'Yes, that's her war wound. It took four months of her in hiding to fully recover. You have a good memory.' He smiled at me, taking my hand. 'Come on, she will keep her eyes shut for now, later will do. She wants to know you, talk to you. Yes, she can talk, and yes she speaks English.'

He laughed and we walked down. As we got nearer we could hear, even feel, her breathing, and I have to say that there is a very distinctive smell, not unpleasant, but strange. I have often wondered how it should be described to you. A mixture of leather with new-mown grass, sweet, with a faint tang of citrus. Yes, lemons. Distinctive and very unusual.

Her head, with large eyes tightly shut, was lizard-like or snake-like. Her muzzle finished with two large nostrils, the edges of which twitched with each breath she took. Large belly-gas noises could now and then be heard and now and then you could imagine her groaning, as if she was aching.

'Shola, we are all here now' Jules said, throwing his arms around her great neck. I was stunned as he cuddled her.

'Myrddin, are we complete?' She half thought it, half said it.

This was another truly frightening moment, a dragon talking. I simply could not understand how it was possible. Jules held my hand.

'Look, Shola can talk a little. But she can listen and she wants me now to tell you all. She has told me – no, ordered me to. Listen.'

Sitting on that hilltop, with thunderclouds beginning to boil in the distance, he began.

'Shola chose you when you were six. You will be the new Myrddin or Merlin, to replace me.' He paused, obviously sensing my questions, raising his right hand in a 'hang on' sign.

'She has been with many, all called by her the same during the years of her life. How old you think she owns up to?' he smiled and gave her neck a hug.

'Eight hundred and seventy next year, or thereabouts'

'Your years. May be right' said Shola. Now I swear that dragons can grin.

Jules, still smiling, continued. 'Anyway, possibly over sixty Myrrdins. A year cannot exist without one. They all have a Shola to help. To represent, to keep lore going, to keep humans meaning anything. Over the next year you will see much more. She may need you, you may need her. This is older and more important than modern life. The two exist but we people forget the original driving forces.' He stopped as if allowing this to sink in.

'Over the year I will need you to see some events, I will protect you, but you must see them.'

Shola thought and spoke to me. 'This is now your duty, and you have had us worried.'

'She means your horse falling, all that worry' Jules said, looking at me. 'It nearly meant everything was ruined. You have to know that your episode has meant that some gifts arrived earlier than Shola planned. You had found that dogs and horses could understand you to a new dimension. That's yours, your gift. Me… well I can a little, not as much or as well as you. But I can shapeshift. I will explain later, but go to your history books. You will see that shapeshifting is recognised.'

Shola moved a front claw and stretched, almost yawning, if that is possible.

'Look into my eyes, look at my face' she ordered.

I looked at Jules, who smiled reassuringly.

'It is time, very safe' he said. He nodded, giving her neck another hug. Then, leaning forward, he gently kissed her neck. I moved around in front of those nostrils, the massive face, the great teeth peeping out from under her lip. Then she opened her eyes; and we bonded.

It was glorious, everything nice you can imagine. A great message entered me of support, companionship, and yes, dare I say it, love. It was the best honour you could wish for. I was gloriously happy and at the same time enthralled by the feeling of power coming from her. She was truly truly amazing in every way.

I found myself smiling, wanting to sing and scream with joy. I could not believe any of it. I found myself touching her hard skin, feeling her scales, while through it all she remained very matter of fact. At times she seemed a trifle bored with my reaction, having I am sure had the same from all my predecessors.

'Now, you have one more thing I am afraid that will be shorter than we intended, owing to that horrible black thing that's brewing over there.' Jules nodded to the thundercloud which had nearly moved over us while things had developed. It was ominously dark, very humid, and almost nightlike.

'Can you get the bag I carried up? It's over there.' He pointed to the base of a nearby hawthorn. 'Even dragons have a job with cumulo-nimbus.'

I picked up his bag and took it to him. From it he pulled out a pair of large overtrousers. They were sticky, as if made of cling film.

'Pull these over your jeans. Don't worry, Shola wants you to.'

I picked the trousers up; they felt extraordinary. The legs held together on their own. I looked at her as I wrestled them over my jeans, to see her looking at the sky.

'We will be fine flying away but we need to get back. Come on, this is my time. On with you both.'

'We are *flying*?' I asked as Jules took my arm and pushed me towards her neck.

'Yes, come on, get over her neck behind me. Those trews will give you loads of grip. Trust us, come on.'

I climbed over her neck, with immense trepidation, behind Jules who was already on, home and snug. I unashamedly put my arms around him. With a massive leap, she was airborne. It was the most thrilling thing you can ever imagine, and I was blown away with what was happening.

The feeling of power was extraordinary. I have often asked horses to gallop to feel the surge of power. This was truly exhilarating. I clung on to Jules' jacket as if my life depended on it. In a way, then and afterwards, I have found that the great thorny lumps that run down Shola's spine are a blessing. You can wriggle down between them and feel safer.

We had been airborne for less than a minute when everything below us, each tree, and road down below, disappeared as if forever. Every hedge, far off building, tree, and sheep was lost, to be replaced with a completely new view. I was stunned.

'Where are we?'

'Strange, is it not?'

Shola flew on, her great wings flapping lazily. 'This is why your people in your time do not carry reports of us. This is an equal but parallel time, you might say. I cannot go back to beyond my lifetime, just back. This is different in time. It is hard for me to explain, but in years ahead your people will find us. It will come. Forward travel is impossible, but backwards is not. You are not going mad.'

Below us a single track wound its way out of the valley. I spotted an oddly-dressed man leading a packhorse. The horse half stumbled along, grossly overladen with what looked like bales of cloth or some sort of fabric.

'He will not hear you' Shola thought to me. 'We are too high and I will not allow it.'

We flew on, and although my sticky overtrousers gave me a safe feeling I began to feel rather sick. As if guessing this, Jules turned his head around to me.

'How you doing, you all right? I felt as sick as a pig the first time Shola flew me, but this is a smooth flight.' He smiled, and with his left hand reached back to give me a playful punch.

'I'm OK' I replied. 'Just feel a bit odd, that's all.'

Shola started to circle higher, giving us a brilliant view down to the sea. Then as she turned, a massive thunderclap sounded, as if on top of us. I looked up to see nothing but blue sky. Shola dropped suddenly, as if in a reflex action.

'Bother,' shouted out Jules. 'We get to hear that, even though it is not really us or now. Shola I think that is it for now. Go for the yard if you can.'

'I beat you to that' she replied, carrying on circling and getting higher.

'She really knows her stuff, eh?'

My sick feeling had past, but I was more than a trifle scared.

'Whatever you want to call it' shouted Jules above another thunderclap. 'When she twitches back into our time, if she is above power lines, it is a little embarrassing. Hence her gaining height to have a safe look first. And thunderstorms are full of dreadful currents.'

As he spoke, as if on call, suddenly we were above the village and his yard and dropping like a brick. I almost yelled with fear. We were in the middle of a tremendous downpour.

'Off' Jules shouted as we landed. Shola's great claws splashed into a great puddle.

'I will call, be safe' shouted Jules to Shola, above the noise of thunder and pelting rain.

'Be safe both of you, I will see you soon' she said, and with this she had gone.

Not taken off; just gone. I looked at Jules in amazement.

'I know, she has twitched away. Come on in quick. We are getting soaked.'

We ran in as quickly as we could as a massive lightning flash lit up the sky, followed right away by a loud thunderclap. Barging through his door, we shook what rain we could off. Both of us were soaked.

'Fire and tea, in that order I think' muttered Jules, going across to his hearth. 'Don't bother saying anything until I have begun filling the gaps in. This is something we will need to do for about nine months, I think. Still, listen. You are my replacement, put simply. A new Myrrdin, By the way, she only uses that name. Yes, she is that old, and yes she will be at your call and you at hers.'

He paused, looking up from the teapot. 'As I have told you before, many years ago, when you were small, she chose you. I have watched you now and then, but she has been always aware. You can imagine the fuss caused by your horse falling.'

He looked at me, but frankly I was still a bit stunned by it all.

'Anyway we have two years, that's all, to get ready. You have a lot to learn in those years and much to see with me. I will teach you how to call her. You will learn every other word first, and then each word in between. You would of course get her on your lap if you put it all together.'

He laughed and I smiled back.

'No, I'm joking, but to call her is serious and must be for a genuine reason. This is a must. Do you understand?'

'Of course. The thought of having such a thing on call is incredible.'

'She is now fully bonded to you. She calls in here.' He tapped his head and looked straight at me. 'She always means it.'

He passed a steaming mug of tea over, which I reached out and took. With the other I helped myself to one of the strange biscuits he offered on a plate. As an aside I now make just the same biscuits, and so does my replacement. More of him in due course.

Perhaps this is a moment to interrupt properly. At this moment of writing I am starving and waiting for dinner to be called. I have read some of my memories and am aware that they get stronger as they get nearer to the present.

My injury, I am afraid, played havoc with my memory. You will have to excuse me. You have no doubt realised that I have also just two years to go. As I wrote at the start, I know my own end, as Jules did and as my replacement does now.

We see many things, do many things, to keep it all safe for you. We have had no choice, the job is given. And what a job. At the risk of repetition I will omit the details, of calls, chants, the minutiae. These are for my replacement, but I will carry on telling you what happened to me. Also I suppose what has happened to every Merlin before and from now on until the sun goes out, or more likely when humans have wrecked their planet.

It was now very dark, but the rain had eased off.

'Come on, you had better go and keep your mum happy' said Jules. 'To be honest I do keep forgetting how serious your fall was. You are doing very well. Well done.'

He got up off his chair very slowly, and groaned.

'Give it a few days and wander down, bring Milly. I can now legitimately begin to teach you some things. By the way, well done for not throwing up.'

I smiled back and began to walk out.

'Very nearly. This is all so weird, so... so.... I don't know what. We'll come in a few days. I am going to get going before the next deluge. Tell me though, why have we only got two years...you going away... what will happen then?'

'Well... I will be moving on, shall we say. No, do not worry now. I'll tell you soon, I promise.'

He said his goodbye and I made it up the track to the bridge. The river had already started to rise and was a thick muddy brown colour. A big lump of wood coursed along, followed by a load of paper. As I half ran up through the orchard another massive peal of thunder sounded, and looking across and up the hill I saw a great flash of lightning.

I burst into the kitchen, home safe.

CHAPTER 10

A SUMMONS FROM SHOLA

As I took off my coat another thunderclap split the air, deafeningly loud and seemingly overhead.

'There you are' said mother, looking up. She and my father were leaning on the kitchen stools, looking out at the storm. A pile of dogs lay undisturbed in front of the Aga. Milly and the others lifted their tails in half hearted welcome. As an aside, I have never had a dog that was terrified of storms, and now of course it is not an issue.

'Back again. Did you meet her?' thought Milly to me.

'Sure, I will tell you soon' I thought back. She closed her eyes, as if sleeping.

'You are so close to that dog now' remarked mother with raised eyebrows. 'Ever since your accident. It's nice I suppose.'

Then her eyes went down to my trousers. 'What on earth are those things you have on?'

She came over to me, pushing her stool to one side.

Like an idiot, I still wore the overtrousers Jules had given me.

'Oh, nothing' I glibly replied, trying to think fast. 'I've been helping Jules with his bees. They're protective trousers.'

I started to pull them off, with great difficulty.

'They look sticky. They're not covered in honey are they?'

'No no. I'll give them back in the morning, forgot all about them.' I scrambled them off and tried carelessly to put them in the boiler cupboard.

When you read this you will think I told an awful lot of lies to my folks. Well - think what their reaction would have been if I had nonchalantly said I'd just been riding on a dragon. I think you can imagine their reaction and the calls to their psychiatrist friends... enough said.

The storm and the heavy rain carried on and eventually we all hit the sack. I did not get to sleep until early morning.

The next day everything was truly soaked. The back lawn down to the orchard was covered in windblown twigs. An old apple tree in the corner had lost half its top, snapped off by one of the gusts. It looked very sad.

Looking down through the home paddocks I could see the river. It was flowing at breakneck speed and a thick brown colour, much deeper than normal and full of debris.

The road that crossed it was shut, as the water had come over the bridge and was gushing either side, carving out a fresh course. All the traffic was being diverted apart from the local farmer's tractor, which as if showing off went through easily, the farmer smiling at all the village children who had gathered to watch and throw things into the gushing water.

I had just finished my toast at lunchtime when I suddenly got the most blinding headache. I should explain that since my fall, and obviously because of it, I never had a 'brain ache'. This one lasted a few moments, then went. In place of it came one word: '*now… now… now*'.

I stumbled out of the house and headed for Jules. It seemed the only thing to do. Of course I had to wade the swollen river as it crossed the road bridge. Luckily here it was not too deep, just freezing cold and a sludgy brown colour.

I should add that this caused great merriment to the kids still gathered watching it. They tried a few sarcastic comments, but shut up when I looked at them, my face obviously distorted by my headache memory.

I found Jules waiting for me

'She called then. That is how. You will know now. The next will be lighter.' He smiled reassurance. 'I have to be honest, that is why she wanted to meet you yesterday. It was a shame the weather was so vile. Every year from now on, at this time, you will join her. You have a task as witness. It is normally about now, but varies a bit, at least within two or three weeks.'

He walked back across the yard to the house and turned to shout over his shoulder, 'Where did you put the trews?'

I had to explain about last night, and where they were.

He turned to look scowling at me. 'Very well, you will have to manage without. I do, as you probably noticed. Thankfully you do ride horses.' He turned, shaking his head, and carried on walking in.

'Come on, you' he said, beckoning. 'And tuck everything in, I mean your shirt, jumper, trousers into socks. Leave no gaps. Come in to the barn. It's important.'

I joined him in the barn and he brought in a large spray can. Grabbing me by the shoulders, he made me stand straight. He then began, rather personally to tuck and retuck every join. He gestured to my throat, stressing that my collar must be done up tight. Then of all things he gave me a scarf for around my neck, soaked with the spray can, and on top of this a hat, which he rammed on.

'Later, I will explain.'

He then started to do the same to his own clothing. We stood there like twins.

'Right, close your eyes, hold your breath, do not move. You will do this to me in a moment.'

He then began to spray me from head to toe in what can only be described as if for chemical warfare. He told me through his mask that it was a very powerful flea killer and repellent.

We went through the doors into the yard, me hoping no one would see.

'Sit there a moment' ordered Jules. 'She comes.'

He cupped his hands, and I heard the faint rhymed calling.

Without delay, making my ears pop with the pressure, the amazing Shola appeared. 'Quick!' she ordered, and with a pathetic leg raising and jumping I was on behind Jules. Then all the familiar sights of his yard disappeared.

'This is normal for about now' thought Shola to me. 'You are needed to witness.'

I looked down at the familiar hills and copses to see that they had changed. The river below us looked bigger, faster and more lined with trees. Away to the south could be seen the twinkling sea. As we got higher I could look north to Beaminster, much smaller, but in the right place. The air was smooth and Shola's efforts minimal. Every time she moved her wings forward in a beat the full force could be felt through my backside and legs... extraordinary, and so strong.

'Yes, we are local' called Jules back to me. 'Look, that is what we call the posy tree down there. We are not going far in distance, but we are travelling in time.'

Shola spoke at this point. 'This was started by a previous Myrrdin. He called me. Needed me. Now I watch and each year need you to witness what I do, need to do, and must do. Sometimes, in fact most years, more than once is needed.'

'This I'm afraid is a horrid wake up' said Jules, turning to me. 'Below us is the plague. I know it sounds far fetched, ridiculous, but we are in the late 1300s.'

'What?' I screamed, 'It cannot be possible.'

'I know, I know, but look down and see. No cars, Just cob houses. Shola said she can go back and she has.'

I do not mind admitting that this whole concept at the time blew me away. I felt sick with worry, thinking of my home, mother, Milly. Now when Shola does this with me I am more prepared, though it is still mighty strange. She cannot go forwards, or back beyond her lifespan. She reassuringly tells me that the boffins will find out how eventually.

We flew on with me clinging even tighter to Jules' jacket. I can remember that at the time I really wondered - why me?

She lazily began to circle until below I realised I could see what I had known from childhood as the posy tree, although when I had known it as a boy it had been riven by lightning or fire, I forget which. I could look down to the west to see a small, church-dominated hamlet which I realised then was my home, Netherbury. To the opposite direction must be the scattered cottages of Mapperton and Melplash. I can remember that as I relaxed a little with the concept I strained to look around. Shola glided on, looking from right to left.

'Why are we here?' I whispered to Jules.

'You will sadly see' thought back Shola. 'I hope this time not for many.'

Jules turned around to me, his finger on his lips.

'Let her concentrate, you will see why she was summoned by our predecessor.'

After what seemed a while I saw a procession coming up the hill.

'They cannot see us' thought Shola to us. She circled lower and looking down I was horrified to see that it was a funeral procession. Two carts led the way with oddly-dressed people accompanying them. On the beds of the carts, both pulled by hairy and pathetically bony ponies were four shrouded bodies. Walking some yards behind was a group of people wailing and along with them holding hands with older people were two children. One I remember was looking around with tear-soaked features, drawing some comfort from a sucked thumb. The whole group looked tired from walking up the hill, and immensely sad. I looked down sympathetically, wanting to help. The whole sight was dreadfully sad.

'They are taking black death victims to the plague pits on Warren Hill' though Shola to us. 'Netherbury will not let more be buried there, all the cemeteries are now full.'

Jules turned again to me, his finger again signalling silence. I nodded, looking down at the group that now had turned off. Below us I could see what were plainly new big burial pits.

'This new ground is the problem' she thought to us. 'It is not protected by the church, by the wall, or what you call holy ground.'

I can remember being thoroughly confused at this point. What on earth was relevant in that? As the questions rose, to my horror on the edge of the pit appeared four hideous creatures. I felt Shola stiffen, her wing muscles becoming tense and more purposeful.

Jules turned, mouthing 'Oh no not again.' He reached back and gave my knee a reassuring double squeeze. I look down with growing horror. The four creatures were truly hideous. They were dressed in jet-black rags and long-haired, with long, ungainly limbs. They looked around, slavering. Now and then they threw their heads back, laughing at the sky, showing hideous yellow and black fangs. Shola has since taken me there many times over the years and I always find the sight of these hideous ghouls scary.

'They want the dead souls' whispered Jules back to me.

Without any warning, and causing us to grip really tight, Shola began to drop on to them, and they now saw her. They pointed skywards and howled in strange tongues. One hurled his great staff at us. To my amazement it was the last thing he did, as a great blast of fire shot from Shola's mouth. The heat and blast were intense. I was watching the ghoul's face as it arrived and saw it register horror and then turn to a crisp, burning mask. As she swooped over a great clawed front leg sliced another of the creatures entirely in two.

She flew in a tight circle and I looked back to see how easily her great back leg stopped a hurled club in flight. Accelerating down, her front legs and claws ripped into the remaining pair, their entrails spilling out. She shot skywards, then turned down again and ravaged their twisting bodies with another fiery blast as she flew over. I remember being truly petrified by what I was seeing. At least that is now my excuse, because as Shola turned sharply again at ground level, I lost my grip.

Try as I might I simply could not stay on. I clutched and grabbed at Jules. He turned to look at me in alarm. I can remember trying to grab one of the spines down Shola's back. At the point when I knew I was falling Shola turned to me.

'*Walk on, get away.*' she thought at me.

As I fell to the ground she and Jules disappeared. I hit the ground on the edge of the pits, winded and badly shaken. How would I get back? Tears rose as the thought of being stuck in the past hit me.

'*Walk on, walk on.*' I felt Shola thinking to me. It was blowing intensely as I landed. I pulled myself up, feeling my aching legs. A smell of corruption and death arose from the pits. I walked around the edge, and immediately met one of the children. The boy looked at me, turned and began to run. Looking in his direction I saw that the other group of mourners were laying two shrouded corpses in the pit. Without thinking twice I turned and simply ran and ran across the shrub on the pit edge over to the wood.

Behind me I heard voices shout. I did not look back but kept on running, feeling my lungs would burst. The land to the wood edge began to drop down, holding large ants' nests on the cropped grass. Just when I felt I could not run any more, Shola appeared on the wood edge.

'Quick, quick,' she screamed. 'They must not see me.'

Without needing any prompting I ran and dived over her neck, lying behind Jules, my legs dangling behind me. I realised that one of the spines on her neck was pressing into my stomach and felt Jules reaching back with both hands buried in my jacket.

After perhaps five minutes Shola twitched back and landed, almost on the spot where it had all begun.

'Mercy that you were safe, quick, get back on properly we need to go back.'

I struggled on to her neck and she twitched back to near the pits. As we landed Jules told me to get my boots off and drop them. He turned, looking at my legs.

'Right, quick, don't ask. Trousers off and, yes - the jacket as well.'

I struggled to get one leg, then the other, up enough to slide my leg out, dropping them and the jacket on the ground. Without further thought we were back over the yard at Jules' place.

'You have perhaps some questions' thought Shola. 'I do not want to be seen, we will meet soon. Myrddin will tell. Goodbye.'

And with that, she had gone.

With my ears popping I turned to Jules, realising that apart from my pants, socks and T-shirt I had nothing on.

'Don't say it. We cannot, dare not, bring 13th century soil and germs to the present. Come quick to the barn.'

Once inside, the ritual of spraying every pore with insecticide was repeated.

'I will say about this first,' said Jules waving the spray can at me. 'The black death was transmitted by a flea, still is. A germ the flea carries causes it. A right lethal beggar. That is why we are done up tight. And you fall off. Well. We cannot transport those germs to now. The risk is total.'

He paused, looking at me with half a smile.

'Make sense?'

I nodded, beginning to feel a bit embarrassed standing there and getting cold.

'Look, she has to go, to help. It is unhallowed ground and believe it or not the dark and evil forces want to take the dead souls as their own. There, I have told you. Bet you used to think it was made-up rubbish.'

He paused, looking intently at me.

'But now you have seen it. If you believe in a force for good, there has to be a force for bad. You have seen it yourself.'

He paused, as if allowing it to sink in.

'Obviously the mourners are not aware. They will have noticed the stronger winds arrive as Shola dealt with them. Bet that made them wonder. They will not believe the kid that saw you, thank goodness. You have had a good demonstration of Shola's power. Is she not truly awesome?'

He stopped and looked at me, putting the flea spray down on the straw.

'Come on' he said. 'Normal medicine, a cuppa and you will have to bung something of mine on. Your parents would wonder!'

He burst into laughter as he crossed the yard. I followed, feeling thoroughly drained by it all.

I am going to interrupt again to say that if you wonder about any of this, go to your computer search engine and have a look. Over the years Shola and I went to the posy tree a few times. It is all there.

Now I am going to have a break from remembering. I need a cup of tea. I am typing this, believe it or not, with a sleeping labrador on my lap. Hardly a lapdog, and she snores. The sarcastic might ask... no, she does not read as well, but chats when awake nineteen to the dozen. She is making now my legs ache and it is late. Tea and bed call. I will continue these memories in the morning.

CHAPTER 11

THE TRAINING BEGINS

I got up very early the next morning, in fact to be honest I hardly slept. I am sure you can imagine why. The previous months, but particularly the last two weeks, had been mind-blowing. I suppose some would say I was in shock after it all.

Going into the kitchen I let the dogs into the garden as quietly as I could. After a while Milly came back in and got on her bed in front of the stove. I don't mind admitting that I lay down cuddling her and telling her as best I could all that had happened.

There is something about wolfhounds in particular which is reassuring, comforting and powerful. She was so matter of fact and logical, and that did me a lot of good.

I can remember that I desperately wanted to talk to Jules, in fact I was bursting to. It was too early, and when later my parents appeared in the kitchen to get their breakfast going, I was grabbed to spend the morning sorting sheep.

At the time we only had a relatively small flock. In the early autumn the lambs were split off from their dams. Then later in the year, and on this morning, the ewes had to have their feet trimmed and be given a dose of wormer. That year's lambs were also gone through to see which would grade for the abattoir.

I can remember my mother saying I looked distracted. I wonder why.

While they were getting ready to go out, I rechecked the hidden clothes from Jules. I had had a bit of luck coming home wearing his stuff because my parents were out shopping.

Up the hill, moving sheep, it was getting colder. The wind blew with an edge to it, forcing me to pull my collar up. The lambs were caught up first, and then pushed from their pen into the adjoining race. I felt each of them on their back and prodded them above their tails on each side, to feel for their condition and decide their fate.

Later in the morning, with a bit of whooping and hollering, they were changed for the ewes. At this stage I was worse than useless. My injury and all that had left me pathetically weak; it took me years to recover some strength.

Each ewe in turn was turned on to its back by my father and its nails trimmed back. Some needed a lot of trimming. Our ground seems to encourage foot growth, and the purple spray is always needed. Finally their ignominy was completed with a mouth full of wormer, shot by me into the angle of their mouths and down their throats.

After lunch Milly and I left the house to walk down to Jules. The wind had become quite strong, lifting the last leaves off the trees. A few last apples hung here and there on the orchard trees and I grabbed one, with a bit of effort. I munched on it as we walked along, avoiding the brown bits, and shared the end with Milly. She trotted alongside me, whizzing off now and then to check out the things that dogs have to do.

We waited for a line of cars and a van to go over the bridge, and then walked around the lane into Jules' yard. Overhead a few rooks struggled with the wind and above them a few wisps of cloud flew along. The upper winds were obviously strong. Everything hinted at the autumn and the approach of winter.

Jules met us as we walked into his yard, emerging from an old stable door. In his weatherbeaten hand he carried an old oil-encrusted chainsaw, and in the other an old hook and bow-saw.

'Morning you two, how goes it? All right after the last bit of fun?'

He grinned, putting everything down to rub Milly's ear. She wagged her tail back, in heaven with his attention.

'Yes, I suppose so' I replied. 'Worried, mystified, amazed, you can say what you want.'

'Right. Got a couple of hours free now? You can both come with me. I am going to start laying a hedge along the top. We can deal with the lot as we go.'

I said all right, and we walked out of the yard, up the hill. I tried to be useful and carried the jerry can with the two-stroke mix.

In the autumn, once the leaves begin to come off, hedges are laid, normally in a rotation around the farm, with each revisited, perhaps after seven years. This part of Dorset often has its own distinctive laying rather than the tractor flaying often done elsewhere.

Working uphill, each upright in turn is more than half cut through with the hook. Then it is gently persuaded to fall along the hedge line. The top is intermingled with the previous cuts. Any uprights then, which were of course horizontal before the fall, are timed off, making the new hedge level. As the hedger advances, a tight, stockproof new hedge is formed. On his way the hedger cuts off and makes flat the mouth of each cut. This helps the rain run out, makes it safer for jumping deer, and importantly makes it look better. Also on the way lots of bramble briars, dead wood, general rubbish and of course the odd unusable bits of timber are cut out and piled to the side. This rubbish is occasionally set alight, and that marvellous smell of burning wood fills the air.

Jules led the way to an old hedge which ran around the hill, separating an old grass field from the yet-to-be-ploughed-in maize stubble. The maize had been cut for silage a few weeks before.

'Right, this is it for the next month' he said, putting all his kit down. He knew hedge laying was something I was not new to, and I was happy to help. In fact I like the result. It is nice to stay tight to the hedge and then at the end of the day stand back and have a good look at your efforts. Lovely, and very satisfying.

Milly wandered about as we worked, always within earshot. She told me that she would always be within range should she be needed.

As we began to clear the rubbish out prior to laying, Jules began telling me what he knew and had done, and also what I should expect.

'Impressed by her power then?' He did not wait for an answer, but carried on.

'Look, I do not really understand why, but sometimes Shola needs a human witness for her deeds. She has called me a bit each year, and will be calling you.'

He paused, picking up his hook to cut through a thick briar.

'You can call her, by the way. It had better be good, though.' He turned to look at me.

'I will teach you, over the next weeks, how you can call her for a favour to be done. It is a perk, if you like to call it that, of your position. You do understand that, don't you? You are my replacement. The new Merlin.'

I don't mind admitting that I did not say much. I let him do all the talking as we worked on.

I did comment that I thought dragons had a bad press and were folklore, not real. I had been stunned, particularly as the burial ground incident had shown her combating evil. He stopped working and straightened up, putting both hands in the small of his back, and gave a groan.

'Look, the problem is that only a handful of people through the centuries have ever known them. You have joined a very select band.' He looked across to me, grinning and raising one eyebrow. He then stopped working to tell me a truly remarkable story, which incidentally I have just told my replacement too. More of him later.

Way back in time, Shola's mother apparently did a noble thing. Jules had persuaded Shola to tell him about it years ago and the story had stayed with him. It seems that when Shola's mother knew her days were numbered, and Shola was young and learning to fly, she wanted to leave her mark on history. She had apparently inadvertently twitched out one day, to be seen by the people of a hamlet and particularly by a knight. They had had what for her was a small tussle, for the knight an immense one. Needless to say the knight had left, but she had called him back. They arrange to meet again, as she was dying. Shola would fetch him.

That day had arrived and to cut a long story short, the knight pretended that he had killed the dragon. He gained immense kudos on returning to the people, taking them to the dead body, acting the hero and affording her a proper funeral pyre. He in fact thought his life through then, revising everything he did; he carried on doing good works from that day until he too died. Later he became better known as St George.

I bet you are as stunned as I was on hearing this. I changed all my perceptions of life. Dragons are capable of great kindness and compassion.

Later that day as we shared a thermos of coffee, we sat on two stumps and took a pause.

'Look, I remember how I felt' Jules reassured me. 'You are bound to think, why me? This is phoney, I want out. Well you cannot. You are now the new Myrrdin, Merlin, a historical figure. Get used to it. You will grow into it. You will see more strange things, be witness to strange events. I suppose you will represent humans in a parallel time which there has always been. Goodness knows, these days with silicon chips, nuclear power and so on, what is real? Necessity has been forgotten, overlooked.'

He stopped abruptly, looking at me.

'I can tell you that in two years you will be without me, on your own.'

He looked at his feet, going very quiet, pausing as if summoning strength.

'Later I will tell you, not now.' He looked up and smiled.

'Over the next two years, or at least what is left, we have a lot to go through. I have got to explain how to summon Shola, to teach you all the useful plants and herbs we can use these days. We have got to meet the other watchers. Yes there are others, and no, they are not like us. Much more importantly, when the time arrives you have to witness with me the rain and wind forces. They are vital too, but I have got to warn you that we will need Shola's strength on meeting, or rather seeing, the wind force. It has scared me in the past.'

He paused again, obviously remembering, the pain showing on his face.

As an aside he spent what time we had together teaching me all about herbal medicines and how they work. We spent days walking around the lanes, over the fields, going from one tree or plant to the next. Milly loped along with us on these trips, chasing the odd rabbit. She never caught one, but it was a useful diversion from the sometimes intense talks from Jules.

I know there is a place for some of the active compounds in old drug sources. Modern pharmacology has produced many exciting and useful drugs, but just because something grows naturally does not make it less valuable. Sadly, in some cases they are forgotten. Many herbal compounds that Jules explained and taught to me over that time I still recommend with respect. They are after all drugs; for example do not forget aspirin from willow, or some antihelmitics from bracken. As I wrote to you in the beginning, such intense knowledge is for my successor, and he has already begun going through it with me.

I should at this point say that Jules, over the next weeks while we laid hedges, taught me how to summon Shola. He hinted weeks before that initially he would teach me every other word. He did just that over the first week. The next week he went over the missing words. There is no way I will commit these to paper. Jules drummed into me that I must never say them in sequence. To summon Shola by accident, or shall we say by messing around, means death.

I can say only that the summons is rhythmic, hypnotic, relatively short and repetitive, and for my successor only.

I stayed that day talking and working with Jules until the light began to go. Picking up all tools and our discarded jackets, we looked at possibly twenty yards of smart hedge laying. All three of us walked back to his yard. I promised that if time allowed I would lend him a hand over the next weeks, and he said that he would carry on my teaching.

CHAPTER 12

THE SICK BOY

I am going to mention now another example of the kindness dragons can demonstrate. After perhaps three weeks of battling the hedge, covered in scratches, hearing the chainsaw howl and using the hooks, one morning Jules seemed somewhat restrained and distracted. The day was one of those typical Dorset autumnal days. The air was still, cold and seemed full of moisture. The far view was restricted by a thin fog to about four hundred yards. Trees could just be made out through it, black sentries. You could never get to this fog; it always seemed to move on. The village was blanked out from the rest of the world.

'I have decided to summon Shola this morning for help' said Jules, rather unexpectedly, as I arrived to have a pre-work cup of tea with him.

'Why, what for? Is something wrong?'

He explained that very sadly one of the children I had met him with months back had been diagnosed as having leukaemia, a form carrying a poor prognosis. He went very quiet at this point and I could almost feel his sadness.

The child was still at home and Jules often called to see him.

He had a crazy idea that for the child, seeing a dragon would be an amazing boost, a treat never matched. This morning being enclosed by the fog to prevent outsiders seeing anything had struck him as an opportunity. He had summoned confidence to do it. It would be a wonderful thing for the small boy. He was sure Shola would agree to let him glimpse her.

We talked a while, putting together a crude plan. I was to act as a sort of guard, for when Shola arrived I knew we would be mentally linked. Jules would talk his way with the little boy and seize an opportunity with Mum out of the way to show Shola to him, if an occasion presented. What an amazing experience for a seven year old.

First Shola had to be onside, so Jules went out on his own to call her to him. He left me in his kitchen waiting.

The mental link with her came almost straight away and my ears again popped with the pressure differences she produces. She summoned me outside, and there I saw her again in all her frightening presence. Her wings folded by her side, she looked up from Jules when I walked into the yard.

'Myrrdin!' was all she said, bending down to listen to Jules, after looking across at me. I remember that I waited quietly, not really moving, taking in her truly extraordinary form. She appeared wet or damp this morning, with her exhaled breath fogging the air. All her claws or rather talons appeared to be blood stained, the stains going up one of her front legs. I was still petrified at seeing her.

Their whispered talking went on for perhaps five minutes, with Jules pointing to the farmhouse just visible up the drive through the fog. Then she was gone, with, I like to think, just a perfunctory look at me. Jules turned to me, smiling.

'OK, she will help, but she ordered me to say that having the nerve to ask her is not usual. She normally asks – no, tells you. She will help if it is noble, I suppose like her mother.' He paused. 'Look, I have watched her for decades now, and you will. Never forget, get complacent, and think her usual, or normal. We are privileged. Like me you must honour this strange position you have.'

I nodded agreement and to this day remember it exactly and the way he drummed it into me.

He told me to take up a position on the edge of the lawn where I could see the drive to the house and across to the conservatory on the back. I was told to keep under the hedge on the right of the drive, so as not to be too obvious. Any problems I could relate to Shola if needed. In fact that day I did not see her again.

I learned later from Jules that a chance did arrive that morning. The boy's mother had been called away to the telephone and left her son with him in the conservatory. The boy was sitting under a blanket having a chat with them both. With mother gone Jules had said that the boy should look across the tractor yard behind the house because he thought he had seen something moving.

The boy had pulled himself up to look out at the very moment Shola appeared. She looked at him, winked, then shot a jet of flame from her enormous jaws and went.

Jules burst into joyous laughter many times later that day as he told me. The lad had turned in astonishment to him, his mouth opening and closing, with no words formed. Jules said 'What did you see? A rat, a strange dog?' He acted ignorant.

The lad's mother had returned, and eventually a rushed, garbled account came out. Mother and Jules looked at each other, the mother little knowing that Jules was not just humouring the boy.

That little boy was given a tremendous boost for his last few months. He never stopped talking about it to anyone who would listen.

Like me you have probably been brainwashed from an early age into thinking dragons are forces for evil, incapable of kindness. How wrong we are. And I bet some still think they are fictional - bad luck, they are all too real.

We carried on laying that hedge on and off for perhaps another month. I managed to slip away from home fairly often. Of course I helped at home as well as I could. In fact I started on my own, laying one of our boundary hedges. The sheep needed daily attention and I did a lot of riding with Caspian, going miles with him.

Milly and I had many walks with Jules meticulously going over which plants were poisonous and which useful, and how to respond to some medical conditions. These days of course, modern science has taken over many early remedies.

From what I remember for those of you interested in such things, the boy had a time in remission, but sadly he did not make another year, Jules and Shola gave him a unique event, a personal sighting and a very real experience for him to savour.

I know I am desperately trying to keep my memories in order for you. At this point of course I now realise I only had Jules around for guidance for just over a year. My successor has the same time now. Thankfully you are not here to ask why we do not start our followers sooner. I do not know why; it is the way things have been done since this Merlin position was formed. I know you think why only two years introduction, but really it involves you being watched - and guided - from when you are six.

I will get on to explaining this in due course, but for now there is a lot to tell you about my last times with Jules all those years ago.

CHAPTER 13

THE STANDING STONES

The autumn arrived very wet, from memory. I carried on seeing Jules on and off as time allowed. He helped on his landlord's farm, and I managed to make myself useful to my parents. They on reflection never questioned me helping out Jules and going off for hours on end.

One miserable wet day and Millie and I wandered into his kitchen to find him, of all things, ironing. He looked up from wrestling with a large shirt of his.

'Hello, how you doing? If you are bored or at a loose end I've got a few jobs' he said sarcastically. 'I have always hated this, I'm useless at it. I put it off as long as possible.'

On saying this he chucked the shirt back on his pile of washed clothes.

'I'll put the kettle on the sticks' he said, turning to me as he walked to the fire. 'Actually I'm glad you are here. One of our annual events is soon. You will need to clear it for a day away, on the shortest day in December.'

He fiddled with a couple of chipped old mugs and an old brown teapot. He then began rummaging around for teabags and of course his seemingly inexhaustible supply of his very own biscuits.

I settled with Millie in front of the small fire, thinking how cold it always was in his place.

'What for, what goes on then?'

He explained that as far as witnessing for humans went, or watching, whatever you want to call it, we were not unique. I was to be the new Myrddin, as per history. However the Welsh, Irish and Scots had similar, less responsible people in their own areas.

He went on to quickly say that Shola was only for me. The other witnesses saw the land-waking lady I saw, but at different times they also witnessed the water ritual I would see later. They did not get involved with the wind ritual, which would be soon after Christmas before the water rite. He paused as if allowing these thoughts to sink in. I must say I was relieved in a way to know I would at least not be fully alone.

After chewing on a biscuit and chucking one to Milly, he carried on. Years ago one of the first Merlins, so he had been told, had built a large stone meeting place. The intention was for the then king to use it, thought Jules. On this he was a bit vague, but he did know that it had been grabbed as a token place for worshipping the new sun, and other possible black magic rites. It was obviously much older, and had roots involving construction from an early age.

The rocks had been linked to healing, were centres for curative powers. One of the early Merlins was reported to have fetched the rocks from Ireland at Aurelius Ambrosia's request. It was to be a memorial to a number of his nobles who had died in battle with the Saxons. Either way, said Jules, it was ancient and rightly venerated for a lot of reasons.

'Yes, but where are we going?' I asked.

'Stonehenge' said Jules, looking at me over the rim of his cup. 'On the shortest day. Which is just before the Christmas stuff.'

He smiled. I sat somewhat stunned.

The shortest day arrived and I walked down to his house mid morning. As far as my parents were concerned I was going with him to Taunton shopping for Christmas stuff. As Jules was known as a somewhat elderly chap in the village I suppose my story was feasible. I shot around that morning checking stock and making sure I was seen to put the effort in.

Jules emerged from his house, walking to his ancient, beaten-up car. He looked rather more dapper than normal, his normal old jumper replaced with an equally old, but smarter, outdoor jacket.

'Righto. In you get, and put your grabber on' he joked as he fiddled for keys.

He had never driven me before, and in fact I had never seen him drive. To say his style was alarming would be an understatement. Fast is not the word. On reflection it might have been his eyes. I had never seen him wearing any glasses.

With me looking forward, gripping the seat edges and making the odd comment, and him peering forward through the windscreen, we joined the main Exeter to London road. Somehow we only collected three hootings from other users. He was really beyond his best-before date for driving.

The main route is only dual carriageway up to Wiltshire, and as the countryside opened up into the big cereal fields I relaxed to his driving. Tractors were still ploughing in stubble, busy as tiny dots on the horizons. We nattered about many things, health (never politics) and my duties following him.

I have to say that we got rid of a serious quantity of chocolate toffees. I have never seen anyone eat so many. He did not stop chewing. I can eat sweets as well as the next man, but his ability was amazing. Maybe they were to help his driving.

As we got nearer, Jules looked at the sky.

'We have to be there for last light. It is only this day in the year you will do this. You will never meet the other three at all during the year. I do not know how their position is passed on to their next when they finish their stint, but it is and you will see their replacement with them once. Sadly then they too die.'

At this point he went very quiet as if gathering strength.

'Look, now is probably the time. You will be without me next year… not because I'm moving away, but I shall be dead.'

'What?' I shouted back. 'How on earth can you say that?'

I turned to face him and he turned briefly to me before looking forward again.

'Look, do not worry. Calm down, it's all right. I've known for years, its Shola's deal.'

He paused and shot a glance at me. 'Look, you have a fixed time as a Merlin. You can call it the job, if you like. Eighty-five years old and then you move on.'

I can remember how the shock as this hit me. The remaining bit of the drive faded from my awareness. How would you feel if you were told exactly how many years you had left?

With the huge grey stones of the henge rearing up on the left, he quietly said

'Look, let me say on the outside it looks like death, and it is for all intents. But Shola has a surprise in store, she tells me. If you are wondering, well, you are reading the diary of a man who is eighty-three.'

He turned into the car park, deserted save for three other cars.

'Believe me, after all these years I am looking forward to the last adventure she has stored up. In any case you might…'

He stopped, scratching his head.

'Yes, you might be involved with her replacement, her daughter.'

I looked across at him, stunned, and shook my head.

'Come on you' he ordered, smiling. 'Let me do the talking. They are a really nice bunch, but you have to make your mark. They are fun, I promise.'

With that he slipped off his seat belt and opened the door. I followed, in a bit of a daze.

Outside the car it was cold. He walked fairly briskly over to the three cars, and after perhaps twenty yards turned his head to me as he walked.

'No names' he whispered. 'Just their country they cover, their responsibility.'

He had his hand up, covering his mouth. As we approached the cars their doors opened and three men got out, all bursting into big smiles. All three were effusive in their greetings. Occasionally you know instantly that you have met nice people, and I felt myself begin to relax straight away.

Each in turn was introduced to me, Jules simply describing me as the 'next', not using my name at all. This seemed perfectly satisfactory for each.

The Welshman had a wonderful soft accent, and dare I say it, and it probably sounds corny, but you could virtually hear him singing as he spoke. He was a small man, probably the oldest of the three, but not as old as Jules. He had jet black hair and a craggy face, with blue twinkling eyes, and nearly always a true smile.

Jules then introduced me to the Scot. He had a large area to travel from and looked worn out. He had thinning blond hair and was tall and very thin, looking as if a well-placed push would have him over. A smile showing near perfect teeth split his face, which was as brown as could be, as if he had just got back from foreign climes. He said very little and did a lot of nodding but when he did talk, I do not know if it was me, he was seriously quiet. Strangely, although he was soft in voice, you never had to get him to repeat. He had the skill to always make himself registered.

Finally the Irishman, who frankly was a wonder. He had jammed on his head a truly decrepit old deerstalker that looked as if it had taken root. Wisps of black hair emerged here and there, over an amazingly veined and craggy face. His voice when he spoke, apart from having a strong Irish accent, was as if coming from a broken box, grating, rising in pitch then falling. Truly strange. He began quizzing me, until Jules respectfully reminded him that over the years ahead I would replace him.

The sun began to set and the countryside around was beginning to close in. Through the gathering dark an endless stream of car headlights moved by. I am able to say, given my own limitations on this account, that as the night begins and the sun drops and finally the black of night arrives, we meet. We have met every year on the same night, for our needs and to confirm our function. We do not pray or any such thing; there is a form of words, leave it at that.

On my first time that night I meekly followed Jules as we walked through the dark to the middle of the standing stones. I stood by him as the others stood around. The moon at that point appeared, with Jules standing with arms outstretched.

This was far from a 'black mass' ceremony. We were after all to see and touch the things that were, and are, important to man. What I am trying to say is that this is not a faith; goodness knows, faith is, for many, real and necessary. No, for us we see reality.

After perhaps ten minutes of standing trying to see in the dark, I heard the screech of a tawny owl. In the next quarter of an hour I was amazed as the group was joined by one owl after another until there were probably forty or fifty of them. At that time I was reasonably expert on bird song, and could make out very distinctly the calls of tawny, barn and little owls. The calling, hooting and distinctive screaming calls of tawny owls filled the air. I did not, nor did anyone else at that point, utter a sound.

To my joy, on Jules' outstretched arm flew in and settled a dark tawny. It landed on his arm and turned to each of us in turn. Though it was now dark you could just make out its large eyes, which seemed to look through you.

The distinct smell of bird-feather dander filled the air, lovely and perfumed. The noise from the owls reached a crescendo and then... well, they simply went. I was astonished by this and looked around the group and at Jules. He now dropped his arms back down and opened his eyes. The Welshman looked at me, saying just 'Lovely eh? Our confirmation, our permission.'

The others nodded, all walking slowly and without talking to their cars, all lost in their own thoughts.

After possibly a couple of hours we all shook hands again and said we would meet in a year. There were a few wishes for a happy Christmas, and no, we have never exchanged presents.

That time of year of course it is dark early, and as Jules drove us back he seemed happier. The bright oncoming lights seemed good markers.

'Good bunch of guys aren't they? In a way it's a shame we are limited to one meeting. It has been like this for generations. They arrange their own replacements somehow. I have no idea how.

'You have just witnessed our permission. Authority, if you like. Our witnessing the White Queen we saw back in the spring and the water nymphs you will see with me soon. They do the same as us, these rights that we see. They do as well. But they do not have any input with Shola. She will be yours only. Of course we have to deal with the wind furies in due course. I think I told you before that without Shola that would be impossible. That is the worst for her. I hate watching, it has been getting harder and harder just over the years I have been watching her. You will see.'

He went quiet again, watching the road. I carried on watching the oncoming headlights go by, not wanting to intrude on his thoughts.

'In the week after Christmas we will see her again. Normally her needs fall that we have some history to witness and almost straight after the wind furies have to be met again. It's becoming hard.' He shook his head. 'I think it is because of climate change, or something happened.'

He almost cursed. It was the most annoyed I could remember seeing him.

Then he turned quickly to me. 'Don't worry, you'll see, leave it to her. She is used to them. She will always win… I hope.' he stopped, and I did not comment.

After perhaps a few minutes Jules put his car radio on. The reception was appalling, but eventually some old ballroom music filled the car as we bowled home. We relaxed back into normal chatter then. It was pretty clear to me that Jules was dog tired, and

I inwardly felt relief as we turned into his yard. He parked up and we got out.

'Have you got any supper?' I casually asked.

'No, I'm fine. Going to the boss for supper.' I have since found out that he rarely, if at all, did this.

'Right, well thanks for driving. I must say it is beginning to make sense now. Or rather more sense. In a way I am glad we are not alone.'

'You will not be alone.' In the light of his front door I could see him smile.

'Look, I get adopted by the boss's family at Christmas but pop in for a glass and bring that lovely Milly.'

I promised I would and we parted.

As I walked back I had lots going through my head, what I had seen, the whole business of it. Shola, the other watchers. Finally Jules having said that his days were numbered. Mine as well. I had been told how long I had.

It was still early when I walked in at home. The dogs in the kitchen gave me an enormous greeting.

CHAPTER 14

A SEA BATTLE

If I am honest, as I write this I do not have a marvellous memory of that Christmas apart from a few things. My parents always engineered a great time. A big fir tree was brought in, smelling wonderful. It was always seasonally dressed, a joint effort by all and everyone. The house was decorated the usual way with sprigs of holly, mistletoe and hung-up Christmas cards that arrived in their scores. People always popped in, for seasonal sherry, whisky, sausage rolls and of course, mountains of mince pies.

The horses got an extra Christmas treat too. My father had a tradition of giving them on their Christmas Eve supper, a shot of brown ale. He was convinced they enjoyed it. Speaking with Caspian over the break, he was right - they loved it.

The dogs of course got seasonally excited. As an aside I do remember explaining to Milly that the barking chorus each visitor got was a touch annoying. Like a star, she got them to play it down a bit - my new communication with her was paying off.

Christmas lunch was the usual massive affair, on reflection too much, but what the hell. Late afternoon saw us all making a slow start, checking sheep, feeding horses, walking dogs and then collapsing in front of the television.

I do easily recall how truly superb and lovely that first Christmas was for me. I was able to tell the dogs and Caspian how special they all were to me. This is a joyous perk that over the years that followed I have treasured.

My father and I did not do the usual hunting on Boxing Day; the meet was too far away. In any case, although my parents were resigned to Caspian and me now disappearing now for hours, the hospital consultants still in charge of my recuperation would have a fit at the thought.

We did go along to watch the local Boxing Day shoot, just for a couple of drives, to meet good friends again and watch the labradors and springers work.

What I do remember was wandering down that afternoon to see Jules. Full of cold turkey, wearing a new, rather itchy jumper from my mother, Milly and I walked down through the orchard. A few people were coming up along the bridle path, and we swapped greetings. A small boy was trying out his new Christmas scooter, pushing it through the mud with a helping hand from a grinning dad. He was making fine progress and I admired it, much to his apparent joy.

Jules' decayed door was half open as we wandered into his yard. I peeped around it to see him fast asleep in a chair by the remains of his fire. This had died down to just a few embers. Trying hard to be really quiet Milly and I sneaked around. I found a few split logs to build the fire back up. He did not so much snore as give the odd snort. He was far away in the land of sleep, looking peaceful in a far away dream.

It was a shame, because I had managed to save enough to buy him a reasonable bottle of whisky as a present. I looked around and used a small table out of the reach of his feet and placed the bottle and a card on it where he would easily see them. Tiptoeing out, I shut the door behind us, at the thought of him waking and finding them, then looking at his remade fire and putting two and two together.

Two days later, well before New Year's Eve was even thought of, I was woken with the same thought I had had months before; a sudden command in my head. An order, a demand. It was really strong this time and as if answering a telephone call, once had acknowledged it it stopped.

I pulled my clothes on. The house was still asleep. Grabbing a slice of Christmas cake for breakfast and an old jacket, I set off to Jules' yard. I also remembered my sticky overtrews. The morning was very frosty and I had to blow on my hands after fiddling with the hasp on the orchard and river gates.

A great plume of blue wood smoke came from the cottage chimney as he emerged, unshaven and looking tired as I walked into the yard. The few puddles in the yard gave off cracks as he walked; it had been cold enough for thin ice to form on the ground.

'Hi, hi!' he waved at me, smiling. 'Got her message then? This call has been moving on about a week a year, since I began. It was originally when he started in the summer, but for some weird reason it moved on. All we had to do was watch and witness.' He grinned. You're a bad lad! And thank you for my present, well received if unnecessary.'

He smiled and took my hands, giving them a playful, friendly rub.

'It was nothing. Just a small thank you for being patient and showing me so much. Teaching me so much too.'

'I'll just get a jacket for now' he said, walking into the house. 'Last time it was fairly warm, but you will need that jacket this time.'

I wanted to ask more, but he had gone in. On coming out, he looked quizzically at me.

'Right, you remember how? We are ready. Call her.'

'No, I can't do that!' I said, shocked.

'You can, and will. I will listen, say it slowly and very carefully as I have taught you.' He smiled, but he was being very firm, with a no-nonsense look on his face.

Realising that this was it, I settled down in the yard and began. Looking across at him, I began the intonation, trying to remember each phrase as he had taught me, with him looking on and occasionally nodding his support.

I have to admit that even now, despite having called a dragon many times over many years, it is still very frightening. There is a point in the call, perhaps in the last few phrases, when it seems to get its own momentum. It takes over, getting its own rhythm, its own power. I was forced down, my eyes tightly shut.

I struggled on, getting more and more frightened. My ears popping with the pressure, I knew she had arrived.

'Well done, he was clear' she thought.

I opened my eyes, trying desperately to not catch her gaze.

'You taught him well.'

'Good. He is not bad eh?' I looked across, to be met by Jules smiling at me.

My eyes looked tentatively towards Shola in all her glory. Fantastic and unimaginable, a tremendous feeling of strength was coming from her. I got the feeling that we were only tolerated, a minor aspect of her being.

She moved, shifting her weight, her great talons ripping heedlessly at the shingle of the yard. Her great saucer eyes fixed me with a look. I felt myself begin to shake uncontrollably.

'Come, we are needed' she thought.

Jules nodded towards her neck and pointed. As I tried to get on, he laughed and pointed at my sticky trews.

' Good, you learned the hard way' he smiled at me, vaulting on despite his age.

Shola turned her massive head around to look back at us. 'We go' she said and everything went.

In what seemed seconds we were over the sea. I do not mind admitting that although I seemed to find her actions easier, I was really glad of my sticky trews as I looked down at the sea. My right hand held on tight to one of her neck spines and my left buried itself in the back of Jules' jacket. I was petrified of falling into the sea.

Away over to the left and behind us, were what looked like the cliffs of Dover. The sea below us was grey, full of white-capped rollers.

'The channel' whispered Jules, turning to me with one hand half over his mouth. 'You will become used to this. It varies a bit each year, but the time is always now. We join after probably a week of effort.'

He waved a hand and for the moment said no more. Then he turned his head forward again. I looked out to the left, at the Downs, cliffs and far off a small hamlet. The sky overhead was an ominous grey, scudding clouds leading us, going to the northeast.

On every hill I could make out a blazing beacon; they stretched far, far away.

He whispered that I should look behind us, at the sea and what Shola was keeping ahead of.

'What do you mean?' I said, trying to turn and get a backward look.

As I twisted around a faint series of booms could be heard, and then from one side of the channel to it seems the other I saw a great mass of ships; galleons, men of war I supposed. Breathless, I fought to turn around fully.

'We will turn' thought Shola.

Her broad wings dipped to the right and she came around to amaze me even more. I was stunned. As she turned I could see what I took to be a British ship wallow in the swell. As it rolled up, a massive broadside fired. I could see the cannons fly back into their restraining ropes, a heavy pall of smoke. A few seconds later, a dull roar reached us. I was horrified, for I could see the result as the target ship shuddered under the slaughter.

The main mass of heavy galleons was sailing in a big crescent shape, or what was left of it, butting into the seas, possibly five or six miles across my view. They were massive men of war, built like wooden castles. In contrast, what I took to be the British vessels were greyhound-like, cutting the sea better, quicker, smoother and blatantly better at cannonry. The firing rate was much quicker, smoother and seemed more structured.

From one side of the channel to the other I could see similar actions, rolling ships, battered masts and split, ripped sails. The smoke from the cannon-fire hung like a mist despite the wind. For me as a young man, inexperienced in life, it was a horrific sight, yet at the same time riveting.

'What is this for heaven's sake? Where are we?'

Jules half turned, lifting a hand. 'I am needed here' thought Shola to me. 'I have to call help… not yet, but soon.'

'I will explain in a moment, have no fear' said Jules. Shola dropped suddenly, causing me to grip tighter.

'Only the wind… it has rough pockets.'

We flew on, watching the horrific sights below. At one point a giant of a vessel was obviously fatally hit, bursting into flames. We hung about long enough to see it eaten by the sea. I could see no sailors in the water.

We have over the years passed over other such events when I could see screaming and writhing men on decks, a few with limbs missing, the decks awash with blood. I do not mind admitting in these memoirs that at times I have violently retched with the sights.

'They have been driven out into the channel, by fire ships. The British sent them in and they panicked' whispered Jules back to me.

'The whole Armada, yes. The Armada flogged up the channel, harried by Sir Francis Drake's ships.' He almost punched the air in a victory sign.

So this was the invasion force of the Spanish Armada. Shola had gone back to 1588, over the English Channel, called by the then current Merlin to help. We were, he thought, about a week from the arrival of the Armada off England. The ships were fought and harried up the east coast, with the idea of driving them north and west over Scotland to make for what they would mistakenly think was safety in Ireland.

How does Shola fit in? Well after perhaps six or seven hours of watching she landed on the beach. Jules and I were ordered off. Jules insisted I understand that I, and in fact he, must remain standing in the sea. Our feet must always be soaked in the surf.

On dropping us off Shola disappeared. I looked at him in fright.

'She will return, don't worry. She has to negotiate, pull acrobatics. If you and I were on board we would probably fall off, or at least vomit.'

He went on to explain that she was arranging for a full-blooded storm to start. She was talking; bartering with a body he called the wind 'furies'. On my obvious frustration at hearing half a story he put a hand up, stopping his scanning of the sky.

'Look don't worry...' he stopped, obviously suddenly lost in thought. 'You will see them again. Sadly they are changing. Harder for Shola. You will see - it will make sense.'

To the south a large cumulo-nimbus began forming, horrible dark dense clouds. Rain began splattering down. Soon we were both soaked. The sea was growing into a storm. Our visibility was reduced as we tried to see through the driving rain, our eyes stinging.

'She has done it again. Ha ha! She always manages it, the darling.'

As if on cue Shola reappeared, dare I say it almost smiling. She was well pleased and quickly ordered us to climb on. To my joy, before Jules climbed on her neck, he leaned in and kissed her, giving her an enormous thank you. I blushed at this outward sign of emotion. This is a practice I have continued. It seems appropriate and right.

Shola turned her head to check we were snug. 'This is always difficult until she twitches out' shouted Jules above a thunderburst overhead. 'Hang on really tight. If you puke, do it over the side or you'll have to give her a bath.'

Now I am not sure why, frankly, it is all still weird, but Shola can only twitch back in the same spot she twitched from. We were faced with possibly the worst flight I had ever had. In all the years that follow it has been the same. It is as if she was flying in a washing machine.

Below us I could see the remaining Spanish ships digging their bows into the sea, decks awash. The British vessels, sailing much better, coped with the seas, still harrying them with cannon broadsides. After what seemed an eternity, we twitched back over a still icy Dorset. Within a moment Shola went. A rough quick 'cheerio' and she had disappeared.

I looked at Jules flabbergasted, beginning to shake. 'Right, in with you now' he ordered, marching me in. To be honest I was not sure if it was seeing mutilated bodies, the enormity of the conflict or just the fact that I was feeling the biting cold.

It was still very early. According to my watch we had only been gone for a morning. Jules spotted me looking and puzzling.

'I know, it gets me still too' he smiled, chucking a blanket at me as I slumped in a chair.

'These furies are becoming a problem, sadly. She is having a job.' He paused, putting tea in his old pot. 'You have seen they were amenable, helpful… now it's getting different. They are stronger. Perhaps we are changing the world for them.'

He poured the boiling water into the pot and rummaged around in his cupboard for two mugs. He produced a tin full of the biscuits he regularly baked.

'I tell you what, before that, a celebratory sloe gin. Your first proper doing. It's not too late. Happy Christmas!'

He chuckled to himself, getting two small glasses and a bottle down.

CHAPTER 14

You can imagine that getting back late morning with trousers still wet to the thigh, covered in salt deposits, smelling of booze, and by then far from unhappy, took some explaining. On reflection I doubt if I succeeded. I spent the afternoon nearly asleep in front of the telly. This was probably a giveaway. Still, it was Christmas, just.

The rest of that first Christmas I cannot remember properly. After what I had seen, no television could compete. I do not mind now admitting that I was probably hopeless company, distracted and itching to tell someone. I spent the time either reading up in history books what I had witnessed, or walking miles with Milly. This extraordinary phase to my life had got a hold. I was lost to it, bemused. I was beginning to realise the enormity of it.

I can tell you that within a week of this event something much nastier was to begin, something that troubled Shola and me unpleasantly, and sadly fatally.

But I am hungry, tired, and cold. I will carry on in the morning.

CHAPTER 15

THE GREAT STORM

I've often wondered how the timing works, but every year, in that first week or two after the Christmas fun, another event calls Shola, related to the wind furies. That first one I watched was truly ghastly; I can recall it too easily. I have no idea why every year at about the same time these events are replayed. Over the years new events arise, new challenges for her and for us to witness. People have no idea how this parallel world carries on. It is probably just as well.

Although the events she is needed for are the same each year, the flavour, timing, force and nature are always slightly different - thankfully.

I had just settled down in front of the fire with a new book given to me at Christmas, lying on the floor with a cushion behind my head. Milly was stretched out by me, enjoying the heat from the crackling logs. I pulled absent-mindedly at the long hairs in her coat as I began chapter one. My parents had gone out, I was on my own and determined to do nothing apart from reading and eating an enormous bar of chocolate.

With no warning, an insistent call split my head. I knew it was Shola, but this one was more insistent. More direct, much more real, and for whatever reason more urgent.

It was pitch dark outside as I locked up, having settled the dogs. Milly asked me if she could come, if nothing else to break her boredom. I explained that it would involve Shola, I had no idea what would happen and it would be better if she stayed put.

Outside it was bitingly cold again, with a light soaking drizzle. I decided to go through the orchard and field rather than the long way around on the road, to save time. The moon and few stars gave a vague light, and to save more time I tried in my limited way when possible to jog a bit.

I had got past the orchard gate and got a bit of speed on in the field when a badger and I got the shock of our lives. No doubt he had been rummaging around on the field edge, trying his luck for worms, mice and the odd apple core, when he was surprised by a charging idiotic human trying to run through his dining room. I was as surprised as he was and nearly ran into him with a surprised yell. He snorted off and I fell in untidy heap. I was not hurt, just surprised, but of course I was now muddy and my knees and hands were soaked. Picking myself up, I walked to Jules from then.

I found him booted and jacketed, obviously ready for something. He looked worried and had a vaguely sad look. Most unusual for him.

'What's up?' I asked, going into his room and over to the fire and putting my hands up to warm them.

'This is always the worst night to see' he said. 'It always has been, but it's getting worse. I hinted at this a few weeks ago. We will let Shola know we are together and ready in a few seconds, but first I have to let you know a few things.'

He then explained that her witnessing had been getting worse for her each year; more punishing, more demanding. He had never seen these beings or entities she had called the Furies, but he thought they must be 'evil buggers'.

They called her at about the same time each year, almost a challenge, a game for them.

He paused, throwing another small log on the fire, and coming back to sit down heavily. With his eyes closed and head bent a little, holding his hands together, he began telling me about last year.

It seemed that just like Shola, the Furies could twitch back in time to anything that caught their fancy, taking her with them. Last year they had gone back to the end of the twentieth century and given Shola am immense tussle while they had set about trashing a great swathe of southern England. He went very quiet again, lost in remembering.

After a while he looked up at me, and slowly continued. Acres of trees were ruined, he said, as if ploughed up, buildings lost, chimneys pushed over, days of cleaning up needed. Just wilful destruction, he continued, quite horrible.

'Makes me wonder how it will end, what will satisfy them' he said. 'There is no doubt in my mind that we, or rather humans, are making them stronger.'

I wanted to quiz him, but kept quiet as after a slight pause he continued.

'You see all this global warming, call it what you will. It must be changing the forces. Our climate is different to when I was a boy.'

He looked across at me. 'I do not know how it will end, I will be long gone any way, which is a blessing.'

At that point, and I had only known him admittedly for only a short time, I had never seen him so thoughtful or mournful.

'Anyway, once a year we have this fiasco to watch.' He pulled himself out of his chair. 'Come on, you call her, let her know we are set.'

I got in some sort of position, getting set, preparing myself.

'Not in here, clown!' he laughed. 'She would bang her head.'

Somewhat embarrassed, I followed him outside.

'No problem' he smiled. 'I have nearly done that myself, lots of times.' He chuckled to himself as he stood waiting.

After a false start, due no doubt to my nerves, I called and she came. To say that she was short tempered would be an understatement.

I am now sure that what was coming up had caused her attitude, but at the time I thought it was something I had done wrong. Perhaps my call, or we had taken to long from her summons. Jules looked reassuringly at me, obviously aware that I was alarmed.

'Come on, Shola, on we get' he said, giving me a boost on to her scaly neck. I wriggled down as he pulled himself in front, using an old vegetable box as a height boost.

'We go!' thought Shola to us, and in that amazing half thought she had gone.

'I am summoned to the year you call eighteen twenty four... local, near the coast. Do you say Lyme...?'

'Lyme Regis?' shouted Jules above the wind. 'Why, what for?' He turned to me, raising his eyebrows. I shrugged my shoulders back, mouthing that I had no idea.

Then I knew she had twitched out, because everything below changed. For one thing there was no silvery scar or road below us, no headlights. I could see the occasional cottage light, and looking south the long line of Chesil beach was easily made out. The sea was jet black and obviously rough, the crashing waves made easily visible by phosphorescence from our height.

It was already windy, making Shola's job of flying tricky. She now and then dropped or made sudden height gains, and the odd shearing turn kept us gripping madly. On the hills to the north of Lyme she put us down.

'Wait and do your watching' she ordered.

Jules said we would and urged her to be careful.

She looked from him to me, did not say a word and left. She remained on view, not twitching out, flying south into the wind and gathering storm.

We looked at each other and began to hunt around for some shelter. If you knew where to look she was still just visible, a black dot in the dark sky. As the clouds parted I could just make her out against the starlit sky. Then she was gone.

We hunkered down behind an old stone wall, looking over the top to try and do our job.

The storm over the next few hours got worse and worse. In the wind we caught shrieking, fearful voices, screaming in worry. The wind was so strong we could make no sense. Carefully we left the shelter of the wall, trying to look through the black at the town below.

We were both horrified; through the rain the odd flash of lightning, the odd bit of moon and starlight, allowed us to see horrors. The sea had risen and was destroying the buildings; we could see people trying to go inland, up beyond the sea. Of Shola we could see nothing, although we both believed we saw her fiery breath in the sky. She had now been gone several hours and I could tell that Jules was starting to worry.

'I am sure she will be fine' I found myself saying, although who was I to say it as a new boy.

We carried on watching the horrific sights below as the dawn began to break.

'Come on, we had better go back where she dropped us' said Jules with a slight quaver in his voice. I did not feel able to say anything but gave him a small clap on the back as we walked.

We stayed there for perhaps another three hours. As the dawn broke Jules kept anxiously looking at the sky. There was enough light about for me to see that he was slightly moist eyed; I too felt a rising sadness.

I kept quiet, not feeling able to say anything. Then… joy of joys, she twitched back in front of us. However, words cannot adequately describe the worn-out state she was in. Blood was dripping from a front leg, which she did not use to bear any weight. Her whole demeanour was sad and worn out. She was soaking wet and obviously wrecked. Her head dropped, almost hitting the ground.

Jules and I gently got on. She twitched to our time straight away, and then without bothering to remain secret she flew back to Netherbury. Thank goodness it was early, with no traffic, and we were not seen.

She crash-landed in Jules' yard and then with minimal explanation to Jules, dragged herself into his open-fronted cart shed. Here, to our shock and amazement, she collapsed into a profound sleep.

Jules and I looked at each other stunned, at a loss what to do for a moment.

'What a situation' muttered Jules, half looking at me, wandering in circles wrapped in thought. 'Come on, we will have to hide her somehow.'

Eventually, over the next half hour, we got her covered in straw. Jules and I lugged bales over, cut the strings and covered her where she lay, with just her enormous head sticking out. Shola remained oblivious to it all, completely sparked out.

We covered her head with an old horse blanket and looked at each other, dreading her discovery.

'Right we will take it in turns to protect her. I'll go and make us something hot. Bacon sandwich all right? Cup of tea?'

Suffice it to say that we stayed put all morning. And then, of all things, Tom Andrews, Jules' boss and landlord, drove into the yard.

'Hell, not now!' whispered Jules under his breath. With very quick thinking he walked over to the opening Land Rover door with a big beaming smile.

'Clear off!' he joked, waving his arms about. 'We've got a present for somebody hidden here.' He waved at the straw heap. 'It's someone's birthday soon, don't know who' he joked.

'Right oh, I get the message!' said Mr Andrews with a knowing smile.

Jules had told me it was his boss' birthday in two weeks. I cannot now remember what Jules had to buy him later to match the size of the heap made by Shola. He managed it and saved the day though. Brilliant.

'Surely it just moved?' said Mr Andrews. He pointed at the blanket.

Jules and I looked around.

'No, probably just slipped a little' said Jules, looking across at me. 'Anyway what can I do for you? What brings you to my humble door?' He ushered his visitor in. When they were safely inside and out of sight, I lifted the blanket to find Shola gone; she had twitched out. I found an old dung fork and lifted out the patch of bloodstained straw, making it harder to imagine it was ever there.

I wandered in, to intimate to Jules that all was in order. I let him know that I would see him some time and gave him a discreet look. Then I said goodbye to them both and wandered off.

Very fortunately, my parents had to leave early that morning to drive to Exeter, and assuming I was fast asleep in bed they had not called to me. My beloved Milly had lain across the doorway to my room, pretending to be asleep, but really blocking the way. I got away with it, but boy, I remember the welcome I got from the dogs and of course Caspian. They were pleased to see me again after a night of worry.

That meeting with the Furies was one of the worst Shola had endured for years. She told me later that on waking from what must have been a virtual coma, she had heard us talking from under her horse blanket and twitched out. In the battle efforts she had ripped a talon, hence the blood. She was sore for weeks.

I later looked up that storm of 1824; if in doubt, you can do the same. Imagine what the results would have been without Shola fighting our position. The storm surge produced that night was over two metres above normal high tide. Along the coast the village of East Fleet was destroyed completely, West Bay had the surging seas, flood the harbour, the river valley and three were killed. At Lyme Regis and Sidmouth houses were lost. There was serious flood damage and many drowned. The famous Cobb was breached and all along the coast many vessels were lost with people drowned.

At Weymouth the lovely esplanade was destroyed, the town flooded and more people drowned. The dreadful effect went further west, destroying many boats at Polperro. At Budleigh Salterton and Plymouth there was massive destruction and blocking of river mouths and smashing stone, with immense damage. The storm surge peaked at between five and six in the morning, which is why

Shola was so late and so worn out.

I have sometimes remembered that appalling night and stopped myself from hitting people I have heard calling dragons just fiction. I am so grateful for Shola's help that night. When this account is read it will make people think.

I slept well that night, completely drained. I bet I was not good company the next day either. In fact I did not meet Shola again for possibly four months, when the spring was well established.

CHAPTER 16

LIGHTS ON THE RIVER

In the weeks that followed the horrific storm, Jules and I met fairly regularly. Always with Milly in tow, we walked miles. On each trip he took in various plants, trees, and bushes again. I had no idea that nature had provided so many remedies, and got well into all the facts, remedies and responses that seemed automatic with him.

Looking back on it I now realise what a clever teacher he was. In a seeming relaxed manner, he got knowledge rammed into my head.

As I have written before for you, I am aware that modern pharmacology has produced many chemical resolutions for medical problems, but we must not lose sight of what is already here. I cannot let on too much of what he drummed into me over those months, but suffice it to say that I have used the knowledge countless times, and now my successor is getting it all.

Jules also spent his time on these walks making me look with new eyes upon all that the natural world has to offer, things we seem to be in a danger of forgetting.

One day in early March he looked really excited, bubbling with life.

'What's happening then?' I playfully asked, throwing some mock punches at him and laughing. 'What happens now? Go on, tell me. You are obviously bursting to.'

He began explaining that what we had to witness was a good antidote to the last horrors. It did not involve Shola at all, and simply represented water forces. He quickly went on to say that this did not mean waterspouts, floods and that sort of thing. It was he felt more in line with water energy, a helping force.

'You will see anyway. It is incredibly gentle, and beautiful, whatever you want to say. I have always felt honoured to witness it, similar to the white queen we saw. I will say no more. You will have to wait. The only slight problem is that it is hellish early. It is mercifully always on the same stretch, but we have to walk a long way. We will have to leave here at three in the morning.

'I'll wangle it somehow, perhaps sneak out' I said.

'You can doss here if it is a problem, anyway' he grinned. 'Next week, always on the same day each year, and here is an odd thing. In all the years this has happened for me it has never ever rained.'

As it happened I was able to sneak out like a mouse that morning. The dogs opened an eye when I appeared, wagged their tails once and went back to sleep.

It was pitch dark outside and it took my eyes a while to adjust. I worked my way down through the orchard and then found the footpath. Overhead I could just make out two hunting bats, their tiny wings a blur. The covering of clouds was being pushed along by a light upper wind, visible by the light from the moon. As I crossed the river bridge I heard a fox begin to bark almost right by me. I made better progress on the road and as I walked into the yard I could see a faint light in Jules' main window.

Now this might seem odd, but on reflection I cannot recall ever seeing anything electrical in his house. As I tapped on the door and went in, I was surprised to see that the light was from an old oil lamp. It hissed gently away, giving a bit of light, not marvellous, but light.

Jules was in the back of the room, in his old chair wrestling with a pair of wellies.

'Oi oi' he half whispered. 'Time for a mug of tea if you want. It's made in the pot.' he pointed. 'Had mine, biscuit too, by it. I'll be five minutes.'

After he closed the door, with no such thing as a lock, we left, following the river down towards the sea.

'The other watchers we met will be doing the same' he whispered to me.

On reflection I have no idea why this event means we have to talk so low. There is no one remotely near and they are all asleep anyway. We were miles from the nearest house, but still it seemed right to be so quiet.

I found the route rather tricky to say the least. It was hardly daylight. It involved negotiating the riverbank and I was still rubbish in slippery mud. The many overhanging branches meant I could not hang on to Jules for support very often. The difficulty was further compounded by the fact that many field barbed wire fences finished actually in the river to stop stock getting around them. All in all you could say the first couple of miles tested my reserve.

Soon the river widened, slowed and deepened, getting on to the wide flood plain. The fields got bigger and flatter, and walking became easier. Jules slowed, looking ahead, and signalling with finger on lips - no talking.

If you are wondering, we only know on which stretch of river we are needed, not the exact spot. We have to walk on until signalled.

There was just a hint of the sun rising, the sky showing the first hint of red as Jules lifted a hand. He bent down and pointed to a large clump of bulrush stalks by the river edge. He then pointed for us to crawl in.

We settled down as comfortably as we could, peeping out at the slow-moving river ahead. In the distance I could make out the street lights of Bridport. The noise of a lorry ground along, and then all town noise ceased. The river slowly gurgled on, and well away across the flood plain I heard a fox bark.

As we waited the sky filled with light, and I could hear in the far distance the sound of a milkman beginning his rounds. In the reed edge a coot started awake, giving its distinctive call. Further down the river I could hear a few ducks starting to squabble with each other.

Then Jules pointed at something that had caught his eye. On the river edge ahead, where it slowed into a deeper pool, a blue flame was beginning to rise. It was flickering and about three or four inches wide at the base. It shimmered, rising and falling, gaining in strength. There was no noise at all, no hiss, no roar, just the soft gurgle of the river.

As we watched another flame began to emerge, noticeably more intense in colour, again noiselessly. This one grew in height, which the other began to match. Soon, to my delight and surprise, at least half a dozen others began to rise, joining in the flickering dance. From the direction of the sea came more flames, as if summoned to the extraordinary dance.

Jules and I watched spellbound as this beautiful dance grew. Each flame was distinct, seeming to take a lead from its neighbour, falling and gyrating to some unheard melody. It was awesome and beautiful. Soon the whole river was lit by the flames.

I have now been entranced by this spectacle annually for many years. But this first time, as it died down and eventually stopped, I was itching for Jules to explain it. We both stayed very still until it had all finished and the river had begun to come to life. Three mallard ducks paddled past, probably the ones complaining to each other before. A water vole plopped in off the bank; I could just make out its head as it swam across the flow. Away across the field a great swirling mass of starlings began moving, looking like a great plume of smoke.

'Come on you. How was that? Unreal eh!' He pulled himself up and offered me a pull.

'You have done it again. What was that? Tell me, come on!'

I struggled to my feet ad he laughed out loud, grabbing my shoulders.

'I remember the first time for me too. Stunning eh?'

He paused, shaking his head, looking at the ground, then at the river, then me.

We started slowly walking back, each now and then turning to look back to where we had hidden. He explained that each year I and the other watchers had to witness the dance. He called them 'water fairies' for want of a term, but spirits, forces or nymphs would have done. He did know that each year they had to dance; it was part of the seasonal calendar. Unknown by many, but needing to be recognised by chosen people, it had to happen. It had in fact been happening since time began, ensuring the continuity of nature.

I can now easily recall, like seeing the White Queen the first time, how enthralled I was, how stunned. I must admit to being in a bit of a daze as we walked back.

It was still early as we walked back into his yard, and Jules asked me in for breakfast. He set about cooking a massive fry-up. We were both ravenous. Never before have the resulting fried egg, bacon, sausage, beans and toast been so well received and devoured.

'Usual mug of tea?' asked Jules, and I nodded back with a mouthful on toast and jam.

'You have seen all the forces you have to now' smiled Jules. 'Making sense? You happy? As you know, with these things you are not alone. The other chaps you met honour their local rights too. You know that only you have responsibility to Shola. I think the other three know of her, but not fully. You will have their respect though.

'Look, I know you did not ask for this, but although I am biased, have been watching you from when you were small, I do think you are adapting to your place. Fine, well done.'

To say I was embarrassed would be not saying enough, but inwardly I was touched by his confidence in me. Perhaps I could rise to the responsibility.

'You have got to give attention soon to your outward life as well though' he added.

We went on to talk over massive mugs of tea about how any kind of career would fit in, given that Shola would always ask and expect a virtually immediate response.

I must say that for a late teenager, it was a lot to be laid on me. Yet it all fitted and worked well though, so far.

As I left Jules shouted after me 'Shola's got a surprise or two lined up for you. It will be sometime in the next month, be ready'.

He smiled and lifted a hand in farewell. I waved back and walked on, lost somewhat in my thoughts and thinking of what I had seen that early morning while everyone else was asleep.

CHAPTER 17

ALONE WITH SHOLA

One of the most frustrating and annoying aspects of the first few years of my recovery was that despite all the physiotherapy, acupuncture and osteopathy I went through, bits of me still stubbornly refused to work properly.

About a month after seeing Jules two friends took me fly fishing for trout, to a local reservoir. The season had just begun and for years before we had gone along at this time, joined by many others - the usual start-of-season melee. But this time it was one long purgatory as my shoulder refused to let me cast.

There is something rather magical watching an accomplished fishermen using a fly rod. The line is weighted to match the rod, and an apparent effortless back swing charges the rod to fire the line forwards out straight. However for me it became dreadfully frustrating, as at best the line fell forward a few yards, however hard I tried. I am sure that any fish that saw my fly must have laughed.

In the end, out of frustration, I walked along to where the bank drops rapidly away, so that within a few yards your fly lands in deep water. On my own I watched the other two catching fish, which ad me even more frustrated.

We had been there for the best part of the morning when I felt the beginnings of Shola's call - and then it stopped. I wondered why. Was I needed or not?

I carried on trying to fish, watching at the same time the swallows hunting for flies over the lake. They flew fast inches above the water, then shot skywards. Two cormorants, the bane of the reservoir fish stockers, hung their wings out to dry on the edge of a jetty. They looked skeletal, long necked and somewhat sinister.

Then a faint call came again; incomplete, vague not demanding but definitely Shola. I did not put anything more to it. I could hardly leave as I had a lift over with the others, and the call did not come again. In fact I did not think of it again until seeing Jules the next day. Then I was able to put two and two together. He had met her planning my next challenge.

I walked down after lunch the next day, taking Milly with me. We gently wandered along, with her trotting off both left and right smelling recent history, as dogs do and we cannot.

Jules was sitting in a decrepit deckchair in his yard, taking the rays, such rays as there were. I found the sight of him rather amusing. He had his old cords on, rolled up to his knees to reveal white legs with big coursing varicose veins. He had stripped to an old vest, revealing a mass of armpit hair and a thin, almost starved, physical shape. On his face was an enormous pair of sunglasses; perched on his nose, they looked ten sizes too big.

'Aha, just the job, perfect timing' was his greeting as he pulled himself up. He gave Milly her usual ear massage and she wandered off to nose about. I thought to her to keep me in sight and not to go too far away.

'Got something planned for you, a good job you're here' said Jules, smiling from under his sunglasses at me. 'You had better tell Milly to come inside with me for ten minutes. She can raid my biscuit tin. I want you to call Shola, she is waiting. You will only be a few minutes with her. She wants you to do something. It will be easy, nice, don't worry.' He put a hand on my shoulder reassuringly.

'You have got though to do this all on your own, that's the deal. Go on, tell Milly. She can come with me.' He turned and started towards the house.

Calling Milly, I explained, saying that I had no idea what was planned. I was sure I would be all right and Jules had said it would be just a few minutes. Then both walked in, Jules turning at the door.

'Go on, it's all taken care of. She is waiting.'

I do not mind admitting now that this next calling for me was nerve racking. I did not have Jules by me, as before, although I was aware of him peeping now and then through his front window.

It took me what seemed ages to get myself prepared, even to the point where I needlessly moved away from a tree, remembering the time I had tried to begin when inside. As if outside she would bang her head.

Eventually I took my confidence in hand, glancing towards the house for reassurance and sitting down in the shingled yard. I do not mind admitting that I felt fear as I began intoning the call.

As the call gathered momentum I became braver. I suppose knowing what to expect eventually steeled my nerves. The last few lines gathered their usual momentum, almost chanting themselves. And then, with a tremendous ear popping, she was there.

I am still in awe of this moment. The feeling of power is

immense; out of deference you are forced to look down. The lemony smell is there and you are aware of an almighty presence arriving.

I did not know what to say, what to do. I was a touch childlike, frightened but at the same time purely joyous.

Shola's front legs were, a little unnervingly, blood-stained again, and as I looked down I could see that caught in her front talons were lumps of wool and sheepskin. Slowly I let my eyes wander deferentially up to hers way. Her tail twitched slowly, heaping up great mounds of the shingle with each sweep.

I looked towards her face and then… we connected.

'Well done Myrrdin' she thought gently to me. 'You have done it, we are one.'

She moved her head to look straight at me; I could see wisps of meat stuck between her teeth, and her breath smelt like a butcher's shop. Despite my brave attempts, my legs had a give-away shake.

'I will carry you now, we want you to see something.'

'But I have Milly here and… I have no trews. I wasn't expecting…. '

She lifted a great front leg. 'You are fine, get on, all is right, all expected.'

How could I argue? I had no option, It was me now, just me.

I walked to the side of her and tried to force my foot up and over her bent-down neck. By wiggling I got myself upright and used both hands to push on her scaly neck. I half wriggled myself back and sat over what I suppose you would call her shoulders, in front of her wings. They moved forwards and lowered and rose in a sort of massive stretch. Through my seat I was aware of her massive muscles flexing. Still today, many years later I find this to be a wonderful sensation.

'We go!' she thought to me, and all normal sights in the yard went.

'Where?'

With no Jules to hang on to, there seemed too much room. I stupidly tried initially not to look down.

As we lazily flew on, Shola gaining height without any apparent effort, I began to relax a little. I found that I could almost link my feet together under her neck. Wriggling down between the spines on her neck, and squeezing her rough neck with my thighs, as if riding, I felt safer.

'Myrrdin called me, once to help. I will show you'

Then she twitched, making my ears pop.

'This is your year, you say nineteen sixty seven.'

We were over the coast and on the horizon, not too far out I could just make out an oil tanker, surrounded by smaller boats.

Shola circled in big lazy circles, my view changing between the land and the sea as she flew. We climbed up into a scattered layer of clouds, which you could almost reach and touch. She flew through one; it was like being in a mist. I looked down, actually beginning to enjoy this, now feeling really safe. Shola picked up on this and begun to fly faster, her wings pumping. The power and speed were wonderful. I almost yelled with excitement.

'Good… you like this. The last six you have not enjoyed things so much.'

'Brilliant, brilliant!' was all I could answer.

'Now we try.'

She closed her wings back against her body and dropped earthwards, picking up tremendous speed. My cheeks and face were distorted and I felt I could not breathe. When I thought we were doomed to hit the sea, her wings opened and we rocketed back up. I whooped with joy and excitement.

'Wonderful, wonderful!' I thought to her, squeezing her neck with my legs.

'You are wonderful!'

'Not just me.' Now I know better about you, we will have fun. I have to go back seven of you since I had one who I really liked. We have to see my call now, look.'

She stayed high, flying over the tanker. I realised that it had not moved, and as we got nearer could see that it was fast on rocks. A flotilla of boats around it had now gone shoreward. From a great gash on the ship's side I could make out a ghastly mess of jet-black oil leaking. With each wave that broke on the injured boat, great gushes of oil spewed out. Looking away from the tanker, I could see a massive slick of oil drifting away to the horizon. It seemed to suppress the waves, and I could just make out a flock of oiled gannets struggling in the mess, their wings beating vainly until they drowned.

As we went downwind the smell of hydrocarbons became ghastly. Without being asked, Shola turned shorewards.

'We need to be clear now. You will see why, Myrrdin asked me to fire this mess. To save nature. I was too late and in any case I am beaten. You will see. This is the ship you called Torrey Canyon.'

As she was thinking this to me there came the piercing screech of a jet fighter arriving in front and to the right of us.

'Now be tight' ordered Shola, as from beneath the fighter I was stunned to see a bomb drop. We watched as it hit and exploded, to be followed almost straight away by another howling jet. It did the same thing, only this time as it cleared the sky above there was a massive blast and a rising pall of thick black billowing smoke.

The blast caught us, even at that distance, and made Shola rock. I clung on tighter.

'You see. Job done without my breath!' I could almost imagine a laugh.

She stayed loitering, more gliding than flying, as we watched the pall of smoke rise. It was so black it caused the sun to be blocked out.

'I will now show one last thing.'

'Have we time? Are we far away?'

'It is no time. I will show you one thing I was asked but could not help at all. We go.'

And with that, in a blink, the sea disappeared.

I found it hard to get it together in my mind as everything went. Then below us I could just make out a bleak land of bare soil. It was hard to see exactly what was going on, as we seemed to be passing through a fog of fine yellow particles. Soon I was having a job breathing, and rummaged around in my pocket for a handkerchief. Risking letting go for a moment, I tied it into a crude mask.

'I will go lower. It is sweeter lower. The Myrrdin for this time, you say eighteen sixteen, ask for help. No sun came… all blocked. A mountain far away blew. I could not help. For one year ruined crops, life was bad.'

She stopped flapping and just hung on the air currents over the barren, ruined landscape. Looking down I could see no crops, nothing growing, just a bare and muddy landscape. Here and there stood the odd clump of sad-looking trees. The land seemed empty, with no cows or sheep evident.

I could not see the sun. As I look up and across to where it should be, just a faint yellow disc was visible. The sky was a murky yellow colour.

'People starving, crops failing' thought Shola. 'Grim. We will go, I could not help here.'

'Yes I cannot breathe too well anyway' I thought back, beginning to get a bit wheezy and my chest feeling tight.

With that thought she twitched back over Netherbury and we dropped into Jules yard. He came out beaming, drying his hands to meet us.

'Good flight? Good five minutes?'

'Wonderful, but not five minutes surely?'

'Yep, actually' looking at his watch 'not even that.'

I swung my aching legs over her neck, went forward, took her neck in both hands and gave her a hug.

'I cannot believe this. It's unreal. I cannot thank you enough for the honour.'

'It gets easier' said Shola. 'I'll call you in you in two months after your white queen watching. I have something then just as important for you to see, also you will meet Typos.'

'Typos?'

I looked around at Jules, who rather mischievously raised his eyebrows and shrugged his shoulders in an exaggerated manner.

'I go, be safe.' And then she had gone.

Strangely, to this day I felt robbed, sad, that she had gone. How ridiculous. I could have become rather emotional. Jules slapped me on the back and we went in together to find Milly fast asleep. She roused as we came in.

'All passed?' she thought to me.

'Yes, all finished. I will tell you both what happened. It was unreal.'

I happened to look up and caught Jules looking at me with a

dreadfully sad expression. On catching my gaze he began smiling. I knew he was miles away, thinking of other things.

He did not say anything, but went over to his seemingly ever-burning fire to hang the kettle on its hook. I remember that I did not enquire, thinking it perhaps more diplomatic not to. He had his thoughts and they were obvious. I hoped he would tell me when he felt it right.

CHAPTER 18

THE WHITE QUEEN RETURNS

I do not know where the time goes; it seems to fly past. I remember this day for the sadness Jules went through. It must have been ghastly for him.

The arrival of spring that year was unusually warm. The hedges greened up, it seemed, in front of your eyes, and the orchard fruit trees were heavy in blossom. The grass already seemed to be forcing its way out, which was fine for the new crop of lambs. We had turned them out on to new grass with their dams. They seemed to spend their time charging about. They would suddenly remember their milk bar and charge back, butting their mothers skywards as they suckled. Within a few moments they would reform into a movable mass, and like all young get up to mischief, exploring and being a general nuisance to their mothers. Spring had come early that year

The day before I knew we were wanted, Jules arranged that I should meet him up on the hill in the afternoon. He was apparently helping with a section of fencing and it would save him doubling back. This meant me walking up the first hill on my own. To this day it still does not bring back any memories of my accident. All traces are gone from my mind.

As the late afternoon sun began to set I looked over the valley at far-off Pilsdon Hill, crowned with its mantle of beech trees. Before it I could just make out the spire of Netherbury church. I spent a while soaking in the view, looking down and across at the sea, but also back inland towards the downland behind Beaminster. It was beautifully quiet up there. Occasionally the noise of a lorry passing in the valley below would filter up.

I looked down and saw Jules manfully walking up the steeper track, his head bent down to the task. As he got nearer I yelled a greeting and he stopped walking, looked up and waved. In a few minutes he arrived, panting heavily, his lips almost blue.

'Oi oi' he gasped. As he flung himself down, his chest was rising and falling.

'God!' he exclaimed, 'I am sure it is getting steeper'.

'Go on, get your breath' I said.

'It is a right old pull up there.'

'We have got ages anyway. Haven't we?'

We sat passing the time, chatting about nothing in particular, before moving off. Jules had recovered.

Jules had a certain trick, and he did it now. He pulled from his pocket a crumpled, off-white paper bag of pineapple sweets and offered it to me. As usual, thanks to the heat of his pocket, the sweets were stuck together in one great mass. And as usual, he looked around for a handy gatepost, went over and banged the bag on it to separate them so I could pick out a single sweet. Incidentally, I would love to find these sweets for myself now, but despite searching I have never succeeded.

We walked on to the top, where a big tractor was preparing a seedbed. The driver saw us on one of his passes and waved a greeting to us. We responded and walked on to meet the small top road.

This time I managed to do the gate, which did not open still, and meant climbing, without any help. We walked up to the manor house before turning off to go down into the valley. By the side of the road great fronds of cow parsley swayed in the wind and wild garlic was growing by the armful. The darkness was drawing on, with Jules glancing at the sky and walking faster.

All around us could be heard pheasants calling, and on the far-off slopes a buzzard was soaring on a column of air from the far off wood edge.

The small lake on the valley floor was very low this year, but the end we had to go around was still thick bog and sticky mud. Jules by now was respectfully silent and I walked behind him, keeping my own thoughts. We walked up and over the further side, picking our way through the brambles and ducking under the holly branches.

Bending low and trying not to fall over on the slippery surface, Jules pointed under a great holly bush. He signalled that he would get under it first, with me almost having to sit on the outside.

We had only been there for what seemed a few minutes when overhead a tawny owl called. The wood settled into night mode, the valley slope meaning we lost the last bit of sunset.

It may have been my imagination but I always hear rustling, which I take to be mice going about their business, and far-off fox calls. The occasional noise of flapping wings came from pigeons roosting against the noise of the light wind in the upper tree twigs.

Jules and I kept quiet until he nudged me. I was ready for this, as below me I could just make out three badgers shuffling along.

Through the dark I was able to make out the way they scented forwards, turning their heads side to side.

To this day I still feel my heartbeat increase in anticipation at such moments. We only had to wait what seemed a few moments for four foxes to appear, running to and fro. They stopped now and then to stand, legs shaking, noses scenting before moving off.

And then… a vision of pure wonder arrives. This time I knew what to expect but I was still stunned. In fact to be honest, I still am, every year.

She is truly beautiful, surrounded by her own light, and walking without sound. Her dress touches the floor over her feet. At her waist is a brown belt and the truly amazing thing is her hair. Long and fine, it flies with energy of its own behind her. As I have told you before, she seems to be throwing things to either side of her.

This time there was a marked difference in behaviour, which although not alarming was bewildering.

Below us, in fact opposite, she stopped. Yes – she stopped and looked up to us. I felt that I wanted to hide, but I was reassured by Jules beside me.

Like the year before, he raised my right hand above my head in a form of acceptance. Her pale blue, intense eyes seemed to penetrate me, in a way frightening. Then she turned her attention to Jules, smiled – yes, smiled - and lifted her hand. She turned and carried on and the musical harmony faded away. I sat stunned.

Jules and I pulled ourselves out. I may not be the most sensitive person, but I could tell from his body language that he was badly upset. We walked on out of the wood, not saying anything.

'Amazing, that. Wish I understood' I offered at his bent back. He lifted a hand and gently waved it. He walked on, and I could hear the odd gasp; he was crying. I did not feel I could or should say anything.

In the dark we met the road on the hilltop, and without a lot of chat walked on the long way rather than going across the hill. As the village lights came into view he seemed a little recovered, although his voice rose and fell a bit until he coughed and gripped it.

'Wonderful. What an honour you have to see it. Remember to introduce your replacement gently.'

He looked at me. In the dim light I could see that his face was tear-stained, his eyes red.

'Look, tell me to mind my business, but are you all right? Can I help?'

He smiled back. 'No. Very kind, but no problem.' He paused, looking at me.

'It's just what faces me… well I suppose you as well, one day. Come on, come in for a cup of tea, eh? The answer to all.'

He gave a forced laugh, smiled at me and squeezed my elbow with one hand. I followed him in. Now I know what was on his mind, I face it too.

We stayed gently talking about nothing in particular, until, noting the time, I realised I had to go. As I stood up, Jules looked at me.

'You will have to call Shola soon, she wants you to see something important.'

'How soon, tomorrow?'

'No, it's not that urgent. In the next month, but…' he paused, looking at me intently - 'On your own… and from perhaps your hill, near your barn. Shift your sheep first, otherwise they will die of fear.' He smiled. 'Let me know how you get on. Wander down with Milly after to tell me.'

CHAPTER 19

A NEW DRAGON, AND A NEW MYRDDIN

The spring carried on blooming with a massive energy that year. Almost daily you could imagine that the grass had grown higher. The new leaves opened on the trees with a rich shade of green. On the road edges around the village the wild garlic threw its white flowers out, competing with the glorious bluebells.

Overhead the house martins and swallows arrived, with their usual excited flying. They sought out their old nest sites with much inspection, flying in and out of the barns and chattering to each other.

We often saw six or seven buzzards airborne over the village at the same time, making their mewing calls, gently flying in big lazy circles. They looked almost as if they belonged in Africa.

My time at home was spent every day preparing seedbeds for our vegetables, with much digging and weeding. The soil needed two passes with our tractor with rotavator attachment until it was a fine tilth. Then, much to everyone's amusement, I could be seen still crawling across the patch, sowing seeds. Even though I was some way past my injury I still found it impossible to get up from my knees without grabbing on a fence and pulling up. I am not much better now, Ridiculous, I know.

I got almost on top of my current jobs, but to be honest Jules' instructions to contact Shola had been playing on my mind. As I am sure you can imagine.

Late one afternoon, I brushed the ingrained mud off my jeans as much as possible, used the garden hose to clean my hands a bit and got ready to go up the hill. My parents were both out, so having a final chat with the horses and settling the dogs, I locked up and left.

It is not much of a walk up the hill, and on the way I gathered my thoughts, and I suppose the motivation and bravery to call her.

Our first field (I did remember my instructions) would not do. It was full of the ewes and lambs, so that barn was not on.

As I climbed the gate a bunch of ewes looked up for a moment. One bleated, but seeing I was not carrying a bucket it put its head back down. With a mouth full of grass it carried on bleating. A far-off group of lambs resumed their mindless running about, and I watched and smiled.

It was actually warm on the hill, with a faint wind blowing. As I looked down into the village I saw the fish-selling van arrive, and a group of children off the school bus. On the other side of the valley a small blue tractor toiled.

Our far fields were served by a long barn, hidden from all the houses on the village edge by a line of trees. I don't mind admitting that I walked about for a while like a chicken; I had to gather mental preparedness. Even now this point takes a certain reserve.

After getting rather cross with myself, waving my arms, stomping a bit, I finally began calling her. I was mentally prepared, which was just as well, for what happened nearly made me soil myself with fear.

For some reason the usual intonation took even more energy at the end to control. It has always seemed to gather speed, unasked, of its own volition. This time it was almost garbled, even though I was chanting it. I wanted to hide, but at the same time I got very excited.

The usual ear-popping was louder and rather painful, making me momentarily having a blinding headache. I shut my eyes until my hearing was normal. Then on opening them I nearly fainted in shock.

For there was not one dragon, but two.

They stood there looking around, snorting. I recognised Shola, of course. She caught my eye and I felt a resurgence between us. She was intensely calming.

The other dragon was smaller. It moved around shuffling its front legs, a small flame issuing from its jaws with an intense roaring noise. The flame, blue in colour, went as quickly as it had appeared.

The new dragon shook its head and almost danced, hopping on its four legs. It then got going through a rearing and bucking sequence. It came to a halt, and a massive fart issued forth. I was stunned, then marginally amused.

This animal was about half the size of Shola, mainly yellow in colour with greenish legs. It was not so heavily scaled, but had tiny spines down its neck. The front legs were more delicate but finished in rapier-looking talons, while the hind legs were already massive. They finished in razor-sharp talons, which were ripping the grass and turf with every movement. Its wings opened and closed along its body, almost shivering in movement.

Shola stood watching, alternately looking across at me.

'This is Typos, my daughter' she thought to me. 'When she is bigger she will replace me. Typos, this is Myrrdin. You know about him. His line will witness you, be there later. Possibly not him, we will see.'

I was stunned; the fact that I was seeing two dragons was crazy enough. To know that Shola had a daughter and that here she was in front of me was frightening and weird. I could not answer, did not know what sensible thing to say.

'All well, Myrddin?'

'Well actually, I'm lost' I eventually replied.

Shola's daughter at this point had stopped jumping about and was standing gently next to her mother, her head tipped now and then to one side, watching me intently. I began to feel a touch embarrassed by the intensity of her gaze.

'She cannot talk your language yet. She learns, all is new. This was to introduce as promised. You will meet many times from today.'

Typos took a step towards me. I shot back, causing Typos to look at her mother. Obviously thoughts were passed, as she then took a step back, turned her head to the ground and closed her eyes.

'It will come. You will have fun, both of you' thought Shola, looking intensely at me. 'She will now go, but I want you to come with me. We need to see someone important.'

Typos seemed to be challenging her mother. After some apparent debate, Shola thought, 'She now comes to watch also. Come, we go'

With orders like this, from something so unreal, what could I do? Walking around to Shola's heaving flanks, I went alongside her neck, which she had lowered right down, putting her chin on the ground. She allowed me to climb on and settle in and lifted her head up. I felt her flex her massive wings.

I looked at her daughter, whose head was just a few feet from me. She was watching intently and turning her head from side to side very inquisitively. For the want of something appropriate to say and do, I simply smiled back. I saw her nostrils go in and out as she smelled me. She had the same leathery, lemony smell about her.

Now you will straight away think this an account of an idiot, but Typos smiled back. Yes - smiled. At that point we bonded. It was the full bonding I had once had with her mother. I felt such joy, jubilation and delight.

Of course, such was my rapport with Shola that all of this was not lost on her. I knew that I had become so, so, so lucky.

'We go, we see' she said. She went, but this time the ground stayed the same.

'You are still here' I thought to her.

'Yes, but not in your now' she thought back. 'We are a bit behind your real time. This is one way we always used to travel.... till some forgot' she added. 'We are behind your time for just a moment, it is only a problem in sun.'

'In sun?'

'Yes. The shadow does not follow the time, it can be seen. We have to take care... again some have failed. Some have guessed us in the past.'

I kept quiet, dwelling on this. It was beginning to make more sense.

We went lazily up and I looked down on the small town of Beaminster. We flew slowly out to the west, following a windy country road. The big hill of Pilsdon came alongside us and far away to the south the sea twinkled.

Typos was flying along, now and then looking back, as her wings pushed her on. She would alternate positions with us, never going in front, just to the sides, above and below.

'Where do we go?'

'Local. We see your replacement, your successor. He is chosen already, he is your next. We may be lucky and see him today. If not we try again, we will see.'

I sat saying nothing, stunned by this news.

We flew on until we were over what I now know to be a small hamlet called Drimpton. Scarcely a crow's flight from Netherbury, it is a small settlement with a pub, village hall and a nice village feel. Shola was scanning below, her great head turning from side to side. Her wings flapped slowly, with Typos keeping out of her way.

We patrolled like this for half an hour; I knew the time because in her passes I often saw the faces of the village clock.

Suddenly she started to beat her wings faster. 'There!' she thought to me. "He is with his mother in their back garden. We have him.'

I tried to look ahead and down. Holding his mother's hand was a fair-haired tiny boy, no more than three years old. They were feeding two rabbits in a run with what looked like bits of cabbage leaves. The lad let go of his mother's hand and half ran, half toddled off to pick up a discarded toy tractor. His mother followed, bent down and scooped him up. Leg wriggling and much laughter followed. She bent down to kiss him on the head. We watched as they walked back into their back door.

'He is William. He will follow you. I will protect him, and after me Typos will protect him. The story continues, Myrrdin to Myrrdin. It is enough.'

One thing I did remember is that we had to be back where she twitched and arrived at the start. She flew back to our field, the two gently flying along, very relaxed and casual. I do remember that I was not very communicative as we ambled back; I was too lost in my thoughts.

The familiar countryside and fields appeared below, and with less ear-popping than usual she twitched back and landed.

'I will call when you are needed' she thought to me. Then, without so much as a cheerio, she and Typos disappeared, leaving no trace.

I walked gently back, lost in my thoughts. I do not mind admitting that in a rather unmanly way that night when I got in, boy, did I need to cuddle Milly.

My parents were back when I got in. They probably put my lack of conversation down to tiredness. I admit that I was lost in my thoughts, and making the excuse of being worn out I went up to bed.

For ages, sleep was impossible. Every time I tried to stop thinking of that afternoon my brain raced back to it. Little was I to know that over the next months my situation would worsen.

Would I have tried to opt out if I had known? Could I, in fact? As I have tried to remember this for you, I have understandably gone over this in my mind.

The answer is of course no, but at times I do not mind admitting the pressure to run and hide has been enormous.

Later I will tell you about further beginnings, but I do remember the next morning feeling worn out and tired through lack of sleep. I went downstairs, creeping so as not to wake anyone.

I shared tea and toast with the dogs, and as the sun rose Milly and I set off through the dew-drenched grass, to see if Jules was awake and up. I knew I needed to talk through things urgently with him.

CHAPTER 20

MY TRAINING NEARS AN END

The fields were soaked with dew that morning. This was bad for me, as of course I did not have my wellies on, just a pair of old trainers. Soon my feet were drenched, and the wet spread up to my socks and trousers.

All across the lower field by the river the grass was marked by the prints of a fox. Randomly wandering, with no seeming purpose, it had been trotting about, possibly to surprise a mouse or something bigger. On the riverbank a moorhen strutted about, and I could hear a duck gently babbling to itself in the reeds.

The river was gin clear that morning, and its usual depth. I stopped on the bridge with Milly, just watching it. The sun was now well up and the hedges were alive with questing birds.

We had to move in off the road as a milk tanker went past. The driver gave a friendly nod of thanks.

We walked to Jules' front door to find it, as usual, ajar. I called out and on hearing us Jules shouted out in French, 'Entrez!' He was obviously in fine form.

'I am sorry we are so early, but I want to talk to you.'

'Not at all old chap, come in. Bung the kettle on, I'm just finishing shaving.'

We wandered in to see him bent over his sink. He had a half lathered face and was hacking at it with an old razor. I could not bear to watch - he was bound to cut himself, I thought.

The fire was going well, as Jules had probably heated his shaving water. I put the kettle on and turned to him.

'I'm not really worried, but a bit lost with it all' I began.

'Go on, fire away, what's on your mind?

While he finished shaving and rinsed his razor, and I made tea for us, we talked. I told him about meeting Shola's daughter and then seeing my eventual replacement. At this point he lifted a hand.

'I know, it's strange isn't it. I remember Shola showing you to me. You were being pushed along in a go-cart by your mother.'

He paused again, obviously lost in his thoughts.

'Anyway, you grew on. I watched now and then, learned more about you. Watched as you grew, and I suppose the rest is history. You will do the same with your chap. The years go frighteningly quick.'

He sat down, holding his mug of steaming tea with both hands.

'Look, as I have said before, you had no choice in this, nor has your next. For what it is worth, I know you've got a good grab of things. You appreciate your responsibility, and will keep a light touch. You will represent the humans at a different, older level, a level most people do not even realise is there. One thing is for sure though, if people did realise they would often be scared silly. Look.'

He pointed at me, smiling but serious. 'Yours is an ancient trust, unknown to but a few. You are not alone. The old forces perform and you witness with others. It just happens that above this you now have the mantle of being the continuation of an old, very old position, responsibility, call it what you will.'

He paused, looking directly at me. 'You and I, with your next, are unique, witnessing many things for the dragons. The sad thing is that you can never tell it to anyone. You will see amazing things, and watch horrible things. This has been going on for centuries. I have no idea why it began, but I do know that you can find stories of dragons all over the world - all over. Importantly for us, our country is littered in history with tales of Myrrdin, or Merlin.'

He stopped, waiting for me to say something. I can remember feeling rather at a loss.

'The position you now have is an honour that you alone will know about. In a way it is such a shame. You cannot share it with anyone, just the one who follows. The other watchers you met with me, I am sure, know you are different. They have never asked me, but I am sure they know we are different. You have got to work out though, how you will earn your bread.'

He looked across at me with a serious face, and raised an eyebrow.

The conversation got lighter, and I suppose after all I had seen so far my mind got a little easier. After all, to put it crudely Jules was alive, and he was strong and I would be like him. Part of me felt honoured, to have been chosen. It just marginally annoyed me that I had had no choice.

'Look I have now got to introduce you to the last new things, forces, if you want to call them that. You are ready for it. It's my last duty, and then I am done. Next week. No - tell you what, we will start now. Why wait, I need to show you heavier stuff. Stuff I suppose Myrrdins have been involved with for centuries and individually have got better, stronger and more refined.'

'The hospital say I still have another three years of improvement' I told him. 'And the university Is keeping my place, so I am done for that. I am worried though - suppose Shola wanted me when I was in a lecture, or working? How does it fit?'

He laughed, turned fully to me and grabbed my knees.

'Look it is not that rigid, I have never had a problem. Although I do remember one time when I excused myself and was gone so long that they were almost on the point of breaking the loo door down.'

We both had a good laugh, and it made me relax a bit more about my future.

'What was Shola's daughter like?' he asked me. 'Fun, like her?'

I was about to tell him when he smartly raised a hand. 'No, don't say, none of my business.' He smiled and I got the point.

It was still early, so with Milly we went outside to wander down to the river. As we walked he began explaining and demonstrating some last things, tricks if you want to call them that. Most of them will remain secret except for my successor, but I feel I can explain a little to you.

When we are chosen we are allocated certain elements – gifts, if you like to call it that. Mine, which after fifty odd years I still find amazing, was communication with horses and dogs. Jules though was given shapeshifting; not just wearing disguise, but appearing transformed. He told me that most of this involved using the background properly, and used the fact that people only look casually when they meet people. First impressions are the norm. People rarely look intently.

He had used this gift a few times. He admitted to me that when he had heard about my accident, he did not want to be seen watching me. He mentioned a rising and falling stack of leaves which he kept going in front of him. He had remained against the road edge, unnoticed by all but the most observant, until the ambulance had arrived.

Over the next few weeks I often met up with him to be shown how a little-known earth force can be used to produce far-off effects. I remembered the way he had stopped a cloud momentarily, months before by the bridge. It scared me witless on one of the first times I met him. Suffice it to say, and I will not tell you more, he taught me how to do this. The first time that I tried it alongside him, I frankly thought I was on the way out. It requires so much mental effort that after that day I have never used it again. Of course I am practised partially with it, and shown my successor, but I have never fully employed it, nor for that matter had to use it in anger.

We covered many miles in and around the village over those few weeks. Milly often came with us, joining in now and then, with Jules drumming into me everything he felt I still needed to know.

I became good at brewing a tea he likes, incredibly strong, over a proper fire. One day he declared a break and showed me how he made his weird but tasty biscuits. He baked or fried them over the open fire on a metal tray. There was a surprising ingredient, which accounted for their strange but wonderful taste, and their somewhat stimulating effect.

Before I move on, I want to say that the names I have used are not the real ones, to protect them. I am not stupid, but do some homework and you will be surprised.

When I think back to that early summer I appreciate how truly kind Jules was to me. I now know that when you are faced with a lad shoved into such a position it takes great skill, tact and kindness to pull it off. We are fortunate with this job that we only have to do it the once, mercifully.

It has occurred to me that I have no idea what would happen if I had said no, or if my successor had declined. Thankfully it did not figure. Anyway I have interrupted my memoirs. I will get back to them, but first two dogs would like their supper. Actually so would I. You go and get yours and I will carry on remembering after.

CHAPTER 21

THE DEPARTURE OF JULES

What follows is still, after all these years, hard for me to write about.

We had been enjoying a glorious early summer. The mornings were unseasonably warm, with light winds, and bright light. Everywhere summer could be felt. Our lambing had gone well, with us losing no lambs at all. They gambolled about without a care; the vegetable seeds were sprouting, and many showing. The horses had their shoes off, and the hay lays on the hill were growing apace.

The guttering along the stable edge was jammed with a variety of weeds, roof runoff, leaves and the odd twig. To try and be useful I rather timidly persuaded my feet up a ladder and spent my mornings trying to clear the rubbish out. My mother had a blue fit when she came home that first lunchtime and found me up a ladder. I will not bore you with her comments about risk, hospitals etc. She was understandably concerned, and once again over lunch I had to do a peace operation.

But in the afternoon, when she had left, I went back up and carried on. Overhead the house martins dive-bombed me as they flew in and out of the stable doors. I worked on, getting nearer the end.

I can recall taking a breather while still up the ladder. I could see down across the valley from my vantage point. Over the river the far house had a lawnmower going, just now and then on view.

Then I looked down to the bridge to see a big black car cruising very slowly up to the entrance to Jules' yard. Curious. After perhaps half an hour I saw it leave again, equally slowly. I climbed down on to the lawn. I was both worried and intrigued. After what I thought was a suitable interval, I called Milly and we walked down the valley edge to see if something was wrong.

The rooks were making an immense noise as we crossed the river, and I thought maybe a predator was harassing them. Looking closely and staring through the trees, I could see no reason for their distress calls. They circled above the rookery calling and yelling, much more loudly than normal.

No cars were present as we wandered into the yard. Jules' front door was, uncharacteristically, firmly shut. As I was wondering what to do next, Mr Andrews came out of the barn at the side of the yard and hailed me. Following behind was his wife Jane, red-eyed and crying.

'Hello there Peter, are you all right?' he asked. He carried on walking towards me, Jane tucked in behind him.

'Yes, fine, been up a ladder, thought I would take a break and walk down to see Jules.'

He looked at me with a very odd look, which I recall to this day. Jane let out a large sob, hiding her face, and turned to walk off to their house.

'I have bad news for you. Come on, we will have a sit for a mo. To the barn, come on you.'

I felt a lurch in the pit of my stomach. I knew what must have happened.

'Jules has gone. He died in the night. I know you two had become close.'

He paused, looking at me. 'He was always talking about you, and very proud of you he was.'

I did not know what to say. It all seemed quite unreal.

We walked to the barn and sat on some straw bales. I could not really look at him; I was feeling devastated. Jules and everything he meant had become my life.

'The cruel thing is that it was his birthday yesterday. Unbelievable.'

'What, he never hinted at that! I had no idea, that's dreadful.'

'Yes, it's true, he was eighty-five. But he was a fit chap. He occasionally looked his age. It just shows you. He was such a nice chap, always useful and dependable.'

'He was eighty-five?' I asked, stunned. I was suddenly remembering what he had told me months before.

'That's right, it's no great age these days.'

He looked at the floor. I sat stunned, not just at my loss but at the thought of what this meant for me.

As if realising my sadness, Milly shoved her head in my lap. 'Later' I thought to her. Her dark brown eyes looked into mine.

'I know' she thought back. 'The rooks outside are mourning'.

I felt awful, sadder than I had ever been. We stayed talking for a time. He promised to let me know what arrangements would be made, but said he was not really aware that Jules had any living relatives. He had never seen any, or had Jules mention any to him. A bit of a mystery, his family.

Milly and I wandered back, not really concentrating in where we walked. At home my parents seemed genuinely sad to hear the news; on reflection they must have known what this loss meant to me.

I felt drained emotionally. Strange as it may seem, Shola made the loss of Jules much more bearable later, putting a different feeling to it.

Jules' simple funeral took place possibly a week later, I do not remember exactly. It was not very religious, with only a handful of people present. I was very subdued; his boss said a few words. I do remember him saying how Jules always seemed to be at one with the seasons. He always knew what was right and was a true countryman. Little did he know how closely Jules was linked in with the natural order.

Afterwards there was the usual drinks affair, which I did not attend although invited by Mr and Mrs Andrews. As I said my goodbyes, Mrs Andrews gave me a hug. Then, leaning near my ear, she whispered 'Carry on his work Peter, it is yours now.'

I looked back to her, puzzled, and said 'What do you mean?' She put a finger to her lips, looking straight at me, then turned as another guest took her away. As she walked across the room with him, she turned and looked at me over her shoulder and mouthed 'be brave'. Then she smiled and was gone, lost among the other guests.

I got to hear later exactly what she meant, and it put a whole new perspective on the Jules I had known.

I walked slowly back, lost in gloomy, sad thoughts, to take my suit off and change into something more casual. I decided to go on a walk with Milly, and we disappeared for a good four hours. I cannot tell you now where we went, but it was a hard, long trip at a good pace. Some sort of order came back to my mind.

My parents were sensibly not intrusive with their questions that night over supper. I was probably not enlivening company, lost in my memories. Now I was on my own. It dawned on me that I had lost my anchor and had all the responsibility. There was no one else.

Then it came to me with a rush. What about Shola? The watchers? The local forces that must be witnessed?

The full magnitude of what I was to do hit me hard, and I went to write in some sort of code the few definite dates I remembered.

My parents left me to sit in front of the television that night; I was not watching it, just using it as a distraction. Jules had known his end, as I now do. It must have been funny to show me everything, get me used to dates, take the newness and strangeness out. He never hinted at his own final date, keeping those thoughts to himself. He had led me to think I had longer, keeping me relaxed I suppose.

I fell asleep eventually that night, throwing the idea around in my head: would I or could I call Shola and what to tell her? Was I brave enough to do it without having Jules in the background for safety?

CHAPTER 22

A CALL TO SHOLA

If I am honest, I did not feel able to do anything for a good week. I was too scared, too worried, too cowardly.

With midsummer rapidly approaching and my memories etched in my mind of the plague pits, I knew I had to call her. The first time with Shola seemed only yesterday.

The sheep were off the hill, having been shorn and folded at home. This meant the home paddocks had their weeds eaten off and a liberal bit of dunging too. Generally the fields were better for it. In the early days this meant the sheep being driven the short distance off the hill to home along the road. The journey meant that someone had to go ahead to close gates, bung up holes and keep them in the right direction. As you can imagine this was often fraught, but sometimes humorous.

Now such transits are forbidden. Foot and mouth disease and other viral infections mean a car-drawn trailer is needed.

The top fields were empty, growing back for winter grazing, which meant I could safely call Shola without the risk of the trauma which seeing her would have caused the sheep. I walked up there and a gentle wind was blowing, making the grass heads dance in the wind.

CHAPTER 22

As I walked around the edge of the field, I stopped to watch a lark overhead. It was hanging on its wings, a dot in the sky. Keeping position it sang its heart out, the wings vibrating each side of it. As I carried on watching it suddenly dropped through perhaps a hundred feet, stopped singing and levelled off, flying about twenty yards with the wind. Here it resumed singing, climbing slowly again as it sang. A marvellous song, rich and intense, joyous.

I climbed over the padlocked gate, trying to gather the courage to call Shola. In front of the barn I stopped, kicking at a dock and trying to gather resolve.

The light wind was warm, carrying the scent of nearby honeysuckle and rich with the smell of the grasses. I was about to do something that seemed so removed from reality that I do not mind admitting I fiddled about for ages putting it off.

Gathering confidence and half thinking I would not be successful, I sat down on the grass, well away from the barn, and began the call. The chant began slowly as normal, with me expecting it to start more insistent and gather its own momentum. I sat quietly repeating the phrases almost to myself. A part of me thought it would not work; Jules was not there. I kept going, not really convinced. Then – yes! It gathered it's own momentum. I could not believe it; I shook with anticipation.

It was real, happening. I carried on with the chant, rising and falling as taught. Then my ears began to hurt and my ears popped. I looked across and there was Shola, in all her fearsomeness. She turned to look at me, shifting her weight from one front leg to the other, her wings settling to her sides.

Though I knew I could look at her, I automatically looked at the ground. My fear was absolute, despite having met and flown with her before.

After what seemed ages, but in reality was only a moment, she spoke.

'Myrrdin, you called' she thought to me. 'You have need. What? Say.'

Like an idiot I began stammering, sounding pathetic.

'Jules is gone, dead. There is just me now, I thought you should know.'

I was straight away aware of her annoyance. I began to be worried that she was angry with me.

'I know, he was with me. His time was finished. What is it you need?'

'What do you mean, with you?'

'He has gone back as he wanted.'

She did not elaborate, but I pushed a little.

'What do you mean, he wanted it? What? Where is he?'

She paused, and if she had been human I could have imagined her muttering under her breath. Her body language, posture and the tone of her thoughts said to me that I had done wrong calling her.

'He wanted to go back to his early time, when his time was finished here as Myrrdin.'

She looked straight at me. I was held by her eyes, locked. I could not have looked away even if I had wanted to.

'You are now, that was plain to you'.

I looked at the ground feeling awkward, wondering what I had done.

'You cannot call for no reason. I am not needed. This is wrong. You have no need of me.'

I began stammering an apology. 'I'm sorry I thought… You should know about him, I did not know what was right.'

I sat down, holding my head and trying not to look at her. After a long time I risked looking up, to be met full on by her gaze. She had me mesmerised, as before, and we mentally bonded again. Her annoyance abated.

We stayed locked for what seemed ages.

'Look, I am truly sorry' I thought, looking at her. Her eyes seemed enormous, bound around their edges by long, soft lashes.

'I did not really know, it is all new to me' I said. 'This whole concept is still very weird for me. Very strange.'

'It is now normal until your time is finished. When your years are finished you can see him again'

'But he died, he has gone?'

'His body, his carrier has, but he has come with me back to his start. His physical form is the same; that cannot change, for him. He remembers now nothing that is ensured by me.'

She paused as if allowing it to sink in. I must admit that I was stunned.

'He has one more life as a reward for his compromise here' she finished, looking at me again. This time I felt something different from her, a sort of warmth, dare I say, a caring feeling.

'I will do the same for you if you wish it' she said, turning her head on one side and looking at me with her intense, questing gaze. 'You can do whatever, when or what you want to return to. I will do it. It will be your last goodbye.'

She turned to snap at a horsefly. I smiled, feeling a little happier, almost relieved. In fact I was so much more relaxed that I found myself smiling at her antics with the fly.

She shifted, turning her body, and moved a little so that she was under some shade.

'You need nothing? I am here for no need?'

'Yes, I have, I realise now, done wrong.' I looked down.

'You are not the first.' She paused as if eyeing me up. 'You like the flight better than all of those before. So this time it is allowed.'

Ridiculous as it probably seems to you, I now recognise that she smiled. I was most relieved. I could feel myself relaxing, and for some ridiculous reason, I suppose out of polite habit, began small talk.

'How is Typos?' I asked. I know what you are thinking and as I remember this I too realise how banal and automatic this is. What nonsense, was I expecting her to say well thank you, or tell me how fast she was growing?

'She grows' was all Shola thought. 'I will call you when I am needed at the pits, until then I go.'

Without so much as a goodbye, she twitched and went. My ears popped and like an idiot I momentarily found myself looking around. She had gone again, and even now, having seen horrid things for her, I find this abrupt disappearance rather disappointing. I suppose to be fair, her job is done, and there are risks of her being seen and so on. Still. We are used to goodbyes.

I walked home off the hill, realising that it was later than I thought. I suppose on reflection that until then all my meetings with Shola had involved an element of time disturbance.

I do remember that I was more comfortable that night with my thoughts than I had been for weeks.

CHAPTER 23

ENCOUNTER IN A STORM

Almost all the time, every waking moment, I waited for Shola to demand my attendance, that first summer. Hour by hour I kept waiting for her call.

I was involved with the usual huge amounts of vegetable and fruit picking. The kitchen was always full of bowls of fruit waiting to be blanched and then frozen, or turned into jam, chutney and pickles. I recall how initially I felt rather inadequate doing this. Don't get me wrong, it had to be done, then as now. But it hardly seemed a career progression for me. Then my still hopeless body or my rubbish speech would remind me that I was lucky to do even that.

In the middle of de-stoning and halving a load of plums for freezer bags, bent over the worktop, a massive call entered my head. It was so unexpected and so strong that I collapsed on one knee. Getting back up, I realised I was going to vomit.

It is probably enough to tell you that the kitchen sink was nearby, luckily for me, not for it. I cleaned up as quickly as I was able, putting the sink taps on maximum, then cleared up the pile of plum stones and shoved the bags into the freezer. Locking the door and remembering to grab the sticky trews, I left the house at a run.

It was windy that day, and the branches of the trees were bent right over. The sky overhead was carrying a heavy cloud cover; it looked as if it would pelt down shortly. Luckily all our hay was off, baled and undercover. The aftermath or grow-back was already greening back on the hill as I walked and ran as best I was able over to the barn. I was so keen to do right and not let her down; I was focused only on getting there.

I must admit to spending a moment getting my breath back and pulling my trews over my jeans before beginning the call chant. If I am honest I did have to summon my resolve as well; not so much as last time, but still…

Before you wonder, yes. I did remember to cover myself in insecticide. I sprayed and sprayed the stuff. I nearly said, as if my life depended on it, which is of course true.

The chant seemed this time to fly along, gathering its usual momentum, and with the usual ear-popping pressure changes the awesome figure of Shola appeared. I had seen her enough to know that today she meant business; there was no great hello. She bent her great head to the ground in cursory acknowledgement. Her neck extended, I clambered on to her scaly neck, settling myself down between the spines in front of her wings. Once I was snug and felt secure she simply twitched. She did not give a warning; she simply went.

I remembered from the first flight with her and Jules where we were heading. Looking down I could fit my modern map on to what I was seeing as I looked down. The church spire of Netherbury was just behind and to our left as we flew up the hill. Shola hardly needed to use her wings, the wind in our face providing lift. She seemed to hang in the wind, making slow easy progress, her great head looking down from side to side. The countryside below us was much earlier than last year, looking asleep, tired, dormant almost.

'We are needed here again, a little later this year' she thought, and I thought back that I understood.

I have no idea how she knows when she is needed from year to year. One year we went three times. I have worked out that she visits to watch and see the need, but as to the exact time, I cannot help or explain further.

As we flew around the posy tree, I looked down to see four horse-drawn farm wagons. The horses pulling them were a shabby lot, and it was obvious from their prominent rib cages that they were heavily worked and poorly fed. They were standing by the track leading to the very obviously fresh-dug pits, not with hay nets, just with a leg tucked up.

Shola worked over above the new graves; there were great piles of fresh earth and a small group of people were standing there. I could see that the dug-over area was much bigger than last time, spreading out to one of the field walls.

A man whom I took to be some form of clergyman was reading from a missal, and all heads were bowed down. In the pit could be seen six wrapped corpses, no coffins, just cloth-wrapped bodies. Over the years I have got used to seeing this, but you can probably imagine that to a young man it was somewhat disturbing.

As I looked down I saw the clergyman suddenly clutch at his book and the robes he had on, and the clothes of the mourners began to flap and shake, in a wind that increased suddenly in strength. A driving rain arrived and even from that height I was able to hear startled cries. Several mourners pulled their collars up and seemed to huddle together in shelter.

At the same moment, Shola thought to me 'Again, again, it happens!' With an amazing turn of strength that pushed me back she dived forwards and down through the driving rain. Squinting to try to see, I peered forward.

The sight that greeted me was truly hideous. A great giant-like figure was climbing up the side of the hill. It was clothed in black billowing rags, carrying a great club in one hand and using the other to haul itself up. Its face was hideous, with a distorted grin, and it was throwing its head from side to side; it seemed to be howling into the wind.

'It comes for the dead souls' thought Shola to me as she dived to take it head on.

The thing, and I am still not sure what to call it, saw us coming and looked up howling at us. Swinging its club in the air in great arcs it looked defiant. Daring us to stop its grim task, it roared at us, jumping in rage, and waving its other fist.

I sat quiet, bracing myself and making myself as small as I could. I had no wish to interfere with Shola's actions, or for that matter to fall off like last time. The driving rain was stinging my face and making watching difficult.

She dropped at a seeming incredibly speed and at the last moment flicked on her side. I had to grip like crazy as she shot a great clawed foot out to rip at the thing's body. We almost juddered to a halt as she made contact, before she freed her foot, flew on and turned almost in her own length. Mercifully I ducked down as I felt the wind from the ghoul's club pass harmlessly by.

The quick second pass was on reflection like magic; while the ghoul turned, wondering where she had gone, she shot a great claw out and very nearly decapitated it. The noise of her claws on flesh was sick-making.

She rocked back up, and looking over my shoulder I was able to watch the ghoul's body convulsed in its death throes. Its mouth made talking movements, its great jaws moving but making no sound. The grass to the side of its neck was changing from green to bright blue as its bodily fluids leaked out.

Shola flew in leisurely style over the mourners, who I could see were now shaking the water from their heads and clothes. The rain and wind had dropped off and it was peaceful again.

'We are done for today' thought Shola to me in that casual matter-of-fact way that she has. We made one or two leisurely flyovers, both looking down as the mourners began to walk off and two men began filling the graves in.

'We go, all done' she thought to me. Those people had no idea how they had been helped, noticing only how the passing storm has soaked them.

The wind and rain had eased right away, as with apparently little effort we made our way back. From height Netherbury church is a really good reference point. Soon the hills behind the village were below us and Shola twitched out and gently and effortlessly landed in front of the barn. I swung my legs off and, rather bravely on reflection, walked to her head. As I made my way, she turned back to me and her great eyes blinked.

'You are fine, I do not feel you there' she thought to me. 'Good rider, light, I feel your legs grip, does not worry. Good!'

I was momentarily embarrassed. Without thinking I put my

arms around her neck again and squeezed.

'Thank you, thank you!' was all I could mutter. Pathetic

'I go now' was all she thought, and then she twitched out and I slowly walked back to the house and normality.

I was and still am in awe of this. I can tell you that every time it was different and I was always bewildered by what I saw.

I have come to appreciate much more about our existence. One day the scientists will uncover more. I realise now that some ancient religions touch on these essential truths, though most seem to deal with the easy stuff, the froth.

Over the rest of that first year I learned many hard truths, which as I remember them I will tell you. On reflection, given my age then, with what I was seeing, it is a wonder I did not crack up.

CHAPTER 24

A SECRET SHARED

I told you a while ago how after Jules' funeral Mrs Andrews whispered to me, saying I should carry on his work. At the time I was stunned. I wanted to ask her what she meant, what she knew, but never got the chance.

One evening late in that first summer after his death, Milly and I were aimlessly having a stroll along the river. All my day jobs were done and we had opted for a stretch before supper. The heat was going from the day and by the river swarms of midges made progress uncomfortable. I was waving my hands in front of my face almost all the time, batting into the clouds and trying to stop them biting.

It got easier as the river flowed into the overgrowth, but then you had to watch where your feet went, avoiding gripping brambles and half-buried flints. The path wandered by the river's edge, now and then making a detour to allow you to go through a gate and at one point over a ramshackle stile.

The path seemed to compete with clumps of nettles, and on entering the main grazing field it was interrupted by poached and now solid mud. A few cows lifted their heads to look at us and then resumed their grazing, their long tongues ripping at the grass. They were comfortable after being milked and ignored Milly and me completely.

As we walked across the fields I saw coming towards us a woman; Mrs Andrews. It would have looked churlish to turn and avoid meeting her, so I carried on walking. Frankly, at that point I really did not feel like chatting to her about Jules. It had been only a few months since his death, and although I knew it was different for him, I still missed him.

Milly and I had earlier walked past the entrance to his yard. The beehives had been moved, there was no smoke from the chimney and a sprinkling of weeds had begun to grow. It had seemed deserted and we had walked on, not really wanting to stop and remember. I had got so used to calling his name, it now seemed so lacking.

As she got nearer she lifted a hand, uttering a greeting. She was wearing a large, floppy straw hat, dressed with blue ribbons and a light blue cardigan over a short summer skirt. Her legs were bare and she wore straw-coloured shoes. I replied to her greeting, lifting a hand. Milly went running ahead, tail going rapidly.

Mrs Andrews bent down to pat her and I could hear saying hello. By the time I got near, Milly had turned to look at me, then continued to sniff about near us, never far away, casting eyes our way now and then.

'Hello Peter, how are you?' she said, offering a hand to shake.

'I'm fine' I replied, passing the usual comments about the weather, the cattle, and general inconsequential chitchat. She had an intense look to her face, but her eyes twinkled.

I wanted to raise the subject of her remarks, but she beat me to it.

'Bet you were wondering what I meant at the house the other

day' she said smiling. 'Come on, turn around and walk with me for a while. I have got to get back and make supper. Just been to see some friends. I've been there all afternoon.'

I called up Milly, turned and began walking alongside her. She took my hand, rather embarrassingly, and I could not help but notice the sweet smell of her scent. As we went she started telling me a little.

Out of respect for her memory I will simply say that she had become very close to Jules and they had known each other for some time years. I suppose she told me enough for me to realise that there was a bit more than just friendship between them, although let me quickly write that she did not tell me anything more personal.

Jules gave the game away, apparently, at a surprise party arranged for his sixtieth birthday. He was not a drinker, but his celebrations were long and his drinks were loaded. He had told her more than he should have. Mrs Andrews looked straight at me and stressed that Jules had told her and only her, of that she was positive. She gave me a firm look to emphasise her point.

'Soon he had to watch the water fairies, that was his job every year' she said. He had not told her anything else and she assumed, that as I was then with him so much, that he had told me about it, and I would carry on.

You can probably imagine the spot I was now in. She looked back at me very intently. Thinking rapidly, I started to laugh.

'Water fairies? How much had he been drinking? Sounds well oiled to me!' I carried on walking, aware that she was staring at me and wondering how I could get out of this.

'I believed him, actually' she rather brusquely replied. 'Even though he had had a few drinks, he never lied. Another thing - he often just disappeared. He would come back somehow, and once I found him tired and worn out. Now where had he gone? Answer me that. He was not telling porkies, I know.'

She stopped talking for a while and I waited, saying nothing.

'He was doing something...' - she stopped mid flow – 'I miss him so much.'

I turned to see that she was not far off crying. Her lips trembled and her eyes were watering. On seeing me looking, she turned her head to one side, lifting a hand.

'It's all right' she muttered. 'I'm just being silly, don't worry.'

She blew loudly into her handkerchief and looked up at me with a rather forced smile. I wondered if I should try to comfort her, but I could only stand there in embarrassment. I had had very little contact with women of any age, apart from my mother.

'Well, I really wish I could help your story, throw some light for you' I lied, hoping my face would not give me away, 'but I really do not know anything about water fairies or whatever, and cannot help with why or how Jules disappeared now and then. He was always there when I called. Seemed normal to me, just a really nice chap. Blooming good biscuit maker too!' I added, trying to lighten the tone a bit.

'Oh Peter, you are as crafty as he was' she said. She was able to laugh now, and smiling with tear-stained eyes, she faced me and placed a hand on each of my shoulders.

'Do not say anything else. Your face, your tone… you are just like him. You're like his twin. The secret is safe with me. Whatever it is you do, carry on, for him and I suppose, for me.'

She looked straight into my eyes, unblinking, holding me still before her. 'For all of us.'

I did not know how to carry on this conversation. Soon we reached the point where her path went off to her house; to my complete surprise she reached out to me, lifted her hat off and kissed me full on the lips.

'Be brave' was all she said as she turned and walked on. Her perfume hung in the air. I stayed rooted to the spot, watching her back as she walked on, without looking back.

New light had been thrown on Mrs Andrews, and on Jules. She had loved him - that was obvious. She knew a little, a very little, about our secret, and had been guessing for years.

Milly and I walked back, our planned walk shortened somewhat. Supper that night was rather contemplative.

At that age, that time, with all that newness in my life, I was desperate to sit and talk with someone. To be fair, I wonder why Milly put up with me.

We walked miles that summer, as it went into autumn, or sat under trees. I must have talked her legs off. We were still limited, we could not use every term and phrase, but in a limited way she was, I suppose, the anchor that kept me going through all the changes in my life. I know she could not understand all I said, but having a listener like her I am sure was a great comfort.

That first summer, on reflection, all I did was wait for Shola to call, as you can imagine. It filled my every waking moment, thinking any moment I would be called. Talk about becoming intense. All I did every day was wait in anticipation.

In fact she did not call until much later, and I do not want you to think she did it all the time. I was called by her twice in quick succession sometimes, but other times not for months. I got used to her calls at last, and stopped throwing up.

I tried in my limited way to be useful at home, filling my days with small farm jobs, a bit of decoration, generally helping out. The one thing that played on my mind that first year was the need to be at Stonehenge in the late autumn before Christmas. I had a problem.

I had only been driving for a while before my accident. With head injuries like mine you have to do a driving test again before allowed behind the wheel. With a degree of luck, a cancellation and a good and understanding examiner, I was mobile again. One problem solved, and then, with a bit of persuasion, I had the use of Mother's car. What it is to have mothers – make sure you worship yours.

The autumn drew on, and without letting on that I was eastbound I had use of the car, and prepared to see the other watchers, on the same date, with immense trepidation. I was filled with doubt and concern as to how I would be received, as I borrowed the car, made my cheerios and set off. It was after lunch and pouring down when I left.

Mother's parting words were 'You're mad doing your Christmas shopping today, you'll get soaked'. I waved at her out of the fogging car window and set off.

CHAPTER 25

RETURN TO STONEHENGE

Normally it was only two hours driving at the most up the road before the henge could be seen, but this time it seemed to take forever. The traffic was slow and heavy for the first half hour and the pouring rain slowed everything up.

I peered through the windscreen, the wipers going nineteen to the dozen. Coming up behind large lorries everything slowed down even more until they were passed. The spray coming off was heavy, and made finding a moment to overtake tricky.

About halfway there the rain eased a little, and with the radio on the rest of the trip went more smoothly. Then the famous stones came into view on the left and my apprehension increased as I remembered my last visit with Jules.

I turned off the main road and drove into the small car park. I was earlier than I thought I would have been, but already there were two cars there. I parked and fiddled about in my glove compartment, really as an excuse to gather my strength and confidence.

I looked in my interior mirror to see that one car door had opened and the man I recognised as' Scotland' had got out and started towards my car. I got out, locked the door and pulled my collar up.

'Hello' he called. 'On your own this time?'

He had an old boiler suit on, a pair of old wellingtons and a heavy coat. As we walked across to the other car, I explained about Jules. He seemed genuinely shocked.

'We all knew that you were his next, but I at least thought I would see him again' he said. He was quiet and thoughtful as we walked over to the other car, which held the Irish person. The door opened as we got to it.

'Have a sit in here. We are one short for now' he said, smiling. We all sat in his car for perhaps twenty minutes, while I explained again about Jules. The conversation was limited, each chap lost in his own thoughts.

'It was good then that Jules brought you along last time' said the Scotsman. 'You going to be all right with this?'

The Irish watcher looked at me in the back. 'Look it is all right, you will be fine, we will sing the chant and you will remember what Jules did in the middle. You know you have to replace him exactly.'

I nodded, but I was nervous and far from happy.

Then an old estate car drove up with two people inside. 'What's this?' exclaimed Scotland, peering through the window as two figures came forward. One I recognised as Wales, but a man a little younger than me was tailing him.

Wales introduced his replacement, having left the warmth of the car. Wales looked anxious, drawn and ill. I wondered if he was feeling well, and it later transpired that I was right to be alarmed.

This was the last time he joined us. His replacement had been brought along for a good reason.

'Come on, it is time, we old hands will teach' joked the Scot. We walked to near the middle of the stones, with the rain now stopped and a weak setting sun just visible through the cloud cover.

'In the middle' said Wales, pointing to me, and we began, or rather they began. I will not, as I said before, elaborate on the chant, service, call it what you will.

I remembered that when I had watched Jules before he had stood with arms outstretched. I caught the eye of Ireland and he nodded at me and smiled, as I rather self-consciously did the same. It was enough confirmation, and as the chant progressed, it may be my imagination but the wind seemed to drop, the rain ceased and the whole world seemed to wait.

As had happened the year before, to my delight, a tawny owl called. Its intense call split the dusk, and was almost immediately answered. Over the next few moments the whole area seemed filled by calls, and then... and then a barn owl alighted on my outstretched arm.

I dared not move, though my arms were beginning to ache. It was light, no weight at all, and when it turned to look at me I was truly stunned by this lovely bird arriving and demonstrating such trust.

Its eyes held me, looking out of its saucer-like face. It clicked the hooked beak a few times and then seemed to look at its feet for a moment. It looked again at me, this time bobbing its head, then looked around, as a chorus of every imaginable owl hoot and call filled the sky.

The calls seemed to go on for some time, though it was probably no more than a few minutes. Soon the owls began to leave; you could see airborne shapes and that unmistakable feather dander smell filled the air.

The owl on my arm turned to look again straight as me, bobbed its head down, opened its wings and flicked off. I did not feel it go; it simply flew off and was gone.

I stood enthralled, realising just how much responsibility these few watchers had. They all came to me, shook my hand, squeezed me by the shoulder, and generally were complimentary and kind.

'Perfect... correct for another year' was the general chorus. The Welshman looked stunned, and I watched as he was taken off to one side and the weight of his forthcoming responsibility was explained.

Slowly we all walked and chatted our way back to our cars. The finale seemed lacking somewhat. We do exchange Christmas greetings, and dare I say it I have taken lately to giving the odd bottle of Christmas cheer. That day, without having the reassurance of Jules with me, I found the other watchers very reassuring. I tried to say a decent thank you to them and a goodbye. They all smiled and gave me reassuring handshakes and bearhugs.

I watched them get in their cars and waited as they drove off. I sat there, going over in my mind what had happened.

My place in history, nature, and the natural order had begun a year before, but it was not until that night that the magnitude of that responsibility set in.

I do not recall driving home that night, but I can tell you that some days as I drive home I am still moved to tears.

CHAPTER 26

ECLIPSE

Please forgive me while I break off from my memories of that first year on my own to recall for you the next time I had any contact with Shola's daughter. This would be one of many that followed.

I have had now numerous dealings with her, but those early joint visits were limited by her age. I believe it was Shola, or it might have been Jules, who told me that dragons can go back, but only within their own lifespan. I have no idea how old Typos is, but she is of an age that meant she could not join Shola in my early days.

I suppose on reflection that this was a blessing. Everything was so new, so mind-boggling and yes, at times, frightening.

I can remember the timing of this call from Shola because believe it or not I was shopping with my mother. I have to be honest, wandering around the shops aimlessly is my idea of hell. It was a hot August day at the end of the twentieth century, the year 1999 and I was being taken to get a belated birthday present, a couple of shirts. This meant of course accompanying my mother around the shops. We wandered from one to another and I had decided on two shirts that met with her approval.

We were walking back to the car, carrying some bags of

groceries as well, when I was laid down by a fierce call. I felt my head would explode. Before I could disguise it, my forever-observant mother saw me stagger. She clutched at my arm, very concerned, and asked what was wrong.

Shola's call passed and I had the presence of mind to act relaxed, dismissing the whole episode, jokingly, as hunger. She looked at me with a sceptical expression. We got in the car, and without a lot of chat she drove us home. She would not let me drive.

The car's vents were fully open as we drove home, but I still remember how hot that August day was. The town was full of holidaymakers' cars and progress out of the town and home was slow. Crawling along, then stopping, it seemed always held up by pedestrian crossings. Eventually we started to get a move on, and I had the job of convincing my mother I was fine. I was painfully aware that to clear off as soon as we got in would be frowned on.

Fortunately, some friends of mothers were waiting for her as we drove in. With the kettle on the boil and lots of chatting going on, I was able to slip out. I simply said to her that I was just going out for a stretch, clutching a sandwich and lump of cake. Mother, with her friends there, she had little option but to ask if I was all right. She looked concerned and told me not to overdo it. Then she let me wander off.

I walked as quickly as I could up the hill and bolted my sandwich, wishing I had grabbed a drink too. In front of the barn wrestling my trews on, I wondered what was in store. I had never had any Shola events occurring at this time in the calendar. Intriguing.

Luckily I had taken to hiding the trews behind stacked hay bales in the barn. They were beginning to show their age, in fact one had a nasty tear. Most times now I do not bother with them at all, finding balance easy enough without them. On these rare unexpected calls I do use them, and when Shola turns sharply they are a real plus.

When I felt comfortable and ready I began the chant, which I do with my eyes shut, to help me concentrate. It gathered momentum, becoming almost self-continuing, and then as before began to rush away on its own.

This time, as once before, it produced in my head a sharp ear-popping. I had to squeeze my nose, and un-pop my ears to get comfortable. I opened my eyes to see Shola there with Typos. They stood looking at me, Typos shifting her weight around. They both looked very businesslike, as if saying come on, work to do, we are waiting.

'You are needed, Myrrdin with us, at this moment!' thought Shola to me. 'We do now… here and now.' She turned her head to her daughter, who was fiddling with the overhanging branch of an elm. Typo had grabbed it in her wicked jaws and was taking steps back. Her hind talons ripped and dug into the turf as her muscles tensed, and with a massive crack and noise of torn wood the limb broke off. Typos spat out the branch and looked up, almost bored it seemed.

Shola turned back to me,

'She comes, in her own time today, to help.'

'Well, that's kind' was all I could think of saying. 'What are we doing? Why are you needed?'

'You will see. There is an eclipse of the sun today, great danger potential. We will be helped as well. You will see. On!' she ordered.

Painfully aware of Typos watching, I walked to Shola's neck to climb on. As I did so, Typos pushed her head towards me, making loud sniffing noises. It was if she was savouring me, checking I had not changed.

'Do I pass?' I jokingly asked, and to my amazement Typos looked me in the eye and thought back 'Fine, no change.'

'She begins, limited, but she begins' thought Shola to me as Typos launched skywards, Shola and me following.

I had now ridden enough to know that as nothing appeared to change below us, we were not twitched back in time, just behind real time. I'm not sure how much, possibly just a moment. It does mean that those around are not aware, although as Shola had explained to me the shadow of us does not change.

'We go away' thought Shola. 'I do not know… we go high to see.'

We climbed up and up, into the layers of clouds and through into the blue clear sky above. Away to the left, perhaps on the flight path to Exeter, was a large jet. It was far enough away not to worry me, and I watched entranced.

'Your planes fly in boxes' she thought. 'It is only the whirly things, or small things to watch.'

I did not dwell on that thought or feel I should interrupt her concentration with questions. It was obvious that twitching back in time, with no planes, helicopters and wires, is much safer.

It got colder and I started to get the suspicion of a headache.

'You work?' she thought to me. 'Not much higher… no air for us here.' I had forgotten that air got colder and thinner with height.

My teeth were starting to chatter. Typos was not as high as us, but looking down I could watch her increased wing rates as she had to work harder.

Looking below her through the gaps in the cloud I could see

tiny towns, and the edge of the land. I could just make out big vessels in the Channel and see the scars of major roads, but I could not make out any traffic from this height.

I pulled my shirt closer around me, as of course I was dressed for the summer's day below. I was grateful for the warmth coming from her neck muscles and tried to wriggle down some more.

'It will be soon' she thought to me, feeling my movements, 'Soon'.

We flew on for perhaps an hour with Shola scanning from side to side. I did not feel that I could interrupt with questions, but I was getting increasingly cold. Typos kept in contact with us, and as we dropped we were soon alongside. Stupidly, and I suppose out of habit as she came alongside, I lifted a hand.

That was absurd. Did I think she would nod in recognition, wave a talon, shout hello? Thinking now about it I am marginally embarrassed.

'Soon she stays' thought Shola to me. 'Your skies are too full further, only we go. We meet again on return.'

Ahead of us, I could make out increasing housing and road cover. On looking further ahead I realised that in fact the skies did in deed look fuller, with planes coming in and going out, I presumed to Heathrow. I kept quiet, other than thinking to her that I would help keep a lookout.

'Fine, soon we are not alone.' I did not have the nerve to ask what she meant, or what we were doing here.

Typos wheeled off, flying much lower and to our left. I watched her as best I could for a while, then lost her in low cloud, coming in below us.

Shola now loitered, flying in lazy circles, and for a moment I was enthralled to see Windsor Castle below us, and then a massive reservoir.

Soon I noticed that it was noticeably darker. I looked at my watch in disbelief; it was still early for sunset. I looked up expecting to see black clouds, but it was still blue, as normal.

'Shola…' I started to think, but she interrupted.

'It starts now. We may be needed. Only the lower bit of the island.'

'What starts?' I thought back, but instead of replying she thought 'We are not alone. They are here.'

'Who are here?'

I could not believe my eyes. Two other dragons were gently flapping up to us.

To be honest I was terrified. It was all mind-boggling; here I was petrified, freezing cold and depending for my sanity and safety on another dragon. Unreal.

'The sun goes for a while. We are needed for defence, and we will follow its path' Shola thought to me as the other two came alongside.

I peeped at them through my hands. I was not brave enough to do anything more. I tried to make myself smaller and less conspicuous.

One of them was mainly black in colour and covered in long white scars. One wing in fact looked like Shola's with a big white scar tissue area, which looked wet. I caught its eye inadvertently and it fixed me with a look. I was horrified to see that it only had one eye, with just a hideous long scar were the other should have been. I looked quickly away to meet the other one's eyes, which were staring at me as we flew.

The second one chilled me to the marrow. It oozed malignant feeling. Predominantly red in colour, it was made with sharper lines, looking fitter and symbolising awesome strength. I found it unnerving. It plainly had nothing but contempt for me. Even at the distance we were apart, I felt very threatened.

We stayed in one place, making lazy circles, as the light began to fade further. Again I looked up, expecting to see a large cloud, but then realised that there was something wrong with the sun. A great portion of it had been obscured.

At last it made sense. This was the solar eclipse that had been heralded on the television over the last few days. With everything going on I had forgotten all about it.

Looking down and across to the east, I saw that the land was in darkness, while when I looked north the light looked brighter.

'One of these is from what you call Wales' thought Shola.

'Yes, Wales.'

'The other is from what you call Germany, the Black Forest.'

'Yes, Germany.'

'We have a risk that the dark ones will use the sun's absence for ill. We watch and wait, it is enough. If needed we will deal.'

It all began to make sense in a way, and the recent plague pit episode with Shola helped to seal my thoughts. It was strange feeling, flying in darkness following a half lit landscape ahead of us, slowly moving east.

I did not feel able to question her. Who had summoned her? What might happen? Having seen her in serious action at the plague pit the thought of two more fighting as well was awesome.

We flew with the failing light as it progressed across the country until it began to increase a little. I was one of the first to see Typos as she flew back in to meet us. At that moment the two other dragons simply twitched and went. Stupidly, I remember at the time being relieved that they had gone and had not been needed, but at the same time I was a little sad. It would have been nice to have had longer contact.

Typos came up alongside and I was aware of mental chatter from her to Shola, relief at not being needed, with perhaps a note of disappointment in her tone. Ridiculously I found myself smiling at it all. Secretly I was very relieved that the threats with this eclipse had not transpired.

I was aware that I was now severely shaking with cold, and I pushed my hands into my armpits in a vain attempt to warm them up. I was very relieved when as we dropped down I began to feel the sun's warmth, and then see the beckoning spire of the church.

As we came over the hill I could see our barn on the edge of the hill, and was horrified to see my father walking with Milly and one of the other dogs around the field edge.

'Not here now, problem' I thought to Shola. On hearing this Typos noticeably picked up speed and a great blast of flame shot from her lips.

'What, where?'

'My father, with our dogs, just there'

I would like to think that Typos relaxed somewhat, and was aware that Shola thought to her. If ever a young dragon was spoiling for a fight, Typos was.

'We go further over when he has walked on' thought Shola as we watched Father. Once he was over the hill brow, both dragons twitched out. My ears hurt almost to the point of making me cry out. My legs felt useless, stiff and frozen. I rolled off on to the grass.

'We go' thought Shola, turning her great head to me. 'Be safe, until next time.'

I lifted a hand and smiled. Typos looked around her mother's great tail and fixed me with a look. Both twitched and went as Milly came bounding up.

'Be quick, he comes!'

With frozen fingers I wrestled with the trews and was annoyed to rip them some more. My legs were refusing to work properly, and I half dragged myself to the barn and stuffed them under some old hay just as my father came in.

'Where were you, I came past here a moment ago?' he demanded.

'I was having a kip in the hay' I lied, rubbing my shirt as if shifting hay. 'I felt really tired and stiff. Must be getting a bug.'

'Mother said you were a bit strange at the shops and you have been gone for a long time. I thought I had better come and find you.' He looked concernedly at me.

'I'm all right, let's wander back.' I acted up calling Milly, although there was no need.

'Right. Now, just have a look at this round the side, what do you make of it? I have never seen anything like it. What the hell do you think happened here?'

We walked around the corner and of course I had to look suitably horrified at the ripped grass and the massive limb that had been freshly ripped from the tree. The leaves were still green and the tree trunk oozed sap from the tear.

'Now what on earth could have caused that? Look at the grass. It seems to have been ripped by forks, or claws, and look at that branch. You would swear those were bite marks.'

What could I do? I showed myself suitably annoyed and suggested yobs, local kids, even giant rats I joked. We walked homeward.

'You are walking oddly as well' said Father. 'I think you've got a nasty bug getting hold.'

I tried to make light of it, saying I would explain later. I thought to Milly trotting alongside. Unless you know dogs, you will wonder what I'm on about when I say she looked at me and smiled.

CHAPTER 27

FALL OF A DRAGON

Now I told you a while ago that my memories were getting easier to recall as they move nearer to the present. This is not entirely true. The next memory is very distinct, but what happened for two years after has gone, forever.

I have tried to remember over the last years, to no avail. I thought the discipline of getting this down for you would help it come back, but it has not.

Having had one bad brain injury as a young man, and then another… well, I will explain. I do know that I must have carried on, but I cannot remember. I will tell you now what I can and how I started again, but that missing bit defies me.

Milly and indeed Typos have filled in the blanks for me. I suppose that if they had not, this letter to you, my memories, would be rather thin.

I well remember the Christmas before. It was marvellous; my parents' house was bursting with guests. Many stayed for the whole break, and many more popped in for sherry, mince pies and general fun. Christmas was one thing my parents did particularly well, and I have very fond memories. The weather that year was really seasonal, Christmas-card like. Snow fell actually on Christmas Eve, only a few inches but it was wonderful. The ground froze solid and the branches of trees were rimmed in frost and snow. Every field had animal tracks, and once the sheep and horses were fed, hayed and comfortable, the traditional feeding, drinking, and meeting friends filled each day.

It was playing on my mind - to be honest it still does - that one of Shola's duties coincided, near enough, with the festivities. It had as the years went on been moving on through the year. Its timing that year meant that it did not really impinge, but happened in the holiday week.

I used the animal feeding and checking excuse, and after wrapping up warm, I left the house. I still found walking on slippery surfaces somewhat tricky. I managed to slip and slide whenever the ground was remotely dodgy. It was nice to be outside as I waited for the call that I knew would come.

I had just finished seeing the sheep after struggling up the hill when Shola called me. I can remember being pleased with myself as I was expecting her call, and it could not have been at a better time. The barn was only a short distance away, and the walk was short.

Very quickly, perhaps somewhat cockily, I settled in front of the barn and began the chant, quite relaxed. I called her this time standing up, and as my ears popped with her arrival, the pressure changes pushed me over. I can remember being somewhat embarrassed as I looked up from the ground to see her eyeing me. Her head was tipped to one side, and I would swear she had a faint smile.

'Can you stand? That is unusual… your position' she thought.

'Fine, I just lost my balance.'

'From kneeling?'

'It can happen. No daughter today?'

'She cannot go back to where I need.' As she said that, I realised what a stupid thing I had said. She must have thought me a forgetful moron.

She shuffled around in the snow and I thought that if a naturalist ever saw these marks they would cause great excitement.

'Come, we go' she thought and with that she bent her head down so it touched the snow. I went alongside her scaly neck and swung a leg over, settling in between the spines as usual. With that she twitched and started hard flying. The air was warmer than at home, and soon, looking down, I could see the waves rolling below. The sea looked grey and cold, with the odd white cresting wave. I could smell the spray even from this height, and heard gulls calling from the shore.

I looked across at the land and this time saw a line of flaming beacons stretching away as far as my eyes could see. I did not have to strain to look behind me this time, as soon her flying took us in line with the leading Spanish man of war. The rest of the Armada spread out behind in a big arc.

Even from our height it was possible to see men labouring on deck. A group of them pulled like mad things on a heavy rope, and at the same time a sail sprang out between the masts, which already carried the classic heavy sails billowed out in the wind.

As they laboured a muffled cannon roared between the land and us, followed by a large splash in front of the ship's bows. The shot had been too long, and looking across I could see, rising and falling on the ocean, the British vessel that had fired it. The rise and fall of the swell had made estimating the shot difficult, but they were closing the gap fast.

CHAPTER 27

Shola dipped a wing and we turned shorewards.

'I am needed to talk to the Furies now' she thought to me. 'We are later than normal. Be careful, remember last year. They are different, younger. You must not touch dry, we are too far back for you.'

'I remember, will be careful, Jules explained.'

I will swear that I heard her cough in despair, but maybe now with the passage of time my mind plays tricks.

Over the surf she flared out, her great legs making big splashes that soaked into my legs. I swung my leg over and gasped in shock. The water was deeper and much colder than I had anticipated. It came above my knees and the next wave came across my groin. I was soaked.

'I talk, will return, I go.'

With that she opened her enormous wings as she turned, missing me by a long way, but I felt flattened by the wind produced by her skywards thrust.

As I watched her fly away, I waded back in a bit, towards the beach, making sure that I really knew the edge that the sea left. Jules had drummed into me that it was vital that I was always in the sea, never touching the beach or shingle on its own.

As I stood being soaked by the bigger waves and getting colder, the seriousness of my situation began to sink in. The time before I had had all the reassurance from Jules, but here I was in another part of the country and back in time.

I was horrified to see along the beach two people walking towards me. I had never been so much at a loss or so petrified. Looking around I realised I had no option but to wade out and duck down into the waves a little. I wanted Shola back, needed picking up. The thought of being discovered was horrific.

As I waded out I watched them approaching. They were huddled in the collars of their tunics. Occasionally one would wave or point in the air. Fortunately both seemed engrossed in conversation.

By bouncing to match the waves I tried to keep my shoulders covered, which was not easy as the waves were increasing in size and the sea bottom was covered in boulders and weeds, pulling at my feet.

As they got nearer I was horrified to see that one was beginning to turn his head my way. Without thinking I took a massive breath of air and went under. The sea was so cold; it hurt my ears and face, the water thundering in my ears. I forced myself down, reaching down to grab and pull on my trews. I forced myself to hold my breath, and tried to keep my legs from floating upwards.

After what seemed an impossibly short time, I had no option but to surface. I tried to stick my head out just enough to take a breath and look along the beach. They were still walking on, wrapped in their conversation. I took a breath and went under again, trying to stay down as long as I could. I did this three more times, until they were far enough away for me to be out of danger. I watched relieved as they crested the shingle and were lost from view.

Although I had shoes on it was difficult to drag myself out. I lay on the edge, getting my breath back under control. I was soaked, tired and freezing, and very quickly began shivering. My body was racked, and my jaws snapped together uncontrollably.

After a while I knelt up, looking skywards. No Shola. A storm was brewing up, the sea gaining visibly in force. Her negotiations had been successful, I assumed, but what good I had been was lost on me, apart from being there and witnessing.

With immense relief I then saw her fly in. When she had landed in the surf I dragged my freezing body over her neck. The warmth from her back and neck muscles was wonderful.

We had to fly back to the point where she had twitched in, and I watched the sea below as I wriggled my cold aching hands under my clothes until they were next to the heat of her skin.

'They did their job, easy this year' she thought to me. 'The easiest for years, strange, not right.'

She was clearly worried; her tone was strange.

'They are not linked to the same lot last year at Lyme?' I thought back, remembering how beaten up Shola had been then.

'They change, something is different, they or their world changes.' I realised it would be wrong to continue.

We flew over the rapidly roughening storm, and I looked down at the remnants of the Spanish fleet being pounded by the few English galleons. With the usual ear popping she twitched back - and I let out an involuntary yell. We were back in a massive storm, with howling wind and driving rain. I looked forward as she fought to hold her position. Her wings laboured strongly against a fierce cross wind. Further forwards I could see that we were a long way short of the barn, and I screamed out a warning as the power lines buzzed within a few feet.

Shola fought the wind with all her strength, and even now I can remember a hideous chorus in the wind. It seemed to pick us up, and to my horror Shola thought to me 'You go now, those wires death, go!'

At that point she flung her left wing down. Losing my balance, I saw that I was possibly sixty feet above the ground as she flung me off. I can just remember looking up as Shola, fighting to fly, was carried into the power lines. With a massive shower of sparks and flame and one last frightful thought to me, she was gone.

If I close my eyes I can easily, too easily, remember her thoughts, her fighting, anger and then fear as she was driven into the cables.

This is the last I remember of this. I have to use others' memories to put together the story from now, for the next two years of my life.

CHAPTER 28

A PAINFUL RECOVERY

I have done this before to you, following my accident with Caspian, but I am afraid to say that from this point until possibly two years later, it has all gone. I have had to rely on others' memories. The hospital consultants tell me that it has gone forever, I will never remember. I must have functioned, as a person, as a son, an odd individual, but what I did for that time is beyond me.

After much persuasion, my long-suffering mother finally told me what happened to me. It took me ages to get any semblance of normality to my life. But I am jumping ahead. Let me try to remember as best I can and tell you all that I have learned from others.

Don't worry - this is the last horror I have personally endured, and with only two years to go until I see Jules again, I have kept going.

My parents were aware that I had gone out that afternoon, of course. They had amusing friends, and kept them entertained in their ways, and time went on. My mother tells me that I did not figure in her thoughts unduly as she got supper ready, fed the dogs and did some last cleaning - motherly things.

As the rain began and the wind increased she began to feel some concern, which was heightened when she heard the first crack of thunder. Soon the storm began, with lightning splitting the sky and almost perpetual deafening thunder.

It sounded to them as if the storm was trapped in the Netherbury valley. This was of course true, thanks to the Furies. It rattled round and round with massive strikes of lightning, heavy rain and deafening thunderclaps.

My mother's real concern began when she tried to call my mobile phone and heard it ringing in the dining room, where I had, of course left it in a jacket pocket.

With a great thunderclap and what seemed at first to be a massive lightning strike all the power went off. All electrical things stopped working and the house was plunged into darkness. Looking out of the windows, they could see that the entire village was without power; even the farm up the valley was black. Much rummaging around enabled them to find two torches in the hall cupboard and Father elected to go out and look for me, leaving Mother inside, obviously very worried.

The electricity board technicians were quickly on to the failed section, their systems narrowing down the fault to a stretch of wire than ran along the side of the village. I met the two technicians years later and without appearing too interested and involved, casually asked them what they found. They had left their Land Rover and were travelling along the power lines, shining a torch as they went; the storm was abating, with just a few rumbles as it died away. The rain began to ease off, and this allowed them to pick up a burning smell. It got stronger as they walked up the hill, their feet and legs getting soaked in the large roadside puddles.

As they approached the hilltop, where the lane narrows to allow passing points, they could make out a strange shape, still smoking and causing the odd spark. It was hooked up in the wire. The burning smell was now very strong. Their first thoughts were that it was a flying machine, a microlight or possibly the remains of a glider. Yet common sense told them it could not be a plane or even a helicopter, as that of course would have fetched the whole lot down.

As they stood on the road edge they telephoned the emergency services and the fire brigade for help - extra muscle, to use their phrase. As they studied the scene the light of a torch coming across the hill alerted them to my father's approach. As he stumbled towards them across the tussocked grass field he came across my soaking, cold, unconscious body. I was unresponsive, not even moaning.

Luckily the emergency services were coming. To get a vehicle to me proved impossible and I needed to be stretchered off the hill to a waiting ambulance and hospital.

I can leave it to you to fill in the gaps - my parents' reaction, the hospital response, the general trauma I caused. I got my money's worth from the Health Service for sure.

The next day at morning light, the power line company found nothing tangible on the wires that would have caused any problem. Scouring below the line, they found what they took to be the remains of a burned cow. It looked unusual, but were not concerned.

As an aside, four years later when a local farmer was making the hedge he found what looked like a massive talon. He kept it for a while and then lost it. I found out about this only much later, before anything could be done. Although what I would have done with Shola's talon apart from a reverential burial I do not know.

As for me, I was in a coma. Yes, my second. For three weeks. Both legs and my pelvis were broken by the fall, and for some reason three fingers were snapped.

No one could understand why I had sand in my shoes. One foot was sharing a shoe with a great frond of bladderwrack seaweed. I was also wearing the remains of a strange and still sticky overtrouser, held around my waist by baler twine, and smelling not of the rainstorm but the sea.

In a way it is just as well that when I came out of my coma and could communicate, I could not throw any light on these things. I simply did not know, could not remember. I spent most of the time asleep.

My fractured pelvis needed plating in several places, which incidentally hurt like hell, and both legs were encased in casts. I spent my time recovering from the anaesthetic, the injury, and generally struggling back to reality. I am sure my parents had frightening times, watching me during those early stages.

The one abiding memory I have of that time in recovery, on the ward and later with the physiotherapists, was that I kept getting blinding headaches. They were often frequent, two or three a day, and intense to the point of me throwing up. The hospital surgeons were alarmed, and kept quoting my previous history. I saw one look at my mother in a knowing way when he did not think I was looking. I had a CT scan in the end, as concerns grew.

I did not know what was happening, but at the time I wished I had. I could perhaps have answered, saving myself and all around me a lot of worry.

CHAPTER 28

Like all trauma cases, of course I slowly improved. As before, my mother told me I seemed occasionally impressed by hospital food and the nursing was caring and attentive. Soon I was helped to stand, and with the casts off my walking training began, at what seemed then a very slow pace.

I was given drugs to help my headaches and consequent vomiting, which after four months was getting less frequent. I had one about every other day, a transient thing, which I dealt with.

Eventually I was given a going home day, and my mother arrived to take me home after six months in hospital. I can recall no memories of hospital, apart from the vomiting. I vaguely knew were I lived, not the exact house but the village. I could picture my horse, just, and the same with Milly. All my other memories had gone, and as my mother slowed and stopped in our yard, it all seemed a touch alien.

My world was to change completely as I saw Milly come trotting through the kitchen door to meet me.

When you read this, do not forget that I am relating to you something that filled my life nearly fifty years ago. Milly is now long dead, but I can still remember her reaction as she lolloped across the yard to me. Her long tail was wagging furiously and as she approached she bent her long neck and head to the ground in welcome. I reached down to cuddle her head and knuckle her ears in the way she loved.

She looked at me with her dark eyes and thought, 'Thank goodness you're back' I immediately shrunk back.

'She spoke to me!' I shouted at mother, moving back and clutching at the car for support.

'I understood. What have you done, what's happened?' I said

to Milly. She whimpered, put her tail between her legs, looking at me and backed in. She stopped in the doorway, almost at the point of growling.

'Don't be silly darling' reassured Mother, holding my arm. 'Nothing is different. Crikey, you and that dog were inseparable. It's fine, Milly. Milly, come on, come here.'

She bent down, calling the hound, patting her knees. Milly slowly crept forwards, her belly touching the ground, making an odd pathetic whimpering noise. I leaned my pair of sticks against the car and bent down, putting my hands down to Milly's head again. I did not say anything loudly, but was horrified as I heard her think to me 'I will explain'. With this she turned, tail between legs, and ran into the garden.

Of course, I had no memory at all of how I had been before.

'I tell you that I can understand that dog!' I almost shouted at Mother.

'Fine, don't worry darling' she said. 'You always were close to her, it probably just seems that way, because you are with her again.' She smiled and supported me back in to see the other dogs.

Milly kept out of my way for the rest of the day. Mother cooked an early supper, and that I remember fully. It is funny how home cooking is always better than anything else.

I was under orders to have early nights, and initially these must have involved a degree of joint effort, as with sticks laid down by the bed, getting me installed initially was tricky.

I will unashamedly use Milly's account of that first night home, as mine has gone. My bedroom door was left open to allow some light in from the hall, and also I suppose in all honesty so that my parents could hear me.

In the early hours Milly crept in, and very quietly, without disturbing me, got up on the bed. I was awoken by her heavy weight holding me down, and reached a hand out to lay it on her hairy head as I used to. I was half asleep, so looking back on it the hound chose her moment well. By the time I was fully awake I had accepted that somehow I could understand her thoughts. Milly told me later that initially I had great fear. It took her a while to calm me and keep me from yelling out. She must have spent the best part of the night with me, and gave me many memories back.

That morning at breakfast, after spending what seemed ages getting dressed, I collared my mother.

'Who was Jules?' I casually asked.

This made her spin around. 'Do you remember him then? How come, what's caused that?' It may be my bad memory, but I could swear at this point she looked down at Milly sleeping.

'Oh, no reason, he is just a name I remember' I tried to flippantly answer. She looked questioningly at me, drying her hands on a tea towel. She explained that he had been an old chap in the village I had got friendly with, had gone shopping with now and then to help. I had helped him with hedging occasionally. I had been upset when he had died a few years before. She had not really known him, but by all accounts he had been a nice chap.

I did not say much - in fact I could not, then. I was beginning to vaguely recall, but he was still lost to me.

She paused, obviously lost in thought.

'Can I gently ask you something then?' said Mother.

Milly says at this point she was awake, pretending to sleep, but noticed me stiffen. 'I am here' she thought to me.

'When you were found, by your father and the other chaps, you had the remains of Jules' bee-keeping trousers on. Can you think why?'

She looked at me out of the corner of her eye, pretending that she did not really need to know. She began to tidy away the breakfast things, loading the dishwasher.

'Was I? How odd. No, I've no idea, what trousers?' I replied, at a loss.

'Oh. Just something, they have been chucked. And for some reason you had a boot full of seaweed and sand' she continued.

Milly says I looked stunned

'Seaweed? Sand? How come?' I replied, stunned, with no recollection at all. This I do remember was hateful. 'That's crazy. We are miles from the sea.'

I shook my head. What on earth was all this?

'Yes. But why were you wearing those bee-keepers' trousers? Had you been near his hives? Come on darling, think. Your father and I have been worried sick.' Her eyes filled as she said this. Milly got up and wandered over to me, shoving her head into my legs in a reassurance. I was completely at a loss, but worse was to follow.

'Look, while you were unconscious you mumbled things, in fact one thing over and over again. Your father taped some of it, which I've got somewhere. The last bit he never got though. You always stopped.'

She wandered off, and began rummaging around in the pile of her paperwork and bits on the worktop. I could see that she was making a determined effort not to cry. I felt awful. I could not help. I did not know the answers.

'Got it, here.' She waved it at me. 'Have a listen to this, it's you being strange.'

She went over to the tape player, dropped the tape in and stood upright, hands on hips, to listen.

The tape began with inconsequential hospital noises. My

heartbeat monitor could be heard, and my mumbling was strange as I had a great tube down my throat. The recording became clearer as tubes were presumably removed. At this point Milly says I nearly collapsed, causing my mother to charge across the kitchen with her arms out. I was chanting, over and again. It faded out and the same bit came back again.

I had no idea why this touched me, why it was important. I knew I wanted it stopped though, knew it was dangerous. I do remember at the time that I was glad it was incomplete. I did not know any more.

Milly picked up on my fear and simply thought to me 'It is to do with Jules, later I will tell what I know.'

I can tell you that later, when my parents went out, I listened to the tape again, and hid it. The chant and the intonations, the harmonies it needed, did not come back to me until much later. As I have said, at that point I knew it was vital in some way, but what it meant I had no idea.

As I convalesced I got bored at times. One day I found an old diary and browsed through it. I was bored with it, until I came to several odd entries, made in some form of code that meant nothing to me. I shoved the diary back in the drawer, to return to it in a hurry later.

CHAPTER 29

SOUNDS AND VISIONS

My progress in walking was painfully slow. It was too slow for me; I am not a good patient. It was awkward, painful and laboured. I was regularly taken to the local physiotherapy department for their help.

Milly and I now spent hours together. It took me ages to accept that I really could, in a limited way, understand her. I wanted to tell my parents how marvellous this thing, this gift, was, but she was adamant that I must not.

I did not question this. To be honest, each day was a challenge, and I suppose on a day-to-day basis it all washed over me.

By late summer, with the leaves still green but in some cases beginning to hint at autumn yellow, and the roads smelling dusty with the heat, I was allowed to walk further. I still walked slowly with the aid of two sticks, which I hated intensely. They were like a badge announcing my disability.

Milly and I laboured along, she getting used to sitting and waiting for me while I caught up. I was often grabbed by local people, who were very polite, encouraging and supportive, but were intrigued by my injury. People wanted to know how I had got there and why I had been covered in seaweed and sand. Word had gone around, probably from the electricity board people. It was a village mystery, and got fed up answering the same questions again and again. It got to the point where I almost hid with Milly when we saw people coming in the distance.

One day Milly and I attempted the hill, up to see our sheep. Their lambs were full-grown now and soon would be split off from their dams, and then eventually go on. There was little I could do to help anyway at this point and the farm jobs had fallen back to my parents.

I looked across the fields over the browsing sheep - and froze. Milly said I became rigid, thoughtless. She looked across to where I was staring and saw that the far barn had my full attention. 'You will call her' she turned and thought to me.

I shifted my balance on my sticks looking down at her.

'Sorry, call who?'

She looked at me and did not say anything.

'Come on say, what do you mean, call who, what? We don't have secrets. Tell me' I begged back.

'We will walk over, at least some way. It will help you remember. I will tell you the little I can' she thought reluctantly back. 'You are Jules now, know that.'

'What? You're barmy! He died.'

'Wait, I'll explain what I can. You, I know, are his replacement. You had no choice - you told me. You and Jules called, were helped by an air horse - I do not have words. You saw many things with him.'

At this point I had had enough and lifted my hand.

'I know nothing of this, I have to sit anyway, my leg's hurting.

We'll go back to the gate.'

As I walked to the barn, I was beginning to feel weird. Something was coming back. I was far from happy and Milly told me later I was going very white, with beads of sweat on my brow beginning to show.

'Was my accident to do with all this?' I challenged her.

'Yes. You were with her then, I am sure.'

'Tell me again what you know from the start, please.'

I eased myself down on to some old bales in the field corner by the gate and she began to explain. It seems that when I began copying from my diaries, it involved her a lot. I had often returned, she told me, visibly excited. Sometimes I came back sick and worn out, looking exhausted. Other times I returned with a far-off look on my face for days, not talking a lot, lost in thought.

I had out of desperation told her, that is, thought to her, a lot, and one day she had been amazed when I had explained to her about the air horse. I had even mentioned it issued a jet of flame, and this was beyond her knowledge. She did not keep quiet but went on to say that since my second fall I could relate to the 'field horse' better. I should find him and retake my talking to him.

She had no knowledge of how the air horse was called until she had heard my voice doing the chant on the tape in the kitchen the first time. Finally she knew I had taken over some functions of Jules, but despite thinking hard could not help. Now I have probably said before, but it is worth repeating, as it is vital to understand me… this hound was an absolute marvel. Without her I would have been lost again.

We walked back down the hill, Milly trotting along, me swinging between my crutches, lost in thought. I must admit that for the next few days I was desperately trying to get my thoughts in order.

When my parents had gone out shopping one morning and been persuaded to leave me behind, I went and found the tape and put it in the player. I was sitting listening to it slumped in an old armchair, feeling slightly sleepy. I had the replay button in my hand and I suppose more out of intrigue began repeating some of it. It was in a really strange language, garbled and apparent nonsense. I worked through it bit by bit, to become slightly annoyed that the ending to what seemed a chant or song was missing. I had no idea how it finished, and I started mucking around pretending I was a black magic witch or similar, as in the films.

Then I started from the beginning, slowly and methodically saying it out loud to see if it had a rhythm or a tune of sorts. To my amazement, intrigue and then utter fright, it took over. It acquired a speed of its own. I did not garble it, but seemed to have no control; the words came at their own pace. At the same time I was filled with a strange sense of joy, fun, welcome.

When the chant finished, I went back to the start and began again. I was now wide awake and laughing, I had no idea why. Then the words finished and the feeling died away. I sat there somewhat bemused, with a glorious excited feeling, but strangely lacking, frustrated, and empty.

I had the presence of mind to hide the tape, just in time in fact, as my parents returned laden with shopping. I had started to help unpack when an extreme headache began. It felt like my head would split. I fell to the floor and vomited up my entire stomach contents. My parents were dreadfully alarmed, and what with cleaning up and ringing the medics for advice, they had a good homecoming.

The headache came back two hours later, not so strong and more transient, when I had been tucked up in bed.

The next morning Milly and I walked down to the bridge and watched the river as it trickled down to the sea. The water was unnaturally low and barely moving. Weeds were invading the riverbed, and the revolting balsam had fully invaded the edge. As you stood still you could almost hear the seed heads popping.

The rookery was very quiet that morning, with just the occasional croak to remind you it was there. There was no sign of the moorhens and the season seemed flat, with very few birds to be heard. Late summer was normally still full of birdsong and birds hunted through the hedgerows for grubs and caterpillars. The fruit trees were not so laden, and the late-season grass had stopped growing. It had great yellow patches, or great slabs of earth in it, like kicked over molehills. Normally I would hunt blackberries, but this year even they seemed missing.

We walked over the bridge, moving in to let a car past, and without thinking strolled on until we found ourselves outside Jules' yard. I stood there looking up at his ruined house. It was obvious that no one was there now. In fact, some of the lower windows were broken, weeds grew in the yard, and it looked generally sad. I started to walk to the door, intending to peep in at the window. I was desperately trying to remember anything at all.

As I stood there a woman drove her car in, too late for me to move back or hide. She stopped the car and began waving at me with a big smile on her face. I knew I had met her before.

'Hello!' she screamed in excitement, dropping her keys on to the drivers seat and rushing around the car to me.

'Peter, I cannot believe you are here!' she cried, standing on tiptoe to give me a big kiss. I smiled back; in fact her perfume had given her away, helped my memory. She was Mrs Andrews, the boss's wife. She had told me about Jules, and I remembered that she had been close to him.

'It has been a long time, what, two years? Possibly a bit longer' she said. She hugged me and then stood back, holding my shoulders as she had before, with a hand each side.

'We all thought you were dead, it was horrid the stories we had. I was worried about the Jules thing' she gushed. She was glowing with excitement.

'What Jules thing?' I said. 'What are you on about?'

'The river thing, you know, that little business you and Jules did. You know, each year?'

As she said this it was if suddenly as if a great slab had lifted my memory, not of the river thing, but the final part of the chant. Perhaps it was being in his yard, or being close to someone he loved? I do not know. But the last bit of the chant came back to me; also the overriding thought that for some reason I must not say it all.

I looked across at her, and she filled in more memories of Jules. She had a wonderful, unstinted smile on her face, which was infectious. Milly implied later that we looked juvenile; if that gives you some idea.

After she had insisted that we meet again, saying again how relieved she was to see me out and about, we parted. I wandered slowly back with Milly, thinking about Jules and what the now-completed chant meant.

We now come the events of an evening a few days later. I do recollect this easily; but even if I had not, Milly never stopped reminding me. She even mumbled and told me again about it as she lay on her last legs a few years later.

We had left the house after supper on the excuse of getting a last bit of air. I felt driven to say the chant fully and see if it did anything for me. It nagged at me, and I seemed held by it.

I did feel now a bit fitter, although still remained wedded to my crutches, and still walked really slowly. We walked up the hill, and to this day I do not know why we then walked to our far barn. I humped an old bale over to sit on and Milly sat by me.

'Sure about this?' She thought to me.

'Nothing will happen, I bet it's not right. Just a laugh' I replied. 'I can always stop, just be there. Don't go.'

'I won't. Go on then.'

I took a breath and began the chant, possibly quicker than I had before, probably through nerves. After a few choruses it seemed to accelerate. I grabbed Milly as security, and felt her move - reassuring. The chant seemed to gather momentum, almost singing itself, forcing my voice to rise and fall. Quicker, rising and falling, it was beyond my voice control this time.

I kept my eyes tight shut, as with a sharp pain in my head I felt my ears pop. At the same time Milly struggled from my hand, growled and then ran off with a high-pitched whimpering. As I turned to see where she had run to, I was aware of something or somebody in front of me.

I turned - to almost die of fear. For there in front of me, in all its glory, was –a dragon.

'Myrrdin, at last' it thought to me. I do not mind admitting that at that point I felt my bowels open with fear. Just as suddenly, many memories came roaring back.

CHAPTER 30

THE RETURN OF TYPOS

I clutched at my trousers to stop my hands shaking, and my feet danced up and down as fear racked my body. I tried to speak and after a stuttering start, garbled out a name that had come back to me.

'Shola!'

I repeated it, and then stopped as the dragon turned its head to the side and a roaring jet of flame came out of its mouth. Its lips drew back, revealing row upon row of large, sharp white teeth. The flame licked at the ground and hay remnants and lit them, in an instant. They crackled into life, giving off plumes of thick grey-yellow smoke.

'Sorry, I'm so sorry!' I shouted as I wrestled myself up and across to the fire. I began stamping it out as best I could, grabbing the remains of an old fencing rail to finish beating it out.

'I am her daughter!' it screamed.

'I'm sorry I do not remember, it's gone, my brain… it's gone' I said as I slumped to the floor, not daring to look up.

'I have seen, watched, all is complete for me' it thought back.

As it spoke the next great slab of thought came back.

'I am Typos' she said. 'We have met before.'

She paused and in that interval I dared to look up. She was enormous, her legs finishing in wicked-looking talons. Her body was covered in soft yellowy-green scales and along her back was a row of spines that got smaller as they went down to her great heavy tail.

Her eyes were like large saucers and jet-black, blinking occasionally, with large eyelids bounded by the softest looking eyelashes you can imagine. Her tail thrashed from side to side, already having taken the turf off. I risked looking up at her face, and as I met her eye I felt an immense comfort enwrap me, a complete joining. I felt her thoughts enter me, and it may sound trite but at that point I felt joined to her and complete again. I was back again, and although my body was still useless, I knew that mentally I was mended. Ridiculous to say perhaps now, but I felt my eyes water with joy.

With no reservations or adverse thoughts I forced myself up again and crossed to her. Putting my arms around her neck, I stayed hugging her for minutes. We were back together and it felt right. Nothing has changed, all these decades later.

'I have twitched back to see' she said.

'What happened? Tell me.'

'It took me many times to find the moment, but you were returning and the Furies waited for her. You were a coincidence. They wanted her dead.'

She paused and emitted a smaller, quieter jet of flame.

'I will be avenged, it's planned, it will happen' she said. She did not elaborate further, but later I will tell you how.

'She was killed by them, you fell, I could not stay longer.'

She fell quiet again, lost in thought and I have now come to realise, she was showing sadness.

'I have tried to call you often, and just recently it is better' she thought. My odd headaches suddenly made sense, as the memory of Shola calling returned. I was so relieved.

'It will be sorted' I began to say, when to my horror I was interrupted by a scream and a woman's voice saying, 'I saw the smoke!'

I spun around to see a woman who lived below the fields, standing there shaking, mouthing and pointing wildly at Typos.

As I turned back with a frightened look on my face, Typos moved with incredible speed. She wrapped the lady in a deadly embrace with her clawed forelegs. The woman passed out, becoming a limp rag in Typos' embrace

'Again' she thought to me. 'Again I will wipe, but you will help.'

'Yes, but surely she knows now?'

'She will forget everything, her mind will be empty. I will go and she will be lost, help her. I will call, from now, when you will witness.'

She looked down at me, and before I could answer, she vanished. The woman fell to the ground, muttering a groan, her eyes rolling in their sockets. I was at a loss. What on earth could I do with her?

I sat by her, thinking fast of all kind of things. She muttered, opened her eyes, looking around.

'Hello, I just found you. You were passed out. Did you bang your head, do you feel all right?' I gently asked, holding her hand. I tried to explain that she lived down below us; I had seen her before. I tried to be reassuring.

Very gently I got her to her feet, and then with a blank look on her face she followed me down the hill. Fortunately she was happy that I matched her slow progress, watching with a concerned, mystified face as I fell repeatedly.

We reached the bottom of the hill in due course and she followed me through the gate. I remembered seeing her before in the village and started guiding her along the street. We had only gone past three or four houses when a man gardening in his front borders said 'hello' to her. She stood blankly next to me, unconcerned and smiling back.

He had known her for some time, it seemed. I explained that I had found her unconscious up on the hill. I could not say if she had fallen, banged her head, or whatever. He took her hand, thanked me for my kindness and led her off. 'Come on then, let's get you home' he said.

In this case discretion was definitely the better part of valour, and I headed home as smartly as I could. Once out of their sight I slowed down and went over in my mind what had happened. I felt whole again, so relieved, and could not wait to see Milly again. All that she had tried to explain to me now made sense.

My mother looked oddly at me as I got in.

'What happened to you then? You're wearing a big grin!'

'Oh, nothing.' I gave her a hug and smiled. 'I just feel much better today.'

I told her I had found a woman on the hill, flat out, and helped her home. Mother knew her neighbours and out of concern she rang them to inquire and sympathise.

I took Milly for a long stretch that night. She explained that being scared witless she had one look and had to flee home. She had run off the hill, squeezing under a gate and jumping a fence in her hurry. She had felt dreadfully guilty and was so pleased to hear the door go as I walked in. Seeing the 'air horse' had simply been too much for her.

I stopped walking and cuddled her. 'It was too much for me too' I said, joking. 'Far too much. But several gaps are now filled, and the chant works. By gosh it works.'

CHAPTER 31

THE LADY OF THE WOODS

The transition from autumn to winter was unusual that year. The days shortened of course, with the light finishing earlier and earlier. The temperatures dropped a little, but not so you would notice. The rain was noticeably missing, with the dust settling only at night, with a slight hint of dew on the grass still in the morning. The river at the bottom of the village did not exactly disappear, but it was so low that I did not see a trout or a crayfish for weeks.

The swallows and martins went early that year, with not a lot of normal massing together. One morning it occurred to me as I looked at the clouds that the skies were empty of them. They had migrated, leaving a sad emptiness in the sky, devoid of their yelling flight.

The home paddocks had a permanent yellowy hint, with the late grass failing to grow following haymaking. It had been a bad year for vegetable growing, with nothing really forming well, and our homegrown potatoes were well down, both in size and quantity.

Over breakfast one morning my mother put the paper down.

'You know, something's wrong with the climate' she said. 'It says here that all over England this has been a bad year. It was the same last year and before that. Little if no rain, nothing has been growing right, and we have the worst crops on record. It makes you wonder, doesn't it?

'I'm not sure' I replied after finishing a mouthful of toast and marmalade. 'Could be. Certainly the fields look grim, and the fruit's been rubbish. It never really got going.'

We chatted generally and I helped clear up. I was at a loose end that day so calling Milly, I put my old coat on and went out. The clouds were beginning to scud along seaward, with a strong northerly behind them. The trees were losing leaves and great drifts of them were building up.

The scented smell of a winter bonfire was in the air; a neighbour had a roaring garden fire going, getting rid of prunings. He shouted out a 'morning' as we passed and I lifted a hand in exchange.

Milly and I strolled on, crossing the lane and going up the hill to check sheep. This had become our daily ritual, and in any case it gave me a quiet time to think. I wanted to believe I was improving; now I had moved to one stick, but my gait was laughable. I found it really easy to fall over, and standing, never mind hopping on one leg, was a joke.

For some bizarre reason, I have no idea what, the dates and code in my diary entered my head. I had only really seen them once since coming back from the hospital. I determined to have a look on my return. Then, as it happened, a car slowed to pass us. As it drew level, it stopped and the window came down. Mrs Andrews stuck her head out with a smile.

'Hello you two, how are you?' she asked, grinning.

'Fine, just walking up to check the sheep.'

She put a more serious look on. 'Look it's not really my business, you and Jules did these things, but have you seen the state of the river? Where is all our rain? You've been out of action now for over two years, perhaps three. Jules has been dead for three years this month.'

'I hadn't thought…' I tried to interrupt.

'You know, all this water business is related' she went on. Something needs to happen. I tell you what, it's a good job Wales and the North are OK. Otherwise we would be starving!' She smiled. 'I am probably being simple, but before Jules died I do not remember problems like this.'

At this point a car came up behind her, so she blew me a kiss, wound the window up and drove off.

Later when I got home, armed with a mug of coffee, I spent ages trying to find a certain old diary. After shifting what seemed piles of old books and magazines, I got it. I settled in an old chair and began flicking through.

My attention was caught by some seemingly inconsequential entries. The first fell in May, without any clue other than meaningless letters, and no helpful comment. I leafed through, and found another similar entry in late summer, with a drawing of a fly lazily done in the margin.

I kept working through, finding some interesting comments about life. Then I found a scrawled note which said simply 'watchers'. It had been written in Christmas week. More comments followed, and then I came to a picture of a river cut out and stuck in for March. Perhaps this was what the 'river thing' meant.

It seemed I had found something, but what it was I had no idea; I could not exactly go and ask someone.

CHAPTER 31

There is a saying that if you give your brain long enough an answer will form, and I do remember very clearly that over supper that night, it came to me. I would ask Typos; she could find out. She said she had found my injury, and her mother being killed. I would ask her. Why not?

In fact I did not have a chance for two days as my parents needed me to house-sit while they were away. I must admit that I was very tempted to call her anyway, but the thought of leaving the animals and the house alone stopped me. In any case it blew like a hurricane, so much so that I feared for the thatch.

As soon as I could get away on their return I slipped up the hill, on my own for sure this time. Milly was adamant about that. I made sure that I had surreptitiously slipped my old diary into my jacket pocket.

I walked up the hill, lost in thought. The diary entries did not joggle any memories, no matter how hard I studied them. I was also frankly torn between worry, even fear, at the idea of calling Typos again, and excitement.

I stopped, leaning on the gate and contemplating my options. The ewes had wandered up to the top gate and lifted their heads to look at me. A few bleated, then returned to heads-down grazing.

Over the valley a buzzard lazily circled, giving the occasional mewing call, and two woodpigeon burst from the hedge with a noisy clatter. A few leaves remained on the trees, and a light wind blew still from the north. The grass in the fields looked tired, as if it was already the winter's end. Little stalks from dock plants stuck up here and there, the leaves themselves long eaten by the sheep.

The sheep were not being fed hay yet, as the grass was holding up in volume. This year we would be hanging on as long as we could, as the hay in storage was much lower than normal. The crop this year had been easy to make, the weather had been easy, but the amount was very low, as the grass had simply stopped growing.

I undid the lock on the gate and went through. In the past I would have climbed over, but now I had my limits. Walking through the top field I gathered my resolve, and even laughed aloud at my excitement. I knelt down by holding on to one of the barn supports and gently lowering myself to the ground.

I closed my eyes, took a breath, gathered my courage and began the chant. It was strange that just calling once had reconfigured the words, intonations and cadence.

Soon it took over, in that strange manner it had, somewhere between worrying, fear and complete exhilaration. The chant filled my head, taking over, and I felt my ear pressure rising to the point of pain. Then, in front of me, I heard her arrival. I was almost pushed over by the air pressure change and had to pinch my nose to equalise my ears.

Then I was brave enough to open my eyes. Once more I was enthralled by her size, vision of power and dominance.

I was not brave enough to meet her gaze initially. I looked reverentially at the ground.

'Myrrdin, you need me?' Dragons do not make small talk.

'Yes, I have a problem' I said. 'The last Myrrdin got me doing something, possibly important, but I am not sure. I have to do them…'

At this point she interrupted. 'He is somewhere else, I went with them to settle him. He cannot now be reached.'

'I know, but I may have help. I put in this book a note, or rather notes against dates in the year.' I paused and looked at her. 'I cannot remember what it means now, I wrote it secretly, in a code. I simply do not know.'

'I cannot, how do you say read, but I can now understand nearly all you speak' she said. She paused, looking straight at me. Now it will seem strange perhaps to you, but her look is enveloping, warming and wonderful. She does not exactly walk around in your head, but the effect is the same. I treasure it.

'What dates in the year?'

She shifted her weight and her great talons dug into the grass, shoving earth up against them. She opened her enormous wings, almost wrapping them forwards over her head. Lifting a great scaly back leg, she stretched it backwards in an exaggerated movement, following this big stretch with her wings. She settled all her limbs back in place and shook, gigantically. It was terrifying, but also slightly comical.

'Well?'

I stopped thinking how to explain, and then had an inspired thought.

'What about if I work out, say either side of a reference point you know, like... what about bonfire night?'

'When the sky is filled with noise and lights' she replied.

'Yes exactly. Should not be difficult, and will give you a reference day.' I paused, looking at her.

Then I had a thought. 'Wait a minute' I said. 'Some places have it on different days depending on how it falls, the weather and so on.'

'I will need one town and what do you say a 'reference' date.'

I could have hugged her.

'Yes exactly, we can use say Beaminster, then count for you in or out.' I thought further to myself, it might vary a bit, but I am sure that it could be worked out.

'Give me a day.'

'What now?'

She looked at me, with a look on her face which if she were human would have meant why not, get on with it. I stood amazed as she settled down stretching her great neck out and shut her eyes. Was she having a snooze? I was dumbfounded. I looked around, making sure no one was coming. I did not want a repetition of the other day.

The diary virtually fell open in May, at an entry that had several meaningless squiggles. A few days later was written 'Beltane, ancient pagan festival'. That will do for a start, I thought.

'Ready then?' Typos thought to me, raising a great eyelash, and with a bound got to her feet. She stood at a magnificent height, stretching, shaking again, then lowering her head to my level. Her head stopped in front of me, enabling me to smell the bad meat on her breath.

'I will count the days back, and perhaps you can see?' I gently asked.

I counted the days back from bonfire night, which luckily that year fell on a Saturday. I looked at her and explained the date. I did not really have the words to say what exactly; but with a last command to wait and stay, she twitched out and had gone. I was left suddenly and ridiculously feeling very alone.

I was at a bit of a loss and pulled out two hay bales to sit on. It was pleasant outside, and although not really that sunny, it was warm enough. I did not bother to look at my watch, but after what was probably only ten minutes, with a great ear popping and rush of wind, she arrived, slightly further away than originally. She turned to look at me and took a few strides over.

'It is urgent, you have wrong' she said; worrying. 'I found you, then your last Myrrdin. I followed him twice, but cannot see what he and you meet. What you do. This is because it is power beyond me. I will take you where you go. Show you. But you cannot go back to see yourself. The power there will not allow. You must know where and wait until next.'

She had seen me and Jules. I was intrigued, but also worried.

'What do I have wrong?'

'Last time you did not go, or before, a sense of failure hangs over' she replied.

'I could not go, I was in hospital then recovering' I exclaimed.

'I know, but there is a wrong, you had to be there.'

I fell silent. What did it all mean?

'Come, I will show you where you are needed' she said.

'What? How?'

'You will ride, like with my mother' she replied.

'What?' I replied, stunned. 'I cannot do that, one day perhaps, but now… I cannot even bend my leg very well, never mind getting on. Anyway if I fell it surely this time would be the death of me. No!'

'You are needed, you will' she replied, stepping to me.

To cut a long story short, I eventually clung to the barn upright and climbed up on to the hay bale seat. Once she could see me higher she came along in line, bending her neck down. Without really thinking straight I found myself wriggling down between the spines on her neck.

'Are you there? You are light' was her comment.

'Yes, but I really must not fall, this is crazy.'

' I will catch, we go… but behind your time a little, our normal way.'

I felt her legs bound and at the same time felt a great comfort, a sense of being where I belonged. I was home again, I felt, as the ground below changed.

Looking down, familiar landmarks arrived and I do not mind admitting that I felt myself getting a little emotional at what was happening. I felt her massive muscles working as with little apparent effort she covered the ground at enormous speed. The wind tore at my jacket and made my eyes water, but the elation was tremendous. I felt very safe and was able to look down without alarm. Wonderful.

I watched the road into the village pass below, and then saw the great manor house on the hilltop. At this point Typos turned to the sea, which from our height stretched from horizon to horizon, and started circling and dropping. Looking down. I was momentarily alarmed to see a group of men cutting down trees in a clearing. I could hear a chainsaw screaming and a tractor engine. I then remembered that although I could see them, our image was history to them, so we did not figure.

'I watched you and the other come here, at sunset, to witness. You will come again, on that date. It must be so. It all goes bad if not.'

I looked down to get my bearings. 'I cannot drive yet, or walk here, it's too far' I thought back.

'I bring' she replied, and I felt great reassurance.

She flew on, and as we circled and lost height our barn came into sight. I felt my ears pop as she twitched back and landed with a great wing fanning. This was all very well, but I could not get off. I had nothing to push against with my better leg, and even with her putting her head on the ground, I had a long way to go.

After much fiddling about and trying to get near the edge of her neck, I rolled off on to the grass and untangled my legs from her neck, I had no option then but to grab at her neck scales and pull myself up. Most inelegant, and I believe it made her give a small laugh.

I am now going to jump a bit, on to the next year, a month before the longest day. It is still, all these decades, later easily remembered, and it still fills me with immense sadness and wonder. Typos and I did other things in between, but it feels wrong to leave this event hanging in your mind. I also want to get it said. It was a very sad but amazing part of my reaffirmed life.

I waited for this day in early May that first year with tremendous worry. The fact that Typos had felt such concern and picked up alarm and possibly fear had played on my mind. It had always been real, a feeling of fear. Although with me in hospital there was precious little I could have done, I was plainly negligent and felt somehow responsible.

We met outside the barn, and after her arrival she looked at me oddly.

'This is more real, more serious than we knew' she thought to me. 'I will take you and go. I cannot be near, too strong.'

'How will I get home?'

'Just be clear and call' she thought back.

This gave me great reassurance, and with careful and frankly absurd manoeuvrings I settled on her neck, in front of her great lacy wings.

As an aside every time I had called her I had been stunned at her increasing strength, almost seeing the muscle groups under her skin. The feeling of health was extraordinary. Sitting on her neck, the power that came through to my legs was phenomenal, and sometimes I could have screamed with excitement.

My ears popped as usual as she twitched just a little way back in respect to our time and leisurely flew up and over the village. I looked back at the sun setting and the rays of light just slipping through a gap in the clouds. To the south the sea could be seen, and a few cars travelled below us.

We crossed the main road and she began going up the hill, towards the manor. A tractor was working the slope below us, with a great plume of gulls following and rooks hanging on.

'You remember the valley?'

'Yes, I think so, I can walk a bit, and you said that sunset is the time.'

'That is right, I have not seen more, just Myrrdin is needed. I will wait.'

She circled, her great head looking intently down at the valley side.

'It is clear' she said. With that she dropped like a brick, taking my breath away. At the last moment possible her great wings fanned out, stopping our descent immediately and sending a great shower of leaves and small stones airborne. I half fell off and stood upright, momentarily lost.

'I go call' she said, and with that she had gone, leaving me on a track which went up to the house, just visible in the half light above the hill. I followed the track down to a small pond and boggy area at the valley bottom. The ground here was very wet and I had to pick my way. I tried to aim for the far side where the ground rose, just a few bushes growing on the top. I could smell in the air the mud and rotting vegetation.

Without getting too wet, but heavily coated in mud, I started up the far side. The ground rose sharply here, great drifts of dead leaves under the beech trees hiding large holes, old badger workings and diggings. On all fours at times, I soon reached the top and could look down into the valley.

It was a fairly shallow feature running west to east, with a grassy floor, dotted with briars, holly bushes and isolated stunted trees. The far side was swathed in a beech hanger and the trees were just starting to show. The floor was covered in bluebells and clumps of cow parsley. Through it all across the floor I could just make out a track which wound along, then disappeared in the undergrowth to the eastern end.

That first time I was at a bit of a loss, wondering what was expected of me, what I had to do, and what would happen. I looked around and saw a dryish lump of leaves by the side of a large holly. Using an overhanging branch to lower myself down, I settled to wait.

As the sun finally dropped the wood came alive with noises, roosting pigeons clattering into position for the night behind me. On the far horizon I heard a dog barking. I pulled my jacket further around me, wondering when something would happen.

Overhead the gentle wind caused the branches to move to and fro gently. In virtual darkness I heard and then saw a deer below me. It walked gently along, winding the air. I was glad I was up above it, out of its scent line.

I remained as still as possible, and then, behind the deer, three foxes trotted into view. They stopped every so often, putting their heads back and scenting the air before trotting on.

Then I heard below me someone shuffling along; I strained myself up, trying to get a better view. My eyes fell on a figure. It was a bent, elderly lady making her way slowly on the valley floor. She would now and then throw things out from a bag at her waist. Her arms made sweeping gestures and her head was bent down, looking at the floor.

As she drew nearer I felt that somehow I would have to make some sort of contact, some recognition, let her know I was there. I shuffled, rustling the leaves. At this she put a hand on her lips and turned her head towards me.

Now I must try to find words to explain what happened next. To this day it is as plain in my mind as yesterday, despite being decades gone.

The little old lady stopped walking. She lifted her head to me and looked straight at me. Her arms stopped moving, and the three foxes were suddenly back at her feet. They ran between us both, one coming up the valley side and stopping just a few yards away. I sat stock still, not frightened but full of anticipation.

Her gaze focused on me, and at that point I was as if the world stopped for a moment. Then the foxes began to bark to each other. They then began whimpering and throwing their heads back. Howling and whimpering, they rushed about. One crawled and whimpered to her feet; she bent down to touch it and it resumed its mad racing about with the others.

From somewhere a delicate blue light appeared, faint at first then stronger and stronger, until the whole valley floor was lit. The light seemed to be locked upon her as she moved. A great crashing noise of undergrowth sounded from the east as four deer trotted into the clearing and came to a halt, looking up at me.

Then, before my eyes, the old lady began to change; to look younger. I held my breath in astonishment as her body became more upright, more youthful, more shapely. Her grey hair seemed to be taking on a new life, beginning to stream out as if pushed by the wind behind her and to change colour to a golden blonde.

I had not really paid any attention to what she was wearing, but now in the blue light I could see a long gown held by a thick brown belt. The drab gown began to change into a pure white cloth.

The lady extended her arms wide to me, and a smile began to fill her face. Her eyes shone an intense blue. I had no idea what to do, but it seemed right for me to lift my own arms out wide too.

Then I felt something moving on my lap. Looking down I was stunned to see that two mice were sitting there. They looked intently at me, sitting on their back legs with their front paws in a praying gesture.

At this point a faint music began, bell-like, with no recognisable tune, but great harmony.

The lady put her arms down, then lifted one hand, pointed at me, turned and dropped it. The deer and foxes ran off and she resumed her progress to the east, turning one last time to look at me. The music and light slowly faded away as she disappeared. I felt the two mice run from my lap and felt dreadfully alone.

I knew I had witnessed something vital, yet I was hopelessly ignorant of what it was. I learned of course, and will explain how it all began making sense. It was a timeless, vital event, which I nearly fouled up for all time.

I pulled myself up, very cold and stiff but exuberant, having seen something so wonderful. I made my way home in the dark until I was on the track where Typos had dropped me. I had only just begun to call her when she twitched back.

'No need, I am near, just think. All well? Do not tell me' she quickly added. 'It is for you, not me, it is your position. Your continuance.'

She has always taken me ever since; I have not missed one. The springs arrive, but I cannot tell you more, that is for the next Myrrdin to know. I will only say that a vital piece of life was complete.

Now I will get back to the date I diverted this account. I hope you agree it was appropriate to tell you now.

Typos took me back that night. It was pitch dark when she touched down and I rolled off.

'One is back, part is complete' she thought to me. It seemed right at the time that I went to her neck and hugged it. What a wonderful thing I had witnessed. I was in a bit of a daze, and at the very least distracted.

When I had rolled off and got to my feet, my diary could be felt in my jacket pocket.

'That was wonderful. What was it for? The natural order? Life?'

'Yours is an ancient responsibility, unknown by others' she thought back.

I pulled my diary out and tried to read the entry by moonlight.

'Now I need to know the others, and what they mean' I said to her. 'They must be just as important. I presumably have to be there.'

I flicked through and the diary seemed to fall open at an entry saying only 'watchers'. Further on there appeared to be entries saying how windy it was, and then of course the river picture. After that night I was bursting to see what these might mean.

My enthusiasm was evident as Typos shuffled from one leg to another.

'Wait, I will see. Give me one of your dates and a reference.'

The date for the entry watchers I could work on from bonfire night for her, but try as I might I could find no more clues.

'I will visit and watch' she thought to me. 'I will try and think as well. It is right, I will call you when happy.' Her stomach emitted an enormous rumble.

I did not feel I could ignore this, but at the same time I was marginally embarrassed.

'Yes, I am hungry too, grub time eh?'

'Grub time?' she repeated. 'What is grub?'

She looked at me, with her head down. I saw that her nostrils were dripping, and her great tongue came out and licked the end.

'Oh, nothing' I quickly said. 'You know, food. It is just a casual term we use.'

'Yes. I need - what do you say - meat?'

'Oh right, that's it.'

Ridiculously, I then moved back a pace, as if she was planning to make a meal of me.

'I had better get back, or they will begin to wonder' I said. will wait for your call.'

'I will call when ready, now I go to eat.'

'Be safe' I said, though it seemed a ridiculous thing to say.

'And you, I go.' With that she twitched out. I gathered up my diary, closed up my jacket and found my way back through the darkness. I got back in as quietly as I could and went up to my bedroom, quiet as a mouse.

After a while of course I had to let my folks know I had returned. I said I had been back for a while and had been reading. Then I looked down at Milly, lying on the floor in front of the stove, to see her looking at me, wagging her tail.

'They did not hear you' she thought to me. 'All well, tell me later.'

I bent down to give her a rub. Wolfhounds are wonderful.

CHAPTER 32

THE CIRCLE COMPLETED

After this, I must have been impossible to live with. The next morning I desperately needed to tell someone what had happened the night before. I did of course realise that this was out of the question and that if I did so I would have the psychiatrists on my case.

It was almost dark that morning; the overhanging clouds were heavy and black. Rain threatened, but never fell. The wind was becoming cold; the last leaf remnants were off the trees.

The air seemed to fill with sweet-smelling smoke as a farm neighbour was laying a few hundred yards of hedge. Each day the fire consuming the brash was refuelled. Through the night it flared now and then, and by the morning a few embers still lay in the grey ash. A handful of leaves, briars and chippings were enough to get it going again.

Milly walked with me to make small talk with the man, and I found myself promising that when I was more able I would help. We walked on and I sensed her excitement as I brought her up to date with all that had happened. She listened, thinking the odd remark to me, but she was a perfect answer to what I needed.

'You need care, the next injury will be bad.' I remember her concern.

'There will not be another, I am sure' I thought back, giving her head a playful rub. I tried to run off, in my mad fashion, bending down to attempt to get her playing. She jumped a bit in the air, her great tail wagging, throwing her head about as if worrying a dead rat.

'I am serious' she stopped playing and thought to me. 'You also have much to do, to catch up. I know Typos is looking at the next diary date. Until then, we have no idea.'

When you are waiting for something it seems to take forever. Each day I waited and waited, getting more impatient and trying to keep myself occupied. I put two and two together and realised from what Typos had implied that my headaches had somehow been her calling, trying to make contact perhaps. If that was the case, how was I supposed to answer? Was I supposed to call with the chant to send acknowledgement, get myself in front of the barn and wait? I had no idea, and desperately did not want to get it wrong.

One morning, it was all answered. I was trying to wash the mud off the outside of my mothers' car. I had nearly finished, with just the wheels still to do, when wham - A massive headache arrived. It was insistent, making me feel sick with its intensity. Mercifully it went, only to return for a shorter duration.

'You all right?' said my mother, who had seen me stagger.

'Yes, fine. I'm going to have a stretch, we are nearly done.'

'Right dear, go and have a sit down instead, or if you are going for a stroll stay near.' She looked across at me as I strolled off.

'I'm fine, don't worry.' I went into the kitchen, followed by Milly.

'I am wanted again, not sure what for, will not be long' I said.

The hound looked at me with those deep brown trusting eyes.

'Right, be careful' she thought, with a bit of false bravado.

'I will, I promise.' I bent down to hug her head. Then I turned and sneaked out of the front door, trying to shut it quietly. Outside on the road, I set off, trying to walk as fast as possible. I was just able to run for a few yards and I half jogged along until I turned to go up the hill. It was impossible for me to run up hills then, but I walked as quickly as I could. My breathing got more laboured. I slowed a little to fight my breath, as I was only too aware that I would need it in earnest for the chant.

I turned into the field, climbed the gate and slowed to a walk, trying to slow my breathing, and took big chesty breaths. In front of the barn, I felt normal and grabbing one of the barn supports I used it to get myself on the ground.

The intonations had only just started when they gathered their own momentum. Almost as if Typos was waiting for my call, it rushed along, and with a strong whistling wind and loud ear popping, she appeared. A massive shower of mud and grass accompanied her arrival. It seemed as if everything stopped; no birdsong, no rustling branches, no cows calling, no sheep bleating. It all stopped, her presence almost demanded it.

'Myrddin, you answered' she thought, looking directly at me. Her gaze enthralled me; it said as much as a thousand words, making normal greetings and speech irrelevant.

'I have found your journeys on that date. It has been harder, a longer way. You have again missed three. You can go back to this one. It is only just missed.'

She stopped as if waiting for my comment. I did not know what to say and was about to ask what it was when she started again.

'Yours is the most important position of them all. I have seen you in the centre receiving authority... confirmation.'

'Confirmation of what, do you know?' I was thoroughly confused.

'Actually in this case, with you, I do.'

She turned her head to one side. On reflection this was probably the closest her facial muscles ever came to a smile.

'We go, you will know more then. This is an easier answer. On we go.'

'I have not got long, before they wonder...' I started saying, then realised that what I was about to say was ludicrous.

'What do you say ?'

'Nothing, forget it, just being stupid.'

'What is stupid?' she asked as I got alongside her neck.

'Nothing, it is gone.'

I had developed a technique where having got level and in front of her wings, I lay down backwards on to them. I could then lift my right leg, swing it over her neck and sit up. She then got up on all four legs. I did feel marginally guilty asking her to lie down in the mud, but it seemed to cause her no concern. It also meant that I did not need to stand on anything. Progress!

'We go, it is longer than before. I have followed you both in time to the special meeting. We go back in this year. For them it will be as now.'

I thought about this as I wriggled down and got snug. I was wise enough now to know that the ear popping meant she had gone back.

'We go back... not far, just a few weeks. That is all we need' she thought.

I looked down and recognised that she had flown out along the main road to London. I saw Crewkerne, and soon the naval airbase at Yeovilton came into view.

'I go up here' she thought, and began circling. I was not brave enough to ask why, but just watched spellbound as below us I saw two naval helicopters beginning to take off. They left in tandem, flying back in the direction we had just come. I twisted myself around to watch them go.

'Tight, we go' she thought. Her wingbeat increased, pulling air in. I felt my eyes begin to water with the cold air hitting my face. Her power lunge was immense and the ground below began to go past faster and faster. I was thrilled by this, and I believe my joy carried through to her.

Her wing beats got even quicker and her stroke longer, throwing great currents of air behind her. She began to dip downward, and the speed was incredible.

'My mother told me you enjoy' she said.

'Enjoy, I love it!' I replied, and began laughing with pure unadulterated joy.

'We stop playing soon. Nearly there.'

I had been so wrapped up in the joy of flying that I was guilty of not really concentrating on our route. I looked ahead to see standing stones on the far horizon.

'That is Stonehenge, I know' I said.

'I do not know what you say. I watched you and the last Myrrdin come here. You are needed, with others. You are now central.'

She flew on, and I watched as the circle of standing stones came into view. The main road alongside was busy with an endless stream of cars. Many had lights on, as it was beginning to get dark and there was a fine drizzle in the air.

My ears popped as she thought, 'We go back to their time'. The ground underneath did not perceptibly change, and looking down I could see three cars in the car park on the road edge.

She flew on to a small dip in the rolling plain, dropped and flared out on the ground.

'I cannot be seen here, not far. You walk.'

'Fine, I will call, when I need you, but what do I do, why am I here? I am at a loss, what do I do?'

'You will be fine, be guided by them. Know that you are central. It is your position. I go'

With that she vanished, and I was on my own. I gathered my jacket about me, pulling my collar up against the drizzle. I could just see the tops of the stones above the hill, and set off to them. I had to climb a barbed wire fence, which luckily was in poor repair and virtually flat, then cross a smaller road that ran to the stones.

There is an atmosphere as you get nearer to this monument, which I began to feel as I got closer. It has a presence, an aura, linked to its past and history. The nearer I got to it the more I felt myself being pressed down by a heavy weight, and walking needed more effort. I got more nervous as the darkness increased and I saw internal lights come on in the cars and their doors opening.

The three drivers stood together, watching me approach. I heard one exclaim, putting a hand across his face.

'Can't be!' I heard one say.

The youngest one started turning as if going back to his car.

'It's all right, stay here' said one of the others, grabbing at his arm and turning him.

'Myrrdin ,is that really you?' shouted one to me. 'How did you get here? What happened last year and the year before?'

All three gathered around me. The youngest one's body language showed great fear.

'We assumed you were dead' said the first man.

Eventually some semblance of order and peace descended, and each man introduced himself, one as Scotland, one as Ireland and the youngest as Wales. This seemed most odd.

'Where is your car, where have you parked?' said Scotland.

'I'm all right, got a lift, no problem.'

'What right here? You were lucky.'

I changed the subject quickly, saying my lift was going to pick me up later. I was aware that all were looking at me curiously, but I did not push the point. Looking across after this towards Wales, I could see his inner torment at these thoughts.

'I need to explain to you that I was in hospital, knocked out, in a coma. I just remembered I had to be here' I lied, hoping to sound credible. 'I really have no idea why, but I will need your help.' I stopped, looking at each in turn.

'That is fine, but you have been central for generations' said Ireland, kindly. 'The watchers are now complete again. We are here to be reverified, it's important. Come, we will do the chant. You are central, it will come back. Perhaps Scotland will whisper to you now and then. Is that all right?'

Scotland duly nodded his assent.

'Come, we should begin, it is time. This way.' Taking me by the hand, Ireland led me to the centre of the stone circle. Then he pushed my arms up.

'Stay as best you can like this, you may want close your eyes, but you will not need to.' He walked back to the others, who had spread out around me.

'You just need to know that this has happened for generations' called out Ireland. You will remember I am sure. Keep still. And when it is done we will talk again. You, or rather you and your predecessors, have been the centre for all time. Stay there, we begin.'

I was somewhat nervous as they began a chant that rose and fell. I let my eyes move from one to another. Wales and Ireland had their eyes shut, but Scotland's were open. He met my gaze with a supporting look, smiling encouragement and carrying on with the chant.

The drizzle finally stopped and I stood with my arms outstretched. After a few moments it seemed the night was split by the call of a tawny owl, strident and seeming to come from the top of an adjoining stone. It flew down, just missing my head and alighting on my arm. I looked across at Scotland, who smiled in support. I looked at the tawny, who turned her eyes on me, clicking her beak. She shook her wings and bent to preen her feathers.

I stood entranced as she seemed to shrink back on my arm, shaking her feathers down. She threw her head back and let out an intense call. This was answered immediately by a myriad more owl calls from the air around the stones. The volume and variety of calls increased in volume.

Ireland looked around the group with a questioning expression. Young Wales looked petrified, rooted to the spot, while Ireland smiled, misty-eyed.

The air was filled with hooting and the smell of feather dander. There must have been a hundred owls. I was in awe of what I had become part of, and looked again at the tawny on my arm. She clicked her beak towards me again and bobbed her head. Her wings stretched out and she noiselessly took off. My arm rose as the negligible weight came off it. I looked towards Scotland and he nodded, smiled and mouthed 'You are fine, it's finished'. The owls were leaving; against the faint light I could see them in the sky, flying off.

'We are back, it is complete again' laughed Ireland.

'Thank goodness, back as we were, we are properly reaffirmed' smiled Scotland. 'After the last two being so empty, thank God you are back.'

He came over to me, putting his arms around me, and giving me a massive hug. Taking a step back, with a hand on my shoulders each side, he looked at me smiling

'Do not ever do that again' he joked. 'None of us had been here as an incomplete circle before. The last two years have been horrible. Promise you will always be here. Be careful.'

'I will try' I joked back, still in awe at what I had seen.

As we walked back to the car, Ireland explained, with all listening, that we formed a timeless acknowledgement of the watchers of the White Queen.

I wanted to ask then about the references to the wind and the river that I had gleaned from the old diary, but thought that this was probably inappropriate. It would wait. Typos would guide me anyway, and if our paths crossed again, at least they were not strangers now.

We walked back to the car, and with a cheery 'goodbye' and 'see you next year', Wales and Ireland left.

'What about your lift home then?' asked Scotland. 'When will he be here? You all right waiting? It's getting cold. You can wait in my car if you want.' He shuffled his feet and then shifted his gaze to me.

'No I'm fine thanks, he will not be long for sure' I said. Then I made one of the silliest mistakes I have ever made.

I will explain that back in my time, which of course for him was the future, there had been a bad train derailment with a few unfortunates killed. As he stayed with me we chatted, and like a complete idiot I heard myself saying how dreadful the train crash had been.

'What's this, what train, I work on the railways?' he said, lifting himself more erect.

Immediately I realised what a daft thing I had let slip.

'Oh sorry, did I say here? I meant abroad.' I tried desperately to change the subject, but I could see that he was not satisfied. He looked at me with piercing eyes.

'Look I will see you next year' he said. 'To be honest I have always felt your position - you are different from us. Enough said, I had better go. Thank goodness you are back. This year was much more reassuring, more complete. Be careful. See you next time.'

With that he shut his car door, started the engine and with one last wave drove off.

I watched his car disappear, somewhat relieved that I had got away with that last stupid remark. I looked around to make sure no one was near and that I was truly alone, with no cars in sight. Then I knelt down and thought the call for Typos, as I had before in the wood at home. My ears popped in the usual manner, but on opening my eyes there was no dragon.

I began to panic. What had I done wrong? My thoughts ran wild. I called again, and in an instant heard her voice saying 'walk'. Of course, dragons can only twitch back to the same place they left.

I half jogged over the car park and back over the fence. There she was, hidden from sight down an incline. I was so pleased to see her that like an idiot I ran the last few yards and gave her a big hug.

'Back again, I am here' she thought to me.

'You are wonderful!' I shouted at the wind.

'What is wonderful?'

'Nothing' I laughed, swinging my leg over her neck.

Later after she had landed, her parting remark left me worried. 'You have no control over the next' she said. 'You will watch, witness, but we avenge my mother. It is the Furies they owe. They are next for us.'

' For us?'

'I have help, you will see. I call. It is this time, they call me soon… they called mother.' She bristled, a jet of flame at her mouth. I wanted to ask much more, but with a parting look at me, she went.

I was left wondering what was planned and what was happening as I slowly made my way homeward. I looked again at the entries I had made, but could get no sense of them.

Christmas must have arrived, and I'm sure it was as marvellous as ever.

I do remember that unusually, that winter stayed amazingly dry. We had a few frosts but no snow and the sky stayed grey, with the sun just peeping through now and then.

It was in the week after New Year that her call came, insistent and much harder than all the times before.

CHAPTER 33

THE GREAT STORM

The call came as I was slumped in front of the fire, reading a book which had been a Christmas present from my mother. I was stretched out with Milly alongside me, enjoying the fire's heat and grazing on a tin of sweets.

To be honest the book was not holding my attention too well, and my eyes rose now and then to the television, which was showing one of those dreadful holiday films we are subjected to at that time of year.

This time I got a warning of the call. There was an initial passing pain between my ears, then all hell arrived, it seemed. It was a blessing that I was lying down, as the call was disabling. I felt my head was going to explode and I felt sick. A few minutes later it returned with a brain-splitting repetition. I waited for it to pass, then I let Milly know and told my parents I was going out for some air and to check the sheep. I threw a jacket on and left the house.

It was a murky late winter afternoon outside, and I wriggled down inside my jacket. Starting up the hill, I was met by a villager I vaguely knew, and despite the fact that my head was splitting and I knew Typos wanted me urgently, I was forced to pass seasonal greetings with them.

I hurried on up the hill, then across the fields to the barn. I was aware that on my last contact with her, Typos had intimated that she was in full control with this, I was just to watch. This implied revenge for her mother. I had no real idea what she meant, but knew that my accident had coincided with her death. Typos had never said more, and who was I to ask such questions?

I arrived as another head-splitting call arrived. I had to wait for it to pass before I could begin, clutching at the barn stanchion for support, thinking that this time I would vomit. Mercifully this passed as her call finished.

It seemed she arrived almost immediately I began, on only the second repetition. I was immediately frightened by her attitude. She seemed to shine all over while smoke and blasts of fire kept issuing from her mouth. She was showing her teeth and her feet were ripping up great clods from the ground. She was clearly very worked up about something. I was not sure why I was being tolerated, and felt inadequate to say the least.

'You were slow!' She knelt down in the open, pushing her great neck and head forward.

'I am sorry. I came as quickly as I could. Leave me out if it is a problem.'

'You are not a problem. Today my mother's death will be paid for.'

As she thought this to me, she threw her head back and a great jet of red-hot flame issued forth. I shrank back, putting both arms in front of my face as some sort of defence against the intense heat.

'She will be paid!' As she thought this great wings were noisily flexed.

I wriggled down between two spines on her neck, almost able to get my feet touching each other, my legs tight against her body.

She turned her great head around to look at me.

'You are fine?'

'Yes' I answered, as with an enormous bound that flung me hard down against her, she took off.

'Where are we going?'

'We go to meet my friends, to help. The Furies say when and where. We go back… not, far to your nineteen eighty six, and local… not far, you will see.'

She flew on, slowly gaining height as she went. Soon the ground below us did not make a lot of sense to my geography, and as it was cold at this height I pushed my hands in between my body and her neck muscles. She felt me moving.

'You are well?'

'Yes, fine' I thought back. 'Who, or what, are you going to see?'

Still she did not answer, and I did not feel able to press the point. I looked down. Far off I could see the Bristol Channel, and beyond it the coast of Wales.

The cloud at this height was broken, and we kept flying into great grey, moist masses. They seemed to have hard well-defined edges, and I was staring at one of these when I heard Typos call a greeting. I looked down and saw a bright red dragon flying straight towards us.

'You have met her before, you will not remember… she remembers you' said Typos.

I sat very still as the red dragon approached and the two conversed with each other.

'This is Y Draig Goch, you met her before' thought Typos. 'She cannot talk to you.'

I looked across and met the eye of the red dragon. Her gaze was petrifying, cold and sinister. She was marginally smaller than Typos and seemed to need to use her wings more. They were perpetually rowing her through the sky. Her great snakelike head turned away from us and looked down.

I felt able to get a better look at her and could see scars on her sides and a great healed welt on her back. Her huge back leg claws hung down, and I could see that they were heavily bloodstained.

As we flew on with her alongside I looked down and saw that we were now well into the Welsh hills. The ground underneath had become more rugged, the roads narrower and more twisting. Far away to the left the sea was shining, and looking this way I could almost smell it in the wind.

'We do not go to what you call Snowdon but a hill near it. You will see. I leave you there for now.'

As she thought this to me I was horrified to see another creature flying to us from the north. Almost at the same time I became aware of both dragons hailing a welcome.

'This is my oldest friend from the north. You will see he differs' said Typos.

'What do you mean?'

'You will see.'

But I already had. This creature looked like a small dragon, but it had no front legs. The large back legs trailed behind it and its wings hardly needed to beat at all, so effortless was its flight. As it got nearer I found myself trying to avoid its direct gaze.

'This is Heptaco, my oldest friend.'

The new creature came alongside us, showing that it had a green upper body, but bright red below. The claws on its back legs caught my eye; they were very sharp looking but all were broken and of different lengths. I caught a glimpse of the animal's face and saw it looking at me with small, hard, pig-like eyes. I shifted my gaze away and looked down. I kept very quiet and still, not wanting to attract any attention to myself.

I have since learned that this frightening two-footed monster is called a wyvern.

'We are nearly complete, our group needs one more' thought Typos. 'We wait, he comes if no rain.'

'No rain?'

'Yes, no rain, he cannot come in rain, but he is more powerful than all.'

We carried on flying in lazy circles, and it was amusing to watch the other two relishing each other's company. They rolled and mock-fought through the sky like two puppies playing in a garden. One would close its wings and drop on the other. At the last moment the lower one would roll on its side and push its clawed legs out to the side. They were obviously pleased to see each other again.

'Now we are complete, he comes' thought Shola. At that the other two, as if someone had rung a bell, formed into line with us. They were quieter, less exuberant.

I was aware that a dragon meeting was going on, and discreetly looked around the sky. I eventually spotted a small dot which was getting nearer at great speed. I watched it closing with us - and let out a yell of fear. This creature was gross, a horrifying apparition. I was so horrified that I vomited noisily over Typos side' this one had three heads. Not only that, it must have been three times Typos' size. Its great wings looked paper thin and made clapping noises as they beat down.

The new dragon was mainly dark green in colour, but each head had a red crest and the skin seemed to be covered in feathers. The three heads all moved independently, each on a huge neck.

I tried to hide my eyes, but when I peeped through my fingers I saw that all three heads were focused on me. I felt the shakes begin in my hands and spread to my entire body.

'You are fine?' Typos thought to me. 'Have no fear, you are safe. This is Tugarin, from Russia. He helps tonight. We teach the Furies.'

As she said this a great jet of flame issued forth and her whole body shook. The others followed suit. A faint smell of fireworks enveloped us.

I looked from one to the other, all in a line, and feared what was coming up. The flying was purposeful now, with the ground speed increasing.

'That hill is called Cader Idris by your people. You are to stay there and watch. We meet the Furies. They are expecting only me, keeping the story of my mother going. We will avenge her. You are safe. You wait.'

All the dragons began circling and Typos dropped off, beginning to descend rapidly. Her great head scanned the ground below us.

'We go!' she thought, heading for a plateau. She closed her wings and dropped, opening them at the last moment in a great fanning stop.

I wriggled off, with some difficulty; my legs did not work too well anyway, and were now very stiff. Half erect, half falling, I got on the ground and pulled myself up with the aid of her neck.

'You must be careful' I ridiculously found myself thinking to her.

She turned her gigantic head down to me.

'I will watch the sky. It is a shame you cannot recall my mother Shola. We fight for her. Stay here, I return. Watch the sky. It begins.'

With a great leap, she took off. I watched as she powered skywards up to meet the others as they circled above.

In a way I was glad to be on the ground, as my legs ached badly. I tried to walk about a bit, looking skywards until the dragons and Typos had gone from sight.

After a while I began to feel dreadfully alone. I flung my arms about and starting singing at the top of my voice, until I quickly realised that I would have some explaining to do if some wanderer heard me.

It was now starting to get dark. My vision down the hill was limited, as the ground seemed to drop away alarmingly. The grass here was almost non-existent, and what there was was covered in sheep droppings.

I had the remnants of a tube of sweets in my pocket and started on one now, aware that it would be sensible to ration them and slow up. As I sucked an acid drop, the sky began to darken and a few spots of rain began. Soon the faint breeze grew into a strong gusting wind, and I took shelter behind a pile of rocks on the edge.

Looking at the far horizon I began to see the sky glimmer with lightning, and then the wind began to increase. Great shafts of lightning and deafening peals of thunder split the dark of the night. Amid the banging and crashing it began to pour down, and with no real shelter I was soon soaked.

Aware that I was in the open and at risk from lightning, I crouched down further below the rocks. It was impossible to stand up. I hunkered down as best I could but the wind was extraordinary, slamming into the hill. It had a sound as if it had been released from hell.

During the odd lull in the wind I looked around at the sky. It was now lit up by great blasts of lightning, giving me a flickering view of the land below.

After perhaps three hours, with all my sweets eaten and starting to feel very cold as well as very alone, I noticed that the storm was beginning to die off; the eye of the storm had moved on. From my vantage point I could see great swathes of lit-up sky to the south.

I started looking skywards, more in hope than anything else, wanting my dragon back. I wondered how on earth I was going to get back, and how I would explain that I had been to Wales. I began to get myself a little wound up.

Then, as the wind died away, my wonderful Typos twitched back, nearly squashing me. She looked completely shattered. Her great head dropped and blood was oozing from her shoulder. One of her back legs seemed to be twitching uncontrollably. Her breathing was heavy and strenuous. She stood exhausted.

'What about the others, are they all right? What has happened?' I shouted at her, my worry getting the better of me.

'Tugarin is fine, but he cannot fly in rain, his wings do not allow. He killed two, he is now gone. Heptaco, my friend, was the best, he killed four slowly. He is always for me my friend.'

'Y Draig Goch… she killed two. Very slowly they scream.'

At this point I do not mind admitting I felt alarm rising. I was linked to murder.

'And you?' I gently thought to her.

This might sound ridiculous perhaps, but she looked at me with an expression of joy.

'I got their leader. I killed him. It was not easy, but I killed him. My mother is avenged, it is done. Now we return. The Furies will not be a problem now.'

So Shola had been avenged, and justice was done. I suppose I got my revenge as well, because when they blew Shola into the power lines, my fall ruined me as well.

In a way I felt rather pathetic. After all, all I had done was watch.

I climbed on board and Typos flew back, very tired now. She mercifully twitched back so that it appeared I had only been gone half an hour.

'Are you all right, do you need anything I can get?' I said to her.

'No. Just sleep. In time I will look at your last date, and call. Be safe.' She looked at me again with that smiling look.

'You too' I called as she twitched out. I walked back down the hill, looking again at my watch, struggling as usual to believe the time effect.

'They all right, all snug?' said my mother as I walked in, realising I was suddenly really tired.

'Yes all present and correct. Any chance of a cuppa? I'm parched. I'll need to change, I lost my balance a bit, got in the river' I lied, hoping there would be no questions.

The next few times I had dealings with Typos I tried gently to get a better understanding of that night.

The Furies, or Harpies, have extraordinary control of the wind. Their power had been increasing, and as an aside I would not be at all surprised to hear that the ocean warming and atmospheric changes man produces have added to their strength.

I learned that every year the current dragon, with their

Myrrdin, has to meet them once, at their calling. They had given Shola a severe fight but she had triumphed, and then they later had taken their revenge. Typos told me that for the moment their numbers had been reduced. She and her friends had taught them a lesson which they would remember. They were expecting only her to arrive, so the other dragons were an unwelcome surprise. Justice had been done, for now.

If you look in the history books as I have, you will find the English hurricane for 1986. It was a horrific event that coincided with the summer bank holiday. It originated far out in the Atlantic and came ashore in a devastating fashion. In Dublin it produced the worst flooding on record, about eight feet of water. It flooded areas of Dyfed in Wales and produced waves of over eight metres in the channel. Helicopters were needed for rescue, and they had a great challenge flying in winds approaching 110 mph.

Three people sadly met their deaths by drowning and five went missing. Structural damage was widespread and many crops were ruined. The great storm of 1986 remains in history a horrific event, famously foretold as a 'bit of rain' by a certain TV weatherman.

It has remained in my mind as an event that would have been even worse if the Furies had not been properly engaged.

CHAPTER 34

AN ENCOUNTER WITH MEWLIC

Something strange began happening to me after that outing with Typos. I started waking two or three times at night with strong memories returning. I would eventually fall asleep, only to be woken, it seemed, within an hour, vividly recalling previous flights and happenings with Shola. These memories were so strong that I woke myself up shouting. Milly barged in through the bedroom door more than once to find out what had alarmed me.

Slowly my memories of the time before my second fall came back, even to the point of Shola fighting to keep out of the wire. My memories of Jules began returning as well. I must have been very fond of him, I realised, and he had taught me so much.

One day around this time I wandered into the kitchen, where my mother was having coffee with a visitor. As I started making myself a drink I overheard the woman saying that a friend had developed a nasty rash. Without thinking, and without knowing where it had come from, I mentioned a herb which was useful in such cases.

The women stopped talking and turned to me. 'How do you know that?' asked my mother. 'Did you read it somewhere?'

At the time I was at a bit of a loss, but weeks of dreaming continued and lots more came back, stuff that Jules had drummed into me. In February that year I kept looking at my old diary as the river picture got nearer and nearer. Typos had still not called and I was getting impatient.

One morning when the sky seemed to touch the ground, Milly and I left the house to have a walk, take a look at the sheep and horses and generally mooch about. I have to be honest and say that with not a lot to do outside, sometimes my days seemed a touch empty. The hospital appointments were finished and the sheep were doing nothing but growing new lambs, needing only needed daily checking. I was not really allowed to use a chainsaw, so I couldn't help much with hedging. The land was fallow waiting for spring to arrive and planting to begin. Riding was out of the question. My mother would have had a blue fit.

We walked across the home paddock and through the gate and stopped by the river. The riverbed had been nearly taken over in places by weeds and grasses from the banks, and the dead stalks of nettles made the edges indistinct.

As we watched a vole appeared, took small sips from the bank, saw us watching and shot back in to cover.

The rookery showed some life as birds were flying back from morning food trips. Their cawing filled the air as they skirmished with each other. They flew up into the Scots pines, where their old nests looked bare, squirrels' dreys.

We had to move in to the side as an oil tanker, arriving to deliver central heating oil for someone in the village, needed all the width of road. We turned and took the track that crossed the fields to Beaminster. This took us past Jules' barn.

While Milly rooted about as dogs do, I stood looking at the now-empty building. Some memories came back.

'You all right?' Milly thought to me. 'We used to go in there for tea. Do you remember his strange biscuits?'

'Yes, come to think of it, I do. I called Shola here… the air horse. I remember.'

I stayed deep in thought, the wolfhound by my side.

'Come on, let's get on' she thought to me.

I looked at her and smiled. 'Right come on then. It's gone, history now.'

We set off, Milly ranging not far ahead, stopping now and then for me to catch up. The far horizon was shrouded in fog. My jacket was soon damp from the moist air.

We left the last few trees and went through a small stile, carrying the remains of barbed wire, and set off across the cow field. The cattle were still in for the winter, but the field carried memories of them. I walked carefully, watching where I put my feet. Later, in early spring, the chain harrow would be dragged over to break these clods up and stir up the grass.

The other side of the field was bordered by an old post-and-rail fence, and as we got nearer I became aware that flying out of the mist, and then circling above us was a very dark-looking buzzard. I saw Milly look up at it, turning her head as it went over.

'I know him, he has spoken to me' she thought, watching the buzzard fan out as it landed on a toprail. It shook its wings and drew them in against its body. Then it pulled its plumage in and bobbed its head.

I was at a bit of a loss, and Milly came alongside my legs looking towards the bird.

'You cannot speak to him, but I am able' she thought.

I stood some way off as Milly went up and stood looking up at the buzzard on the rail. They remained together focused on each other for perhaps ten minutes, occasionally looking towards me, nodding.

The buzzard was large as buzzards go, his feet on the rail looking disproportionately small. His plumage was predominantly dark brown, with paler feathers at the throat giving him the effect of wearing a necklace. His wings as he opened and closed them were lighter in colour underneath, and I saw gaps where new flight feathers had to come through.

I felt bold enough to begin slowly walking in, stopping perhaps just a couple of yards away.

'This is Mewlic, he knows your story. It is in his spoken history' said Milly.

'What are you saying, what do you mean?'

'It is a long story. Your first fall is important. They knew you would be the next Myrrdin.'

She stopped; the buzzard must have interrupted.

'They know of all your predecessors and your next chosen. They watch from one family to another as the years go by.' She paused, looking at me.

'You were chosen to carry on. Your fall from the horse, nearly spoilt it all. I have that story now to tell you. It is complete.'

The buzzard moved from one foot to the other, obviously butting in with her thoughts.

'His people are assigned to watch all your people' said Milly as the buzzard prepared to fly. 'They keep the stories by telling them to each generation.'

Mewlic took a last look at us both and launched himself into the air. He circled above us, then flew away towards the hill, to be lost in the fog.

'Well?' was all I could say as Milly looked up at me.

'I will tell you all, later' she thought as we started homeward. Later she did so, and I have faithfully recorded all that history at the start of this message to you.

The significance of my position I suppose then became more real to me. My successor will, I am sure, feel the same.

A few weeks later, another call came from Typos.

CHAPTER 35

THE WATER FORCES

I had been expecting the call from Typos for days. I had been reacting to the slightest headache and becoming almost paranoid. The last couple of times I had found the calls rather debilitating; on reflection, they were not long, but they were highly unpleasant. I had nearly always suffered a blinding headache with vomiting.

As the date in my diary with the river picture got nearer, I got twitchier. The waiting got more and more intense, and this must have altered my personality, as mother at one point as me if I was feeling all right.

I had taken myself into the orchard and was having a small fire to burn up the prunings. It had taken a lot of effort to get a hot base to it, and at last I could begin to feed it in earnest. The flames crackled through and the smoke, when it was not making my eyes water, began to plume off. Dark blue with a great smell from the apple wood, it rose almost straight in the windless air.

With Milly watching and chewing at the end of a stick, I was lost in my work. Then as I straightened my back for a stretch, the call began. I staggered a little, making Milly look up.

'Does she call? Are you needed?'

She stopped chewing and looked up at me. Her tail gently wagged a few times as she watched.

'Yes, I am wanted' I replied, gathering up the jacket I had taken off. 'I will not be long I am sure, stay here on guard. I will turn the key.'

Everyone was out, either at work or shopping. I settled the dogs and set off at a smart walk for the barn.

I had to wait before calling her, as a tractor was working in an adjoining field. I waved at the driver, hoping he would not switch off for a natter. Luckily he just waved a greeting and carried on. He turned at the headland and began a parallel pass away from me.

Down behind the hedge, and trees, hidden by the barn itself, I felt safe enough from prying eyes. I lowered myself to the ground, hanging on to the stanchion upright for support. I guessed later, that she had been waiting for my call, as almost straight away she arrived.

'Myrrdin, we can begin' she thought to me on arriving. I have mentioned before that each time I see her anew I am overawed by her growth. This time was no exception; she looked double in size. I realise now years later that she had now reached her full size. Her coat, scales and everything about her skin had sheen, and as she moved the muscle groups underneath were obvious. Her eyes were saucers that held me in their gaze. Once their gaze held me, it was as if she was walking around in my head.

'You have missed again, as before, you have to amend.'

'You found the day, and what I do then. What does the river picture mean?'

'That I do not know, but every year has been the same day.'

She turned her head to watch a group of pigeons fly over. 'You have been the same day and the same start. I have watched you and your previous do the same.' She paused, looking at me.

'But it is the same as before. I cannot see, the forces are too strong. They block. I see your start.'

She stopped and looked at me, lowering her head and turning it to one side.

'I cannot help more, it is nearer though. This river here, down below.. I have in one year past nearly seen you to the sea.'

'What, this here?' I exclaimed, pointing down into the valley.

'Yes, and early, how do you say, before first light.'

She stopped thinking, but kept looking at me. I stood there relieved that this call, was local.

'Always the same day, every year, I have found your need. Now you do.'

'Yes. Yes. I will, no problem, I will.'

'Now for this moment I can go, I will call when you are needed.'

All I could say was the usual 'be safe, see you soon'.

'Why?' she quickly said back. 'You have need?'

'No, it's just a term.'

She turned her great head on one side, fixing me with a look, and with a final 'be safe', she twitched and went.

Now I do not mind admitting that in a strange way, I was getting rather fond of her visits, and I hated it when she vanished so quickly like that.

I walked back home and went to find my old diary. The river picture was for three days' time. I thought long and hard about taking Milly with me.

Later I explained to her what was happening, my possible need. We agreed that maybe she could come with me, but as we got further along the river, she would hang back a bit. Our rationale was that she might have been walking herself in any case, but obviously, as she was not human, it would hopefully be allowed. I was glad we reached this joint decision. I was not worried about what I might see, but to have a 'mate' with you was a plus.

The alarm that I had muffled under my pillow seemed to go off the moment I fell asleep. I had lain awake for ages, so much going through my head that sleep was initially impossible, tossing and turning. It seemed that I could not get comfortable, and then the chirring under my pillow arrived.

The house was pitch dark and cold as I went to make a quick cup of tea and rouse Milly. She was up and stretching when I walked in, having heard the alarm too.

After the kettle had boiled and the best part of a packet of biscuits had disappeared, I pulled my boots and jacket on. Then, turning all lights off and very quietly locking the door, we set off across the orchard. Luckily there was still a little moonlight, and on the horizon the sky was starting to change colour. A vague hint of pink red heralded the arrival of dawn.

As we walked down to the bridge an owl screeched and a far-off fox barked. The river was just flowing, and having my wellies on, I was tempted to wade in and make quicker progress than on the weedy bank. I could hear Milly now and then, make an almighty splash as she jumped in. With me keeping two hundred yards ahead, we made our way on. I kept looking ahead, for what I had no idea.

Soon the tree-enclosed river opened out on to the flood plain. Up ahead on the horizon, I could make out the neon lights of the nearby market town.

I surprised a drinking deer by the river's edge, which turned to look at me, and then galloped off. The river at this point was starting to flow a little, making the odd gurgling noises now and then. I stopped and stood for a while, watching the sky becoming redder.

Ducks could be heard talking to each other in the rushes on the edges, and I heard a plop as a large vole jumped in. I could just make out its shape and the slight bow wave it made as it swam.

I turned towards the sea and was intrigued by what I took to be a small flicker of burning marsh gas on the far side. The river seemed to slow as I watched a small flame come in my direction and stop. It seemed to grow a little, unaffected by the flow around it. I could hear a faint hissing noise, and saw it come towards me again. It stopped on the river edge.

I watched flabbergasted as before my eyes it grew in size, and then began to move back to where it had originated. As it moved back, one, then half a dozen new flames spurted up. They grew in size until they were about four feet tall and seemed to dance to each other. Rather unnervingly, they all began advancing to where I stood.

I resisted the urge to step back, expecting at any point to feel their heat. Weirdly, I felt nothing at all, though the hissing drowned out the gurgling of the river. As I watched one flame broke off and moved quickly towards the sea. It had only been gone a few moments when I was truly stunned to see a large, purple, flickering flame coming upstream. It moved towards me rapidly, growing to possibly ten or twelve feet high, then stopped in the shallows. It stayed dancing there, joined by the others.

The blue light from the flames bathed out that of the rising sunlight, and I noticed that it had gone strangely quiet; the dawn chorus had stopped. The flames built in intensity, and then slowly one by one began fading, leaving just the biggest. This started rotating on the spot, and then began to move away. It stopped on the far side, without appearing to burn the rushes. It bent towards me, and then silently stopped – and disappeared.

I stood rooted to the spot, feeling both stunned and honoured. It had been an unreal experience and I simply did not know what to make of it.

It has been like this now for the last few decades, although the big flame has never come from the sea to join the little ones again.

I began to walk slowly back. Milly rejoined me.

'I watched it all from the other side. They danced to you' she said.

'I know, I know' I mumbled.

I was a little overcome with it all, and what it obviously meant in terms of continuation. I knew I had to be there, to witness it. I realised that it was part of a timeless, vital ritual.

We got back to the house still very early in the morning, but as a treat I cooked her and I bacon and eggs.

'You cooked her what?' I hear you ask. Yes, you read right, we both deserved it. The rest of that day passed in a blur.

EPILOGUE

I have tried to remember in some sort of chronological order how I began with this honour. I did not ask for it, but as you have read, we are given no option. It has meant that I have seen some amazing sights, and some ghastly ones.

I am lucky in that I have had a lifelong chum many would die for – as I nearly did. I am also lucky in that my relationship with wonderful dogs and horses is one many would dream off (right now my dogs are getting fed up with me beavering away at these memoirs and have told me to feed them).

If you doubt the validity of these memories, go to your history books and read again; Shola and Typos are there.

As for now – well, I am going to have a week or two away from this. I have to tell you about lots of things; Typos being called to fight your corner without any of you knowing, and my new Myrddin, my replacement.

As I have hinted, I have only two years to record the last few years' fun, and then I will see Jules again. In the meantime I will wrap this lot in a plastic bag and put it all in a sealed tin. I have recently had two big diseased elms drop so I will put the tin under the logs in one of the unused stables.

You wonder if I still share my life with a horse? Oh yes. A hound? Again, yes. You will not believe it, but as I type these closing words, Typos is calling. I must go to her.

Wish me luck.

ND - #0413 - 270225 - C0 - 229/152/16 - PB - 9781909304567 - Matt Lamination